Restlessness filled her. She told herself it was because the babies were moving around, making her uncomfortable. But it wasn't just that. Her mind was restless for an entirely different reason.

And the reason had a name and a face.

Dennis Lincoln.

Every time Nicole closed her eyes, she saw his face and relived their kiss.

Body tensed, she stared up into the darkness. She was being adolescent. A pregnant woman shouldn't feel this way. And *she* didn't want to feel at all. Not anymore…

Marie Ferrarella earned a master's degree in Shakespearean comedy, and, perhaps as a result, her writing is distinguished by humor and natural dialogue. This RITA® Award-winning author's goal is to entertain and to make people laugh and feel good. She has written over one hundred books for Silhouette, some under the name Marie Nicole. Her romances are beloved by fans worldwide and have been translated into Spanish, Italian, German, Russian, Polish, Japanese and Korean.

MARIE FERRARELLA

Happy New Year—Baby!

This Time Forever

Silhouette® Books

Published by Silhouette Books
America's Publisher of Contemporary Romance

To Sandy Lee, my almost daughter.
Love, Jessica's mom.

SILHOUETTE BOOKS

ISBN 0-373-80933-6

HAPPY NEW YEAR—BABY!

This edition published by arrangement with Harlequin Books S.A.

Visit Silhouette at www.eHarlequin.com

Printed in U.S.A.

Chapter 1

When Dennis Lincoln opened the door, the shower stall exhaled a cloud of steam. The mist hovered about him as he stepped quickly out of the cocooning warmth of the shower onto the tile. He shivered. The rest of the bathroom felt cold.

The headache he'd had when he went to bed still throbbed lightly just outside his temples. Dennis carefully toweled the excess water out of his dark blond hair, then draped the damp towel over the silver rim of the shower stall.

He'd stayed up until past two in the morning, watching the miniature surveillance cameras he had set up. Neither the one in the carport area right outside her door, nor the two within her apartment had picked up any activity. Looked as if it had been a slow night for both of them, he thought. A slow night in a succession of slow nights.

Which was why it was now time for phase two of the operation.

Phase two had been set in motion yesterday with a simple

purchase from Mike's House of Affordable Electronics. Much more than fifty-two inches of sound and screen, the TV gave Dennis a way to meet his quarry. It gave him an excuse to strike up a conversation, get into her apartment *with* her permission, and subsequently into her life. Right now, it seemed the best way to find the answers.

Or, he thought with a wry smile as he glanced in the mirror, if she knew the questions.

Not exactly the way he'd envisioned his future ten years ago, clutching that hard-won law degree. But it suited him.

Even if it didn't suit his face, Dennis mused as he pulled a comb through his wet hair. No one looking at his affable, guileless blue eyes and quirky half smile, complete with dimples, would have ever guessed what his true occupation was.

Which was exactly what made him the best candidate for the job. It allowed him to make contacts, form quick relationships and get to the heart of the matter where a more abrupt, blunter man would have struggled weeks for a toehold.

He'd been here, settled in at Sandcreek Apartments, for over a week now. That amounted to exactly eight days, and thousands of feet of frustration, if counted in video tape.

So far, the cameras and the tap on her phone had yielded nothing out of the ordinary. If she was involved with the Syndicate the way her late husband had been, the involvement was covert. They hadn't attempted to make any contact with her.

Dennis couldn't continue to sit on his hands and wait. Waiting always irritated him even though it was the hallmark of the job. He had to become friendly with her, to cull her favor and her trust.

It shouldn't be too difficult, he judged as he passed the blow dryer over his damp hair with wide, even movements.

Nicole Logan looked as if she needed someone to talk to and he intended to be the one she opened up to.

Blessed with a light beard, Dennis shaved quickly, then rinsed off his razor. His father's razor, he thought absently, looking at the ancient, double-edged shaver. Just about the only thing, besides his hair color, that the old man had to pass on to him before he died.

A razor and an armload of responsibilities Dennis had been too young to understand at the time. Understanding and acceptance came much later.

Placing the razor into the medicine cabinet, Dennis walked into the bedroom and crossed to the rack where he had meticulously laid out his clothes the night before. Image was important. He had to look the part of an up-and-coming tax lawyer on the cusp of tax time.

Something he might have actually been, he thought, slipping on his trousers, had things turned out differently.

But they hadn't, and he never looked back. Not once. This job had instantly given him what he had wanted. A way to take care of his mother and younger sister. His mother had died two years ago and Moira was on her own now, but he still remained with the Department. The money was decent. Having few needs of his own, he spent most of it on his sister.

Up until she had died, he'd used it to spoil his mother, to pay her back, at least in part, for past sacrifices. But that wasn't the only reason he was here. He enjoyed the job. It satisfied his latent lust for adventure that had come to the fore in the last decade.

The same lust, he knew as he shrugged into his tapered mauve shirt, that had gnawed away at his father. Except that he knew how to channel it and Harry Lincoln had not. In the end, his father's avarice and his yearning for more had led to his death. A casualty at the altar of the god of gambling.

Dennis buttoned his cuffs slowly, trying to shake off the thought. Lately, his line of work was taking a toll on him that it hadn't before. It wasn't quite as exciting, quite as interesting or as satisfying as it had once been.

But then, he was on the other side of thirty now, not twenty. Things changed.

What didn't change, he reminded himself, stepping up his pace, was that Sherwood was waiting for results. And it was up to him to deliver them.

Dennis tucked the tails of his shirt into his tan slacks, getting his story straight in his head, should the woman in 176 ask questions. Any questions. Hesitation might raise suspicions and then all his work would be for nothing. Not that he'd invested a great deal of time into this particular phase of the operation, but there was over six months of groundwork that he had put in that he didn't want to see go up in smoke.

Especially now, with the last bit of information Winston had given him. His partner had told him that Paul Trask was the key figure in the gambling syndicate the Justice Department was looking to place behind bars. Paul Trask. That made it personal.

Dennis forced his thoughts back to the moment at hand. He favored simplicity. That meant keeping his cover as close to his own life as possible. There were less mistakes that way. Less room for slipups.

He laughed to himself, though there was no sound. His own life, what was that? It seemed as if it had been an eternity since he had laid claim to having a life outside the Department. An eternity since he had shot hoops with his buddies at the gym or taken in a movie with Moira.

Right after this was wrapped up, he was going to apply for some vacation. God knew he had racked up enough time without using any of it.

Pressing the button on the tie rack his sister had given

him as a joke, Dennis made a quick selection. He hated ties, but they were required—a necessary evil for the image he was projecting. Measuring the ends against one another, he began forming a knot. What sort of a demented fool had conceived of tying a noose around a man's neck and then compounded the insult by calling it a fashion statement?

No question about it. Right after this was over, he promised himself again, he was going to pick up the threads of his life and see about weaving them into some sort of a recognizable tapestry.

Adjusting the knot, Dennis grinned at the simile. Dimples sprang up to both cheeks. Moira would have been proud of him. A Contemporary Literature instructor at UCLA, she was the creative one in the family. He was the practical one.

He'd had to be.

Dressed, with his jacket on his arm, Dennis strode through the living room toward the front door. His goal was not the carport where his vintage Mustang was housed, but the apartment next door.

Her apartment.

She hadn't left since she had come in around six last night. A silent alarm he had rigged beneath her doorsill would have instantly warned him if anyone had come or gone during the night.

Technology certainly made his job easier. But it still didn't replace good old-fashioned legwork. Something he was about to implement.

He'd asked for the big-screen television to be delivered today. It was an extravagance he was paying for out of his own pocket instead of the Department's. The set would eventually find a home within his sister's house. His own studio apartment was hardly large enough for the bed and the table that were in it now. It was far too small to accommodate the set.

Besides, Moira had a fondness for old movies. The set

would be his belated Christmas gift to her. After it did its work. Which was to wangle an instant introduction to the lady next door.

Otherwise known as his assignment.

Nicole Logan wrapped the blue-and-white-striped towel around her dripping dark brown hair. She arranged it into a turban as she walked out of the bathroom. The ends of her bathrobe hardly came together anymore, much less overlapped.

She was outgrowing everything at such a rapid rate that if she didn't give birth soon, she was going to wind up wearing circus tents, she thought glumly.

The shower stall was beginning to make her feel claustrophobic. When she turned within it, it seemed as if her stomach was always brushing against the opaque sides. It took everything she had not to feel despondent. With every passing day, something else was either too small or too tight.

Nicole looked down at her protruding stomach. It certainly looked a great deal larger than her sister's had been just before Marlene gave birth.

She sighed, shaking her head as she went to her closet to try to find something to wear that didn't bind. The way she was going, this baby was going to be the biggest baby born on record.

Everything felt cramped.

And right now, it was also painted in shades of dark blue, like her mood.

Shedding her robe, Nicole got dressed quickly. She purposely avoided looking at herself in the mirrored wardrobe doors. That had gotten to be too much to bear. Though her face mercifully hadn't gained any weight, the rest of her certainly had. The woman reflected there bore little resemblance to the one she had been a scant eight months ago.

Had she ever really worn a size six?

Nicole settled on a cream blouse and a kelly green corduroy jumper which still left her room for growth. The very thought made her shudder. Only when she was dressed did she finally look at herself. The festive color didn't help lighten her mood.

Maybe it was because of the holiday less than a week away. From where she stood, Nicole could see the Christmas tree she'd put up in the living room. She supposed it was hopelessly sentimental of her, but Christmas meant something special. Or it should.

But here she was, twenty-six years old, facing Christmas widowed, pregnant and alone.

No, that wasn't quite right and she knew it, Nicole amended, struggling to get hold of her emotions. She wasn't alone. She had her sister Marlene and that meant quite a lot. Marlene was always there for her. She always had been.

As for being a widow, well, she hadn't been married to Craig in the true sense of the word for some time before his death. Apart from an occasional stopover after he had started winning in a big way on the racing circuit, Craig had distanced himself from her and their life together.

Nicole went into the kitchen to fix herself a cup of tea. Maybe that would help. At least it couldn't hurt. Measuring out a cup of water, she set the kettle on the burner. As the element began to glow red, she felt her eyes begin to smart.

She brushed a hot tear from her cheek. All she managed to do was clear the path for another to come rolling down in its wake. It sped faster because of the trail that had been forged.

Hormones, she thought. Just hormones making her feel sorry for herself. Right now, her emotions were stretched out like a giant rubber band and some unseen hand was mercilessly plucking at it, making it twang first one way, then the other.

The feeling was driving her crazy.

This just wasn't like her. She wasn't the type to sit around and wallow in self-pity like some indulgent, self-centered, pampered brat. She was the one who always fought back. The one who stood up for herself. The one who took risks in order to make her point. She had refused to allow her father to relegate her into a neat little niche the way he had tried to do with her sister. And when James Bailey had seemed to have gone out of his way to ignore Marlene and her after he had divorced their mother, Nicole hadn't begged for his favor. Instead, she had dug in and stood up to him.

And gotten slapped down and then disowned for her trouble.

The kettle screeched, steam billowing out of two tiny holes like smoke emerging from a fire-breathing dragon. She poured water over the waiting tea bag, then dunked it mechanically, her mind skirting the past.

Her father hadn't liked her spunk, he had been annoyed by it.

But Craig had admired it.

A bittersweet smile played on Nicole's lips. Or, at least Craig had said he'd admired her spirit. She tossed away the tea bag, then picked up the mug, cradling it in both hands. The apartment felt cold. She husbanded the bit of warmth she was holding.

Nicole looked down at the dark liquid in her mug and thought of Craig's eyes. They'd been brown like that. Brown and warm and heart melting. Set off by a sexy smile that had broken down all her defenses and clouded her judgment.

How could she have known that it had all been a big act just to get his way? That someone who she had thought was a freewheeling rebel was really just as self-serving as her father had been? Coming from completely opposite directions, Craig Logan and James Bailey managed somehow to walk down exactly the same road.

A road that ran right over her heart.

Needing to feel loved, craving it with every fiber of her being, she'd finally let her guard down and allowed herself to be vulnerable. Or maybe Craig had managed to seep through the walls she had set up around herself. However it had happened, she had fallen blindly in love with him. So blindly that she didn't realize that Craig was in love with the idea of marrying a rich girl and not in love with Nicole.

The word *blind* seemed appropriate. He'd been a blind date, arranged by her roommate. She'd gone on the date reluctantly. Three dates later, Craig had deftly utilized her dissatisfaction with school to get her to drop out of college and run off with him.

A month after she'd met him, Nicole had become Mrs. Craig Logan, convinced that the rest of her life was going to be wonderful. Craig was exciting, a risk taker, someone who wasn't afraid to live on the edge. He was everything her father was not, flamboyant, entertaining, attentive. Any way she looked at it, Craig Logan was just too good to be true.

That should have warned her from the start. But she had been too wrapped up in him and their life together to realize that.

Craig wanted to be a race car driver, setting his sights on becoming the next king of the raceways. The inheritance she'd gotten from her paternal grandmother helped fuel that dream for Craig. It had paid the bills as well as bought the car that he needed to race. She'd been frugal with the money and there was still some left. It was part of what she was living on now.

At first, life with Craig on the road had been very exciting. They went from town to town, following the circuit, making love in dozens of different hotel rooms. It was exhilarating. And so different from the life she had led as James Bailey's rebellious daughter.

Cynicism curved Nicole's mouth as she sipped her tea. Yes, it had been exciting. For about three years. And then it started getting old. Very old. The excitement eventually petered out. The very things that had made it all seem so spontaneous, so glamorous, began to tarnish it. She never had a place to call her home. Never felt settled.

But she tried to tough it out and kept her feelings to herself because Craig seemed so happy. He thrived on the circuit and he was good at racing. If he gambled a little too much, well, that was just his way of letting off steam, he had said.

But one day, sitting alone in a hotel room in Nevada, Nicole took a good look at her life and realized that she didn't have one. Not one of her own at any rate. She had Craig's life and that wasn't enough. She needed something to do besides cheering him on, besides watching the racing groupies bat adoring eyes at him.

When she talked Craig into putting down roots, at least part of the time, near her old home, she had hoped that they had hit upon the perfect compromise.

Fool, she mused now.

But at the time it seemed all right. While Craig continued on the racing circuit, she had remained behind and gone back to college to get the degree she had abandoned for him. She went to classes and attempted to ignore the rumors that returned to her with unsettling regularity. Rumors of Craig and his women.

She'd done what she could to hang on. For a while, she'd even talked herself into believing that it was all hype and that Craig couldn't help it if women threw themselves at him.

It was never the throwing she minded, Nicole thought now. Men like Craig always attracted women and it was to be expected. That went with the territory. It was the catching that bothered her.

It became clearer and clearer to her that Craig was doing his very best to catch every single pass thrown his way. And the money, there always seemed to be huge sums of money going out, more than she thought there should have been. More, she felt, than was coming in. It went to support his lavish lifestyle. She never saw any of it beyond the diamond ring on her hand. As time went on, Nicole became torn between attempting to ride it out and leaving him.

And then, one quarter away from graduating, she'd found out that she was pregnant. It would mean putting her life on hold again, but the thought of a baby excited her and calmed her at the same time. She was going to be a mother, someone's mother. It meant the world to her.

When she told him, Craig had been far from elated about the prospect of becoming a father. That had hurt her more than she'd thought possible. But, with Marlene's support, she had tried to bear it, secretly hoping that once the baby was actually part of their lives, Craig would settle down a little.

Nicole pressed her hand against the huge mound before her as fresh tears followed in the trail left by the others. All that was in the past. A spinout six weeks ago had made the rumors and their future together all moot. Craig was gone. The car had caught fire and there hadn't even been anything to bury. She'd held a memorial service for him and gone on with her life.

She supposed, a lump growing to insurmountable proportions in her throat, that nothing had really changed. She was still here, in this apartment, where she has been during Craig's times on the road. Her plans for her own future hadn't changed. She still intended to be a teacher once the baby was born.

It was just that…

Just...

Oh God.

Nicole closed her eyes, unable to put into words why she felt as if her life were over. It wasn't. She was twenty-six, with a college degree whose ink was barely dry, awaiting the birth of her first child. Life was good, the future was bright.

So why did she feel as if she'd gone skydiving into a bottomless abyss?

Nicole set her mug down on the table. She'd finished her tea without realizing it. Without really tasting it. As she looked down at the empty mug, the buzzing noise in the background registered.

Someone was ringing her doorbell.

Nicole remained sitting at the table. It was a little after eight-thirty. No one came around at this time of day. It was too early. She knew that Marlene was home with her baby. She wasn't expecting anyone and there was no place she was supposed to be. She only worked four days a week at the art gallery. Friday was her day off.

The doorbell rang again, setting her teeth on edge. She wished whoever it was would go away. But that didn't seem likely from the insistent buzz.

Placing her palms on the table, Nicole pushed herself up. Crossing to the door, she looked through the peephole. Nicole blinked to clear her vision. It was the man in 175. The one who had just moved in less than a week ago. What did he want?

"Just a minute." Nicole stepped back and flipped open the locks that she had installed herself. She took a deep breath and hoped she didn't look as awful as she felt. "Yes?"

Dennis had his speech all prepared, but the faint tear stains on Nicole's cheeks stopped him cold.

"You've been crying." Why? he wondered. She hadn't

gotten a call and no one had been by to visit. He watched a fresh tear careen down her cheek. "And you're still crying."

Embarrassed, Nicole rubbed the telltale streaks with the heel of her hand and sniffed.

"No, I'm not. I'm answering the door." She blew out a breath slowly, trying to regain her composure. She knew the man by sight. Curious, she had gone so far as to read his name off the mailbox which was right next to hers, but they'd never exchanged any words. She wished that he hadn't picked now to start. "Is there anything I can do for you?"

Dennis hated tears. It reminded him of all those evenings when he'd heard his mother crying after she thought he and Moira were asleep. He'd never acquired an immunity to them.

Make use of every opportunity, he'd been taught. Sometimes it was harder to remember than others.

He smiled apologetically. "I'm sorry, I didn't mean to walk in on something."

Oh God, sympathy. She couldn't handle sympathy. That would only make her cry more.

Nicole tossed her head, narrowing her eyes. "You didn't."

She felt like an idiot. Her nose was probably red. Nicole wished that he would say what he had to say and then leave.

"Crying jags are common for women in my condition. Look," she said abruptly, cutting herself off, "you didn't ring my bell because you wanted to take a survey on how emotional pregnant women are. Is there something I can do for you?"

Touchy. Obviously not a shrinking violet. It made him feel better.

Dennis glanced down at the key in his hand. "Yes. I'm your new neighbor, Dennis Lincoln. I'm expecting a delivery today, and I can't be here to let the deliverymen in. I called the rental office, but they and maintenance seem to have disappeared off the face of the earth and I can't get anyone to house-sit.''

He paused and looked at her. She wasn't about to volunteer, he guessed. That made him feel better, too. Though it was part of his job, he really didn't care for taking advantage of kindhearted people. Besides, he reminded himself, she'd probably been in on it with her late husband.

''I know it's a huge imposition and this is the last minute and all, but are you working today?''

Dennis already knew the answer to that. He'd had Nicole's complete schedule down pat before he ever moved in.

Nicole shook her head. ''No, today's my day off.'' The day stretched before her, suddenly very large and empty. ''I was just planning to put my feet up and watch my ankles thicken.''

Dennis glanced down at her feet. She was barefoot and had the kind of feet that reminded him of ''Cinderella'': small and dainty. Her ankles were slender and graceful.

''They look pretty good from where I'm standing.''

The compliment, given so spontaneously and guilelessly, made Nicole laugh softly. It felt good. It had been a long time since she had been given a compliment. She smiled at him.

''Thanks, I needed that.''

His smile grew. ''Any time, Mrs. Logan.''

She had no idea why, but for a moment, she entertained the idea of inviting him in. Maybe she was just lonely, or hungry for a kind word. That wasn't like her, either.

He looked as if he was in a hurry.

Just as well, Nicole thought, she wasn't in the market for any new friends. ''What is it that you're having delivered?''

''A big-screen TV.'' Dennis nodded toward his apartment. The door was standing open. "My old one gave up the ghost just before I moved. When I went to replace it, I decided to treat myself to something that I've been wanting to get for a long time."

She knew how that was. Except, in her case, it had been an education, something she had regretted turning her back on in the name of love.

Nicole cocked her head, unable to resist the temptation of looking into Dennis's apartment. From where she stood, she had a clear view of the small living room. It appeared very tastefully furnished, but it was missing something.

Nicole looked at him, curious. "No Christmas decorations?"

It was an oversight he hadn't thought about. Moira normally took care of that end. He never bothered with decorations at his apartment.

Dennis glossed over it casually. "I haven't gotten around to it yet."

It sounded like procrastination to her. Something else she was well acquainted with. Craig did it all the time. Had done it, she corrected herself silently. Had done it. "It's only a few days away."

Moira would really like this woman, Dennis mused. "I don't generally let things go until the last second. This year, however, things have gotten so hectic I seem to be leaving my whole personal life on hold until the last possible moment."

Nicole nodded. He watched, intrigued, as a smile crept into her eyes. They were an interesting shade of indigo.

The comment reminded her of something Marlene might have said. "I have a sister like that. I'm thinking of getting a tranquilizing gun and shooting her with a dart for Christmas."

Her smile broadened when she thought of Marlene. Now, with a brand new baby and maybe even a potential man in her life, perhaps Marlene would finally slow down to a trot instead of a gallop.

Radiant, he thought. There was no other word to describe the way she looked when she smiled other than radiant. Except, perhaps, for ethereal.

Not that that entered into the situation, he reminded himself.

"So you'll let them in?" He held up the key in front of her.

Nicole took it in her hand. "I'll let them in."

"You're a lifesaver." He jerked a thumb behind him. "I'll just tape a note on my door, telling the deliverymen that the key is with you." Dennis hesitated for what he felt was the appropriate amount of time. "You're sure you don't mind?"

Nicole pocketed the key in her jumper, her fingers still curved around it. She shook her head at his question.

"It might be the highlight of my whole day."

The sad look had returned, undermining her smile and chasing it from her eyes. He was tempted to ask her what was wrong.

But that would be getting ahead of the plan.

"Thanks, you're a doll." He turned toward his apartment, then stopped, realizing that he hadn't told her the approximate time. "The store said the deliverymen would be by between eleven and three." That was asking her to stay put for four hours. "I know it's a huge imposition—"

Nicole waved away the concern she saw etched across his face. "No problem. Like I said, I wasn't planning on doing anything today anyway. I'll see that it's delivered in one piece."

"Thanks. I appreciate that."

Dennis turned and taped a note to his door. Nicole watched, surprised. "You were rather sure of yourself, weren't you?"

He turned to look at her over his shoulder. "Hopeful," he amended. "Always hopeful."

She smiled sadly to herself. Hopeful. She'd forgotten what that was like.

Chapter 2

The moment after she had agreed to wait for the delivery, she'd regretted it. There was nothing Nicole hated more than having to wait for something or someone. Whether it meant sitting in Dr. Pollack's office, waiting to be seen, anticipating a delivery, or standing in line before a movie theater, waiting always made her feel fidgety and impatient.

But Dennis Lincoln had looked particularly needy and she was free for the day, so in a moment of weakness, she had said yes.

Now she was stuck with the situation. Sighing, she decided not to waste the day completely and went to work on her ongoing conversion of the small, second bedroom into a nursery.

She had just finished painting one wall when she heard a distant, rumbling noise, like the sound of a truck approaching. Setting down the roller, she looked at her watch. She'd expected the deliverymen to arrive later than the allotted time frame. It was just fifteen minutes into the first hour.

"Nice surprise," she murmured, wiping her hands on a rag as she went to the front door.

"Mr. Lincoln isn't home," she called out to the burly man stepping out of the passenger side of the delivery truck. "But I can let you in."

A kindly smile negated the impression his leathery features created as the deliveryman looked at her condition. He shrugged shoulders that looked as if they belonged on a much taller man. "All the same to us as long as someone signs for it."

The thinner of the two men hopped onto the back of the truck. He angled the television set onto a dolly and then pressed the hydraulic lift to bring them both down to curb level. As he maneuvered the set up onto the curb, Nicole unlocked Dennis's door and pushed it open.

She meant to wait outside. But idle curiosity goaded her on. Succumbing, she walked into the apartment. Nicole looked around slowly. For a man, Dennis kept a very neat home, she thought. There weren't any boxes piled up, the way she might have expected since he had just moved in. Everything looked picture perfect.

"Where do you want it?"

The burly deliveryman's question brought Nicole back to the present. "Oh."

Nicole looked around, debating. Dennis hadn't said anything about where he wanted the set and it wasn't the sort of item that could be easily moved around. Once it was set down, it would be there for the duration, unless he had some strong friends.

There was an empty space facing the sofa. She noticed the cable outlet on the wall a few feet away.

Nicole pointed to it. "There, I guess."

The burly man nodded. "Looks good to me." He and the other deliveryman moved the set into position. Within moments, the cardboard packing was being removed.

While his partner took the flattened cardboard out to the truck, the burly man took out a clipboard and presented it to her. He jabbed a short, stubby finger at a space on the bottom of the form.

"Just sign here, madam, and we will be out of your way."

Nicole wrote down her name, then paused. The deliverymen were probably expecting a tip. She felt in her pocket for a bill. It was empty. Nicole frowned. "I'll just go get my purse—"

The man took the clipboard from her as he shook his head. "No, that's okay. You buy the baby something from me."

He laughed under his breath. Walking out of the apartment, he called out something to his partner. The other man peered out of the back of the truck and laughed as well, but it was a benevolent sound.

Nicole remained in the apartment a moment longer. She was tempted to look around a little more. It wasn't right, but then she'd never slavishly tread the straight and narrow path. If she had, she would have never run off with Craig to begin with.

She approached the closet between the living room and the master bedroom, wondering if it was as neat as everything else or if he was the type to stuff everything out of sight. After a momentary debate, decorum won over curiosity. That and the fact that if the closet was crammed with possessions, they would come tumbling out if she opened the door. She didn't want to spend the next half hour trying to stuff everything back.

Nicole let herself out, locking the door behind her. The delivery truck was just pulling out of the complex. The day looked much too nice to remain cooped up in the apartment with cans of light yellow semigloss paint. Nicole pocketed

Dennis's key and decided to pay a visit to her sister and her brand-new nephew. She needed her spirits lifted.

The sun was fading from the sky when Nicole returned. Walking through the door, she kicked off her shoes. She'd bought them for comfort, but now they pinched. Her feet felt swollen, just like the rest of her. Not that she could see her feet to verify that.

Nicole sighed, trying to take heart in what she'd seen this afternoon. Three weeks after delivery and Marlene looked great. Miraculously, her figure was back to what it had been before she had gotten pregnant.

She opened the refrigerator and poured herself a glass of orange juice. Nicole fervently hoped she'd look as good as Marlene did three weeks after she delivered. Even six weeks after she delivered.

There was something different about her sister, Nicole mused. A definite change that transcended appearance. That undercurrent of urgency to prove something, to constantly achieve something had dissipated. Marlene was a different person now.

Miracles, it seemed, still happened.

Suddenly too tired to make the trip from the kitchen to the living room, Nicole sank down in a chair beside the kitchen table and nursed her glass of juice.

If Marlene still seemed a little tense, she thought, it was because she was really trying hard to be the perfect mother as well as a successful businesswoman.

Nicole's mouth curved, but there was only bitterness in her smile as the word *mother* echoed in her mind. It was small wonder if Marlene felt lost. Her sister had no example to follow. Neither of them did. There were no warm memories of a mother's love to remember, no examples of selfless caring to emulate. They had no real-life experiences to serve as reference.

Nothing other than what Sally had provided as their housekeeper. Sally, who had staunchly remained with Marlene after James Bailey had died, was gruff and spoke plainly, but she had a soft spot in her heart for the motherless children they had been. It was Sally who had given them the only attention and affection she and Marlene had ever known. Still, Sally was no substitute for the real thing.

Nicole looked into her glass, tilting it and coating the sides as she thought. Though they never spoke about it, Nicole imagined that Marlene felt exactly the same way she did. That ever since Laura Bailey had abandoned them, there had been something missing from their lives.

Something very important, no matter how hard she tried to deny it.

Nicole felt her eyes misting again.

Damn, what was it with her today? Everything was making her cry. She hadn't thought about her mother walking out on them in years.

Nicole exhaled loudly, bracing her shoulders which under the present circumstances wasn't easy. She wasn't going to allow memories of her mother, or lack of her mother, to prey on her mind now. As far as she was concerned, her mother was dead. Laura Bailey had died the day she had accepted her husband's generous monetary settlement in exchange for leaving her children's lives forever.

She set down her glass and sniffled. This weepiness had to stop. Being pregnant certainly had its downside. Wiping her eyes with her handkerchief, Nicole curved her other hand around her belly. Though she adored the baby she carried with every shred of the love that no one had ever bothered to tap into, Nicole absolutely hated being pregnant. Almost from the very beginning, it had felt as if she were dragging around an old-fashioned steamer trunk filled to capacity with rocks. Rocks that shifted and moved independently of her. Luckily, she had Marlene to lean on. Marlene had given birth in the beginning of December and knew what lay ahead.

Unlike Marlene who had anticipated the delivery with some trepidation, Nicole couldn't wait to give birth and be done with it. She was passionately looking forward to shedding this elephantine weight she was struggling with. Naturally thin, she had never carried any excess weight until now. And as for her emotions, they had never been in such a state of constant flux as they had been these past months. Minor things taxed her patience and as for the major ones, it was almost beyond endurance. It was a struggle just to get through the day.

Rising, Nicole saw her reflection in the chrome trim on the stove. A pregnant woman was supposed to glow. If that was really true, then someone had failed to issue her the requisite mother-to-be glow kit. Par for the course. If her ship ever came in, she'd probably be standing in the airport at the time.

Damn, she had to shake this mood.

Nicole wandered back to the refrigerator and opened it again. There wasn't anything in it that hadn't been there that morning. It was filled with healthy food. Nothing tempted her. Marlene had asked her to stay for dinner but Nicole had taken a rain check because she wanted to be alone. Why, she hadn't the faintest idea.

Or maybe she did.

Nicole dearly loved her sister, even though they had approached life from different paths, and there wasn't anyone else's company she enjoyed more. But Marlene seemed caught up in her child and even in Sullivan, the brother of the man who had donated his sperm to create Robby. Nicole felt as if she were intruding.

She felt, she thought now as she listlessly shifted food on the top shelf, like an A-number-one grouch right now.

Nicole let the refrigerator door slip from her fingers. It

sighed shut, eliciting an echoing sigh from her. Maybe she'd just catch the news on TV and then go to bed, even though it was early. With any luck, she'd feel better tomorrow.

She'd just walked out of the kitchen when the doorbell rang. Automatically, she glanced at her watch. It was past six o'clock. She wasn't in the mood for visitors. Lately, she mused, she wasn't in the mood for very much. Except for fudge ripple ice cream, and she was all out of that.

The doorbell rang again. Resigned, she crossed to the door. Standing on her toes, Nicole looked through the peephole, prepared to send whoever was on the opposite side of the door on their way.

She sank back on her heels. It was Dennis Lincoln. Now what?

Nicole flipped the locks and opened the door. She left one hand guardedly on the jamb, unwilling to invite him in. "Hi. Is there anything wrong with the television set?"

She'd been crying again, he realized. Her eyes were red rimmed and slightly puffy. Against all regulations and safeguards, something protective stirred within Dennis. He did his best to ignore it.

Dennis shifted the paper bag he'd picked up at the Chinese restaurant. Filled with small cartons of different entrées, the heat radiated through the paper, warming his hands. Following Nicole over the course of the last week, he'd learned little except that she had a fondness for Chinese food.

"No, the set's fine. Great, as a matter of fact." He grinned like a kid with a new toy, which was just the way he figured he was supposed to look, if possessing an oversize TV set had mattered to him. "Maybe you'd like to come over this weekend and watch something—with your husband if he's around."

Every muscle seemed to instantly tighten in Nicole's face. The profile he had on her said she and her late husband hadn't been close in the past couple of years, but they'd obviously been close at least once in that time. He glanced at her stomach. Still, he could see that he had just pulled the scab off a raw wound.

There were times when the job left a bad taste in his mouth.

Nicole lowered her eyes. "I'm afraid that won't be possible."

The stillness in her voice underlined the awkward moment. He didn't want to amplify her pain. Dennis glossed over the moment. "I guess he's not much of a TV buff. Well, then, perhaps you'd like to—"

He didn't know, she thought. There was no reason for him to know, of course. It was just that Craig's death had been such a part of her life in the last month and a half, she unconsciously assumed everyone knew.

She cleared her throat. "My husband's dead, Mr. Lincoln."

He let the appropriate concern register on his face. It wasn't difficult. There was something about the pain in her eyes that drew it out of him naturally.

"Oh God, I had no idea. I'm so sorry." She was really devastated about his death, Dennis thought. Logan had been a damn fool not to have appreciated her. "When did it happen?"

She took a deep breath, distancing herself from the words. "Almost six weeks ago. He was a professional race car driver. His car spun out on the track and hit a wall. They clocked him doing one twenty." Craig had died just as he'd lived. Quickly. There should have been comfort in that, somehow. There wasn't.

"I'm really sorry. I didn't mean to remind you, I mean—"

Nicole waved away his tongue-tied words. There was no need for an apology. "That's all right. The story only made page three of the sports page. There was no reason for you to know.'' She lifted her shoulders in a halfhearted shrug.

After all, it wasn't as if her new neighbor had been an acquaintance. And not even Craig's friends had come to pay their respects when Craig died. She didn't recognize half the people who had attended the funeral. They were people who had populated his new life. Craig had changed from the darkly handsome, gregarious young man he had been when he had started out on the racing circuit. Success had changed him. Or maybe, it had just brought out the man he had actually been.

All water under the bridge. It had been a long time since she had been head over heels in love with Craig. In her heart, Nicole mourned the man she thought she had fallen in love with, not the man who had died. There were times when she believed that the Craig Logan she thought she had known never really existed except in her mind.

This was the point where Dennis was going to be sympathetic. He had planned it this way. But as the words rose to his lips, Dennis felt uncomfortable with the role he was playing. Whether or not she knew about, or condoned, her husband's involvement with the Syndicate, this had to be a rough time for her.

''Listen, if there's anything I can do—if you need anything—help around the apartment, something like that, I'm pretty handy when I find the time.''

Nicole shook her head. ''I'm fine, really.'' If she needed anything, she'd call maintenance before she'd knock on his door. He wasn't anything to her, even if he did have kind eyes. ''Oh, before I forget.'' She dug into her pocket. ''Here's your key.''

He took it from her and she stepped back, ready to close the door. Her gaze fell on the package in his hands. There was a translucent stain on the bottom of the bag.

"Well, goodbye. I don't want to keep you from your dinner."

"You're not, exactly." He looked down at the bag. "This was my way of saying thank you for this afternoon. I bought dinner for two. You and your..." His voice trailed off, purposely lost in an implied apology. Dennis offered the bag to her. "Chinese food. Since you're alone, maybe I could join you if I manage to have the feet in my mouth surgically removed."

The aroma was tempting. It had resurrected her dormant appetite and his manner was disarming in a soft, puppy dog sort of way. Still, she hardly knew him. Nicole shook her head. "I don't—"

He wasn't going to give her the chance to say no. "I don't have anything nearly this good waiting for me in my refrigerator."

"Then maybe you'd better take it." She pressed the bag toward him, but he didn't accept it.

"Old custom, never take back a bag of Chinese food. It's bad luck." Then, before she could protest further, he opened the bag in her hands and looked in as if he didn't already know what it contained. "Wonton soup."

She loved wonton soup. Nicole struggled to remain strong. She pushed the bag back into his hands. "No, I—"

"With sweet and sour pork, lobster Cantonese and Moo Goo Gai Pan." He raised his eyes to hers. She was weakening, he thought. Dennis felt pleased, but there was a faint trace of guilt as well. "I've also got fried rice and appetizers."

Nicole could feel her mouth watering. What would it hurt? He looked harmless enough.

"I wasn't sure what you'd like," he continued. "Other than the fact that everyone likes Chinese food."

She felt her mouth curving in a small smile. "You took a survey?"

His grin grew larger. "No, but I never met anyone who didn't."

There were probably people somewhere who didn't like Chinese food, but she certainly wasn't among their number. Nicole glanced at the greasy bag. "It looks as if your Moo Goo is trying to make a break for it."

The bag was threatening to tear. Dennis spread his hand protectively over the bottom. An edge of the carton was already beginning to protrude. "I need someplace to put this down."

She nodded toward his door. "Your kitchen comes to mind."

Dennis glanced over his shoulder. "Sure, if you'd rather eat there. My cleaning lady was just in yesterday, so—"

That would account for the neat state of the apartment, she thought.

"No, I meant that you should eat it in your kitchen." She really didn't feel like having company. Talking about Craig had brought memories back to her. Memories that hurt.

He raised the bag. The blend of aromas was doing its own selling, but it didn't hurt to push just a little. Obviously his attempt at conversation wasn't enough to gain entry to her home or her confidence. And now he'd need to hire a cleaning lady. "It's a lot of food for just one person and leftovers have a habit of turning a strange shade of green in my refrigerator before I get back to them." One look into her eyes told him he had her. "Besides, I'd feel better about putting you out this morning."

She could almost taste the egg rolls. "Well..."

He went in for the kill. "And I was raised to believe that neighbors should be neighborly. This will be my chance to do something neighborly."

It was becoming obvious that if she didn't agree to have dinner with him, he would stand here, talking all night. She supposed that there was no harm in sharing a meal with him.

Nicole stepped back, allowing him access to her apartment. Being on her own terrain would make her feel a lot better than being on his. He sounded like someone with small-town values, but you never knew.

Neighborly. Now there was a word she hadn't heard in a long time. "Exactly where were you raised?" The door thudded shut behind her and she deliberately left the top lock opened. It never hurt to be careful.

If she'd employed that prudence earlier, maybe she wouldn't be in this predicament now.

No, her pregnancy wasn't a predicament, she corrected fiercely. Just the beginning had been.

Dennis placed the bag on the kitchen table just in time. The rest of it ripped away. The carton of fried rice in the bottom of the bag made unceremonious contact with the tabletop. His hand greasy, Dennis automatically reached for a paper towel from the roll above the sink.

"I'm from Houston," he answered as he wiped his hands. It was only one of many cities he and his family had passed through, but it was as good as any to tell her. He looked around for someplace to discard the paper towel.

Nicole opened the cupboard beneath the sink and indicated the small pail there. "That would explain the twang."

He grinned as he tossed the crumpled towel away. "What twang?" he asked innocently, purposely thickening it for her benefit.

"Yours."

"I don't have one," he informed her with a straight face. "I've been in California for the last eleven years. Whatever accent I had has long since been washed out by the surf."

"You drawl," she contradicted. "Just a little." And she had to admit that she found it rather cute. He made her think of lean, tall Texans and other things long buried in childhood fantasies. "I think it comes out most when you say 'ma'am.'"

She watched, intrigued as he made himself at home in her kitchen. It would have annoyed her if he hadn't done it so effortlessly, so guilelessly.

Dennis took out the cartons from the bag one by one and placed them in a semicircle in the middle of her table. He laughed. "I'll have to remember not to say it, then." Carefully, without being obvious, he took in his surroundings as he worked.

Her apartment was a true mirror image of his own. What was on the right in his apartment was on the left in hers. The only difference was that her apartment was a great deal more cluttered than his. Housekeeping was not a high priority for this woman. Somehow, it seemed to fit her.

The bag emptied, Dennis deposited it into the garbage, then turned to her cupboards. Taller than Nicole by almost a foot, Dennis reached up and took out a stack of plates before she had a chance to stop him or do it herself.

Nicole stepped back from the table as he began to set it. Wariness crept in. He seemed a little too comfortable in her apartment. She didn't want him getting any wrong ideas. Men had a habit of thinking that widows were emotionally needy and vulnerable. The last thing she wanted was for a man to think of her as vulnerable.

Turning, Dennis saw the look in her eyes. It was the same kind of look a hermit had when he discovered poachers on his land. He could almost guess what she was thinking. Dennis shrugged, making light of it.

"Sorry." Taking out the utensils, he placed a fork and a spoon beside each of the two main plates. "I'm used to doing for myself."

She just bet he was. Nicole stood behind her chair, keeping the table between them. "Even in someone else's apartment?"

She certainly wasn't trusting, but then, maybe she didn't have any reason to be. "It feels like mine, only in reverse." As an afterthought, he drew out a napkin from the holder and tucked one beneath each set of utensils. "It's like I tumbled through the looking glass."

Or through his camera lens, he added silently. He'd certainly seen this scene often enough in the last few days. He avoided looking toward the small transmitter he'd positioned on the far end of the top of her refrigerator. Through it, he could see the entire kitchen and part of the living room. There was an identical transmitter planted in the nursery, letting him see that room and the small hallway beyond.

He gestured at the set table. "Besides, you look as if you've had a long day and you're tired. My guess is that you could do with a little pampering."

She hadn't done very much to speak of, but he was right about her being tired. Carrying this baby around made her feel as if she were working a twelve-hour shift in the coal mines. And it was nice to be waited on for a change. Usually, she just heated something up and ate it straight out of the pot.

Rather than argue, she sat down at the table. Dennis got busy.

Wisps of steam curled above the soup as he poured it into the two bowls. It smelled heavenly. It was as if he'd read her mind. She raised her eyes to Dennis's face. "You don't have to do this, you know."

He conceded the point, but he added, "And you didn't have to let those deliverymen in for me, but you did. One favor deserves another and this is the least I can do."

Counting the appetizers, there were six small white cartons. Carefully, he deposited the contents of each one on a plate, adding a fork on the side. Within minutes, the cartons were cleared away and the table looked as if it belonged in a restaurant. Only then did he take a seat opposite her in the small breakfast nook.

He was waiting for her to begin. Feeling slightly self-conscious, she dipped her spoon into the soup. "You do that well." She nodded at the table setting.

Dennis grinned as memories returned to him. "Old habit. I worked as a waiter to put myself through college," he added in answer to the question that rose in her eyes. That much was true. "There are times I look down and still expect to see one of those half aprons tied around my waist."

She took more than her share of lobster. Realizing what she'd done, Nicole began to place some of it back on the plate until he stopped her.

"Enjoy it," he urged.

He made it difficult to resist. "How long did you work as a waiter?"

"Five years." Passing up the lobster, he took a spoonful of the fried rice and then topped it with a helping of spicy chicken. In her condition, she would avoid it.

Nicole thought of how harried Marlene had been, going to college and working for their father in her so-called "off" time. "Must have been hard, working and studying at the same time."

He shrugged. At the time, it had been well worth the struggle. "When you want something badly enough, you find a way to get it. Obstacles don't matter. Making the goal does."

Now he really did sound like Marlene. Nicole stopped eating and studied the man sitting across from her. "And what's your goal, Mr. Lincoln?"

He gave an exaggerated shiver. "Please, call me Dennis. When you say 'Mr. Lincoln' like that, I feel like I should be wearing a stovepipe hat and tugging at my beard."

Though he was tall, he was muscular and his hair was a dirty blond. He wore it on the longish side, which led her to believe that whoever he worked for wasn't a stickler for decorum.

She didn't particularly want to be on a first name basis with him. That left the door open to becoming more personal than just nodding at one another in passing. And she had all the friends she needed. Or wanted.

"You're the wrong coloring. And you're not gaunt enough." His eyes were still on hers, waiting. Nicole paused, then relented. "All right, Dennis, what is your goal?"

He told her what she wanted to hear. What he might have wanted for himself if he led a more normal life. "What every man wants. To have a good job, to be a success at what I do. To have a family." That sounded a little too perfect. He paused, then added, "Eventually."

The honesty surprised her. He was probably too busy sowing oats everywhere. With his looks, he wouldn't lack for takers. "But not now."

"No, not now," he affirmed with feeling. "I still have a long way to go before I ask someone to marry me and share my life."

Nicole looked down at her plate and wondered where the lobster Cantonese had disappeared to. Could she have eaten it that fast? "Maybe she'll ask you to share hers."

If she was looking for an argument, she wouldn't find one here. "Even better. An independent woman."

Nicole sombered as she raised her eyes to his. "You're patronizing me."

Definitely accustomed to being challenged, Dennis decided. "No, I'm feeding you." He deliberately drawled. "Like it?"

Maybe she was being too edgy. Maybe he wasn't anything more than he claimed to be, just a nice man saying thank-you. In her case, that would be a first.

She helped herself to the rest of the lobster. "It's good."

Mentally, he took another step forward. "I bought this at Sun-Luck's." The restaurant was a popular one at the local mall, one he had seen her enter earlier in the week. "Familiar with it?"

Nicole started at the name, a myriad of emotions crisscrossing through her. It was at Sun-Luck's that she had told Craig that she was pregnant. It was her favorite restaurant. Once it had been *their* favorite restaurant. Nicole had picked the familiar surroundings to break the news to Craig.

He'd walked out on her, leaving her sitting with strangers staring at her.

"Yes," she answered, her tone flat. "I'm familiar with it."

But not in a good way, he thought. His curiosity was piqued, but he let it pass. He wasn't here to satisfy idle curiosity, he was here to do a job.

Dennis divided one of the egg rolls and offered her half. Nicole looked at it as if she were regarding a peace offering. After a beat, she accepted it. He couldn't recall ever seeing such wariness in a woman before.

"So," he continued pleasantly, as if attempting to smooth over the rough spot he had inadvertently created, "are you planning on staying here?"

The garden apartment complex was occupied predominately by singles and childless couples. Having a baby here set her apart, but then, he had a feeling that Nicole Logan was accustomed to standing out.

Nicole sat up as straight as her condition allowed. "Yes." The conformation was defiantly uttered.

He picked his way through the minefield carefully. He didn't want to say anything that would alienate her. "Good for you. Then you've turned the second bedroom into a nursery?"

What did he care what she did with her second bedroom? And why was he here in the first place? In her experience, men who smiled the way he did and came bearing gifts were after something.

And she had absolutely nothing left to give.

Her voice was tight, her cadence measured. "Yes, it is."

This was going to be a lot more difficult than he thought. "Hey, whoa, that wasn't meant to be a call to arms."

She placed her fork down, her appetite disappearing. "Why are you asking me these questions?"

Had he come on too strong? Or was it just that she was naturally wary of strangers? The profile he had on Nicole Logan labeled her gregarious. It didn't seem to jibe with the woman sitting before him.

"It's called making conversation, Nikki," he answered mildly.

Nicole stiffened instantly. Craig had called her that. And she didn't want to be reminded of Craig anymore. "My name is Nicole, not Nikki. Or, in your case, Mrs. Logan." She rose from the table. Letting him in had been a mistake. "Look, this was very nice of you, but—"

The doorbell rang, cutting into her dismissal. She turned and looked accusingly at the door. It was getting to be like LAX in here.

Hand to the small of her back, attempting to contain the ache that had materialized there, the one that always came these days when she sat too long, Nicole crossed to the door. Exasperated at the interruption and annoyed with herself for allowing Dennis into her apartment in the first place, she forgot to look through the peephole. Instead, she yanked the door open.

There was a good-looking, well dressed older man standing in her doorway. He looked vaguely familiar, though she couldn't place him. He smiled at her, but his eyes were deader than the promises that Craig had made to her.

"Mrs. Logan?" Dark blue eyes swept over her as the stranger said her name.

Instinctively, Nicole wanted to back away, but she remained where she was. She was vaguely aware of Dennis rising behind her. Nicole looked at the man's chiseled profile and tried to recall if she had met him on the circuit during the days when she had traveled with Craig.

She couldn't remember.

Bingo, Dennis thought, recognizing the man as the owner of one of the casinos the Syndicate numbered as their own.

Holding the door ajar, Nicole stood blocking the man's way. "Yes?"

The man's smile was cold, isolating her. "I'm here to collect what's mine."

Chapter 3

The man made her feel uneasy, but years of experience had taught her how to mask her feelings. Nicole lifted her chin.

"I'm afraid that there has been some mistake made, Mr.—"

If she was attempting to be defiant, it made less than no impression on him. "Standish." The name rolled smoothly off his tongue. "Joseph Standish."

The name meant nothing to her. The dislike Nicole felt was immediate and intense. If the man continued to look vaguely familiar, it was because Joseph Standish, if that was really his name and she doubted that it was, reminded Nicole of the type of people Craig had taken to hanging around with the year before he died. Dangerous people.

People she didn't want anywhere near her or her unborn child.

"Mr. Standish," she acknowledged coldly. "I'm afraid that I don't have anything of yours."

His lips parted slightly in what could have passed for a smile if it hadn't been so mocking. His tone remained mild and all the more chilling for it.

"Oh, but I'm 'afraid' that you do, Mrs. Logan." His eyes swept past her and the man behind her to look at the apartment. It had to be hidden here somewhere. "Mind if I take a look around?"

Nicole's breath caught in her throat. He was going to push his way in. She didn't want him touching her things. She squared her shoulders. "Yes, I do mind."

Whether she minded or not didn't matter to him. What was on that disk that Logan had managed to steal did.

Dennis took a step closer to Nicole, his eyes locking with Standish's. They were as flat as the eight-by-ten photograph he'd been given at his initial briefing. Dennis had seen more warmth in a tray of ice cubes.

"Is there a problem here?"

Nicole was weary of fighting her own battles, but used to it. So much so that she automatically resented any interference. Still, she had to admit that a small part of her felt better having Dennis here beside her. It made her feel less vulnerable.

Standish assessed the man behind Logan's widow with a speed that had become second nature to him. Tall, rangy, the man didn't really appear as if he'd pose much of a threat, but then, you never knew.

"The only problem is you butting into a private conversation."

His eyes flickered over Nicole. Even with that swollen belly, she was something to look at. Probably had been a hot little number in bed. Too bad Logan hadn't spent more time at home in bed and less at the tables. This trip would have been unnecessary, then. Standish hated loose ends almost as much as he hated unpaid debts. He had thought that things had been all tied up with Logan's death—until they couldn't find the disk.

"My business is with Mrs. Logan."

Since she didn't know him, that meant whatever connection Standish had, had been with Craig. That was all behind her now. She didn't want any part of it. Nicole looked at him coldly, even as her heart hammered.

"I don't have any business with you." Turning the doorknob, she started to close the door. "So if you'll please leave—"

Standish's hand shot out like a rattlesnake striking its prey. With his palm splayed against the door, he prevented her from closing it. He had no intention of leaving yet. He hadn't gotten to where he was by allowing people to walk away from him when he wasn't done with them. And this was far from finished.

His words were measured and sharp, like hail falling against a tin roof. "You're right, you don't have any business with me. Your husband did." His eyes remained on Nicole, cutting the other man completely out of the picture. "Too bad he had to die so young. My condolences."

Nicole felt as if she were looking into the eyes of Death. "Thank you."

"A few weeks before he died, he took something from me. Something I'm very sentimental about." He smiled, showing off two perfect rows of teeth. "I was hoping it was here."

She hadn't seen anything out of place amid the things Craig kept here and if Standish was sentimental, then she was a choirboy. "What was it?"

He had no intention of telling her. "I'll know it if I see it. Don't trouble yourself by looking, I'll just—" He began to enter the apartment.

She didn't want this man here. Like a militant soldier,

she barred his way. "You'll tell me what it is, or you'll leave."

She was going to be trouble, just like her husband, Standish thought. He hated using a gun. It was far too messy and personal, but he had no qualms about eliminating what was in his way.

"After I look around."

Very gently, Dennis pushed Nicole to the background, his body a buffer between her and Standish. "The lady said to leave."

She saw something that frightened her flicker in Standish's eyes. Damn Craig and his stupidity. What had he gotten them into?

She placed her hand on Dennis's arm, silently telling him that she could handle this. "Craig kept very little of his things here, Mr. Standish. He traveled a lot. Maybe whatever it is that you're looking for was left behind in some hotel room."

Rooms in seven different hotels had all been systematically torn apart. "I've already eliminated that possibility. He was here before his last race."

For a total of about ten minutes, she thought. Bent on partying before the big race, Craig had left her behind like so much lead weight. Even so, she hadn't been able to bring herself to go through Craig's things yet. She'd meant to, but every time she started, the pain of memories prevented her.

Nicole sighed. "Leave your number and I'll call you if I find anything, but I doubt—"

"Don't doubt, Mrs. Logan. He had it. I know that for a fact. I suggest you find it, Mrs. Logan." Each time he said her name, she felt as if he were laughing at her. "And quickly." His glance lowered from her face to rest on her abdomen. "Unfortunate things have been known to happen, even to ladies in your delicate condition when they don't cooperate."

Numbed by the barely veiled threat, Nicole curved her hand protectively over her belly. Words failed her.

Dennis shook off her hand from his arm, pushing himself directly into Standish's face. Though the same height, he guessed that the other man had about five years on him. And a few more pounds. The slight bulge under his coat was what he used to even things out. Dennis knew he could disable him before he ever reached for his weapon, but that wouldn't be in keeping with the image he was trying to project for Nicole.

"She said to leave." His voice was as low, as deliberate, as Standish's. "I think she meant now."

There was nothing to be gained by a physical confrontation, at least not one with a witness. Standish was accustomed to picking his places. There would always be time enough for that later, if necessary. Trask said to keep the body count down to a minimum after Logan. Trask was getting old and soft, but for now, he still ran the Syndicate and had to be obeyed.

Standish inclined his head, addressing himself to Nicole. "Fine. I realize that all this must have taken you by surprise, Mrs. Logan. I'm not an unreasonable man. But I do tend to grow impatient if I'm kept waiting too long. I'll be back."

He paused to consider a time frame. "Say in a week?" He had no intention of waiting that long. His eyes skimmed over her girth before he stepped away from the door. "In the meantime, if I were you, I would give very serious consideration to what I said."

Hands shaking, Nicole slammed the door closed behind Standish. Only then did she give in to the fear that had taken hold of her.

"Oh, God," she whispered.

She looked as if she were going to faint. Dennis quickly took her arm. Her skin had turned almost translucent and her hands were clammy. "Are you all right?"

Nicole passed her hand over her face. What could Craig have possibly taken from that man? It couldn't have been money, Standish would have asked for that outright—wouldn't he?

She didn't look at Dennis as she replied. "Not really."

Dennis guided her to the chair in the kitchen, then placed a hand on her shoulder, gently urging her into it. "Why don't you sit down?" He studied her face, wondering how to handle this new turn of events. Either she really didn't know the man who was just here or anything he was talking about, or she was one hell of an actress. "So, what are you going to do?"

"I don't know." She shrugged helplessly. She could call the police, but what good would that do? There wasn't really very much information she could give them. They usually responded after the fact, not before. "It was probably just an empty threat."

Men like Standish didn't make empty threats. It was bad for business. "It didn't sound very empty from where I was standing."

"No," Nicole whispered, "it didn't." She looked up, suddenly realizing that she had said the words aloud. She tried to gloss over the situation. "Craig periodically got involved with people who wouldn't have met with approval at a Daughters of the American Revolution meeting."

Dennis nodded his head toward the door. "So then this is nothing new for you?"

"I didn't say that." Nicole took a long, steadying breath. She could handle this. She'd handled everything else until now. She just didn't know how yet. "They've just never made house calls before."

God, what a fool Craig had been. Could she have really been in love with him? Could she have really been so damn blind and missed all these defects when she had agreed to run off with him?

She knew the truth now. She hadn't been running away with Craig so much as running away from home. And her father.

Nicole ran her hands along her arms. She felt cold, even as the heater was turning over.

"It wasn't enough for him to have it all," she murmured, half to herself, half to Dennis. "Fame, women hanging on him, money, it wasn't enough." Sadness rimmed her smile. "He wanted more."

She looked at Dennis, who was patiently listening to her. Why, she still hadn't figured out. Just as she didn't know why she was even saying this, except that it had been bottled up for so long and he was a stranger, not a friend. Sometimes it was easier to talk to strangers.

"There were a few pockets of time when he gambled away more than he earned, even with all the endorsements coming in."

They'd come, she remembered, courting the new king of the track, and he had eaten it up. Anyone else would have been set for life. But not Craig. With him there had been this huge hole that no one and nothing seemed to be able to fill.

She sighed as she looked at the door she had slammed in Standish's wake. He'd be back. She didn't know what she was going to do when he came. She was almost positive that she didn't have anything that might belong to him. "I guess this is one of those times."

She looked so small, so vulnerable. It made Dennis forget for a moment that he wasn't supposed to get involved in anyone's troubles.

"So, what are you going to do?" he repeated.

For a moment, she'd forgotten that he was here. She'd been talking out loud to herself. But he was here, and he shouldn't have been. She distanced herself from him. "That's my problem."

He'd had a feeling she'd say that. Feisty didn't begin to describe her. Though it got in his way, he had to admire that. "Living next door to you kind of makes it mine."

The logic escaped her. "And just how do you figure that?"

Dennis grinned at her. "It's that neighborly thing again."

As she had said, it wasn't his problem. It wasn't anyone's problem but hers, courtesy of Craig. She'd find a way out. Tomorrow, when she was less exhausted and could think clearly. After all, she couldn't give Standish what she didn't have. He had to be satisfied with that—didn't he?

Nicole blew out a breath as she looked at Dennis. "There's such a thing as being too neighborly. Don't worry about it."

The woman had more courage than brains. There was no doubt in his mind that she hadn't seen the last of Standish. "Do you want me to stay here tonight?"

Nicole stared at him. Where had that come from? She was exhausted and hugely pregnant. That should have turned anyone off.

"No." As soon as she turned him down, something small within Nicole wavered, afraid. She buried it quickly. She was a big girl now, and had been on her own for a long time.

The offer seemed like the right thing to say. Besides, though he was next door, he didn't like the idea of her remaining alone for the night. Standish might decide that a week was too long to wait and return in the middle of the night. If the man entered through the door, it would trip the alarm system he had rigged, but if he entered through the sliding patio door, Standish could harm Logan's widow before he had a chance to reach her.

"Would you rather stay at my place?" He kept the suggestion low-key. "I've got a sofa that folds out in the den. You could have my bed."

God, he almost sounded chivalrous, but she knew better. No man was altruistic. They always wanted something in return. "No."

She was being difficult. It only stood to reason that she'd feel better with someone she knew. "Do you have any other place to stay?"

"If I wanted to." Her eyes met his. She saw the question he was about to ask. "I don't want to. It'll be all right," she added with an assurance she only hoped was true. Maybe if she said it a few times, she would eventually believe it.

He'd hidden his surveillance equipment while the delivery was being made, but he was going to set it up again as soon as he left her. And it looked as if he were going to be staying up late tonight. He knew that Dombrowski would cover for him while he slept, but somehow, that didn't seem good enough just now.

Dennis noticed a pen in the corner of the counter. Leaning over the table, he pulled out a blue napkin from the plastic holder and wrote seven digits on it.

"Here." He held out the napkin to her.

She stared at it, making no move to take it. "What is it?"

It was like trying to lead a mustang to water. He was getting kicked for his trouble. Dennis took her hand by the wrist and placed the napkin into her palm. "My phone number."

She wasn't helpless and she didn't accept aid from a stranger under any circumstances. Despite the meal they'd shared, that's what they were. Strangers. She didn't know any more about him than she knew about Standish.

Except that he didn't make her blood run cold, the way Standish did. And he smelled good.

"Why would I want that?"

This one put a new spin on stubbornness. He wondered if it was her pregnancy that had her behaving this way, or if she had always been so bullheaded. "So you can call me in case you have any strange visitors in the night that don't go 'Ho-ho-ho.'"

Nicole frowned at the napkin, but she didn't crumple it and throw it away the way he half expected her to. Instead, she folded it in half as she looked at him.

"Why would you want to get involved in this?" she challenged.

There was nothing in it for him. She had long since passed the point where she was dazzled by a sexy smile and a drop-dead body. And if she had once wished for love and acceptance, well, that had fallen by the wayside as well. The price tag was too high and the returns too low on the emotional investment that was required of her. Love was a highly overrated emotion. So what was he doing, offering to be her protector?

She was suspicious of his motives. He wondered if she had something to hide, or if she was just being prudent. If that was the case, he couldn't say he blamed her. Craig Logan might have been a winner on the track, but he was a real loser otherwise. He could understand her being leery of men.

"Let's just say I've always had a secret fantasy about rescuing a damsel in distress."

Nicole's frown deepened. Did he really expect her to believe him? "In this case, the damsel probably outweighs you."

Dennis laughed. She was large, there was no disputing that, but she was also petite and that exaggerated the image. Having seen a photograph of Nicole before she had become pregnant, he knew exactly how stunning she could be.

"I sincerely doubt that. I hit the scales at 185."

And all of it looked pretty solidly built from what she could see. Nicole shook off the thought. She was being adolescent. "If you think I'm telling you what my scale says, you're more naive than I thought."

Naive, now there was a word that wouldn't have described him, not since he was nine years old. Children of gamblers grew up quickly.

He leaned against the doorjamb and smiled engagingly. "And why would I be naive?"

She glanced at the remainder of their meal. "For getting involved with a pregnant widow whose late husband seemed to have ran afoul of the wrong crowd."

He lifted a shoulder and let it drop casually. "What's life without a challenge?"

She didn't need a challenge. She needed a little smooth sailing for a while. Maybe forever.

"Life is challenge enough," she murmured, looking out the window. She hoped that Standish would keep his word and stay away for a week. Maybe by then she'd be able to find whatever it was that he was looking for.

It would have helped if he had been more specific. Dennis saw the worried look flitter through her eyes. "Are you sure you don't want—"

"I'm sure," she said abruptly, cutting him off before he could try to change her mind. This time, she might just let him. "Thank you for dinner."

He enveloped her hand between his. It felt small, frail. Her manner had almost made him forget just what a delicate woman she really was. "The pleasure was all mine."

He was being incredibly polite. Her mood at dinner had been rather surly and then Standish had made his appearance. All in all, it didn't make anyone's listing of top ten evenings.

"Then I would say that you have a very low threshold of pleasure, Mr. Lincoln—"

He arched a brow. "It's Dennis, remember?"

She sighed and nodded. "I remember."

"And my threshold isn't low at all." He had a feeling that she had very little to smile about. Maybe he could do something about that. His smile widened beguilingly. "Maybe we can discuss that threshold some time."

"Maybe," she agreed, closing the door behind him. "But I wouldn't hold my breath if I were you," she added quietly.

Nicole tucked the napkin with his phone number into her pocket and went to clear the table.

Surveillance equipment in place, Dennis maintained vigil until two in the morning. He knew that Dombrowski had spelled Winston in the converted VW van that was inconspicuously parked in the carport. Two sets of eyes were better than one.

Accustomed to snatching catnaps whenever he could and able to run on next to no sleep, he managed to get a few hours in the recliner beside his monitors. Even then, he slept lightly, anticipating the telephone ringing at any moment.

It didn't.

When he opened his eyes again, it was a little past seven. Immediately, he looked at the monitors. Nothing had changed in the parking lot. The same cars that had been there last night were still in their designated spots. The second monitor showed only an empty room. Nicole wasn't anywhere in sight.

Dennis sat up. Rotating his shoulders and stretching, he was instantly awake, instantly alert.

That was due to his training. By nature, he wasn't really a morning person. His sister Moira was one of those. Bright and cheerful before her first cup of coffee. He didn't understand it.

He needed a cup of coffee now, he thought. A strong one.

Still wearing the jeans he'd had on last night, Dennis padded out to the kitchen. He turned on the coffeemaker and opened the front door to get the paper.

As he bent over the mat, reaching for the newspaper, he heard her.

There was a gasp, followed by a cry of anguish and then a few choice words that could have only been evoked under duress.

She was in trouble. Damn, how had Standish managed to get in without either he or Dombrowski seeing the man?

Moot point, he admonished himself.

She hadn't called him, but then maybe she hadn't had the opportunity. Maybe she had been overpowered instantly. It was the only thing that made sense.

Adrenaline pumping, Dennis banged his fist on Nicole's door.

"Nicole, are you all right?" he demanded. There was no reply. He pounded on it again. "Nicole, open the door!"

It was a fire door. He could dead lift twice his body weight, but there was absolutely no way he could force the door open. But he could break open a window.

Dennis turned away from the door and toward the kitchen window when the door swung open.

She stood in the doorway, wearing a pink dress that was far more cheerful that she was at the moment. The apron that no longer fit around her waist was slung over her right shoulder.

Exasperation filled her voice as she snapped, "No, I am not all right and why are you yelling like that?" He'd scared her half to death, banging on her door. She thought it was Standish.

Her sharp tone faded a little as she realized that he was wearing only his jeans and that he had failed to close the snap. It hovered more than an inch below his navel, adhering to tapered hips that belonged in an exercise video. She'd already guessed last night that he was muscular, but she hadn't realized just how well developed those muscles were.

His torso had almost perfect definition. If her hands weren't already damp, they would have become so.

"What's wrong?" Dennis demanded as he looked beyond her shoulder into the apartment. There was no one there.

She wiped her hands on the edge of the apron. "You're the one yelling and banging, you tell me."

Whatever the problem was, it wasn't Standish. "I heard you gasp and cry out."

Her brows drew together as she fisted her hands where her waist used to be. "What are you doing, standing at my door and listening?"

"No, I was getting the paper." He raised it to substantiate his story. "When I heard you gasp I thought that maybe Standish had forgotten how to count and turned up. I was worried," he added for good measure. It irritated him that it was partially true.

What he said made her feel guilty. He didn't deserve to be the target of her waspish tongue. It wasn't Dennis's fault that her garbage disposal had decided to pick today to throw up. Lately, that seemed to be the way her life was going.

She sighed, dragging a hand through her hair, her expression softening. "Well, you can rest easy. No one took a contract out on me during the night. Except, maybe, for my garbage disposal." She glanced over her shoulder. "It seems that it's not up to grinding chicken bones anymore and has sought retribution by clogging up my sink."

The tension created by the spontaneous flow of adrenaline began to ease from his body. A grin lazily crept over his lips. "They run independently of each other."

She didn't want logic at a time like this. She wanted an unclogged sink. Annoyance raised its hoary head again.

"Well, something is clogging up my sink." She gestured toward the kitchen floor angrily. "I was rinsing out a frying pan and suddenly, I've got a lily pond in my kitchen."

Not waiting for an invitation, Dennis walked into her

apartment. Barefoot, he picked his way gingerly across the wet floor to the sink. He flipped the switch closest to the door and was rewarded with a whining noise that sounded like a car slipping a gear. A moment later, a wisp of smoke emerged from the midst of the rubber covering over the in-sink eradicator.

He shut off the disposal quickly. Squatting, Dennis opened the cabinet doors beneath the sink and looked in. He began moving aside an army of cleansers as he worked his way to the wall.

Nicole tried to bend down and peer over his shoulder. The ache in her back curtailed the effort. "What are you doing?"

He found the cord and followed it to the plug. He worked it free from the wall. "Unplugging your disposal before you have a fire."

She looked down at the floor. It wasn't exactly a lily pond, but there was enough water to remove the wax shine. Suddenly, she felt overwhelmed.

"The water would put it out," she said wearily.

Dennis rose, brushing his hands off on his jeans. "Got a mop?"

"Of course I've got a mop," she said defensively. Just because she wasn't a neat freak like Marlene didn't mean she was an utter slob. "Why?"

Justifying everything to her was getting a little old. "I want to dry the floor before one of us lands on our butts."

He said "us" but he meant her. She could tell by the way he looked at her. She didn't need someone inferring that she was a klutz. "Well, leave and then you won't be in danger."

He only laughed and shook his head. "Nicole, you are definitely a challenge to be neighborly to."

All right, so she was being grumpy, but she couldn't help it. She was always grumpy when she was tired. Stubborn about maintaining her independence, she'd remained up most of the night, listening to every noise that didn't sound as if it belonged. In a garden complex of 203 apartments there were a lot of noises that sounded as if they didn't belong.

She gestured toward his apartment. "It's Saturday. Why aren't you watching your new TV?"

He had a simple enough answer for that. "I don't watch cartoons."

"You don't have a VCR?"

He thought of all the electronic equipment in his apartment. Equipment trained to document her life. For the first time, he wondered what she would have said if she knew.

"I haven't hooked it up yet," he said evasively.

"Well maybe you should do just that." Her tone was dismissive. Nicole picked up the telephone receiver. "And I'll call maintenance about this."

Confident that she was sending him on his way, she tapped out the numbers to the rental office.

Amused, Dennis crossed his arms before his chest and leaned a shoulder against the wall. He knew it wouldn't be long. Briefed on everything surrounding her complex, he knew that maintenance had a reputation of always being somewhere else when they were needed.

Three minutes later, Nicole sighed and hung up the phone.

"Nobody there?" he asked innocently.

She slanted an annoyed look at him. "Just the machine." But she had a feeling that Dennis already knew that.

Dennis hooked his thumbs on the loops of his jeans. "I don't think it's been programmed to fix disposals." This couldn't have worked out better if he had planned it. "So, do you want my help?"

She hated asking, but it was either that, or start washing dishes in the bathtub. "Yes."

With a satisfied nod, Dennis turned toward the door. "Okay, just let me get my tools."

She picked her way carefully to the broom closet for the mop. "And get a shirt while you're at it."

He turned in the doorway, surprised by the request. "Why?"

"Because you're too distracting running around without one." She saw him raise an amused brow. "I might be pregnant, but I'm not dead."

"Nice to know." He disappeared inside his apartment.

Muttering under her breath, Nicole grabbed the mop and began drying her floor.

Chapter 4

Nicole had barely put the mop away before she heard the quick, light rap on the door. She looked up sharply, her heart rate accelerating. Damn, this wasn't fair. She didn't want to feel like this in her own home, frightened by every sound. Even dead, Craig was still messing up her life.

She approached the door cautiously. "Who is it?"

"Mr. Fix-it."

The feeling of relief at hearing Dennis's voice was simultaneously overwhelming and annoying. She shouldn't have to be afraid like this. And she shouldn't have to feel as if she had to depend on anyone for anything.

Swallowing an oath meant for Standish, Nicole opened the door.

Dennis walked directly into the kitchen. He was carrying a small, rather new looking toolbox and, following her suggestion, he was wearing a shirt. It was a faded blue pullover that was missing a button at the throat.

The shirt didn't help. Rather than serve as camouflage, it

accented his muscles. The banding at each arm was clearly straining on his biceps. Both were beginning to tear at the seams.

Nicole sighed without being completely aware of why.

Dennis glanced at the floor. She'd managed to get the shine back. "Nice job."

He placed the toolbox beside the sink and flipped open the lid. A small assortment of tools was arranged inside, black handles all facing in one direction. He rummaged through them.

"You know," he quipped as he took out the wrench he was looking for, "my place could stand a once-over."

Some women worked through their problems cleaning. Nicole could never understand that. To her *cleaning* was a problem.

"Sorry, my mop's retired." She thought of his apartment. It was a great deal neater than hers was right now. Saturdays were reserved for cleaning. It was getting so that she dreaded Saturdays. "Besides, don't you have a cleaning lady?"

"Not for long." Dennis opened the cabinet doors again and began taking out cleansers, stacking them over to one side. "Ophelia is a grandmother five times over and rabidly looking forward to spending more time with her grandchildren." He was making it up as he went along. There was no cleaning lady, but someone like the man he was portraying would have had one. Dennis thought of his mother, who had spent years cleaning up after other people so that he and Moira could have a decent life. Spinning the rest of the story was easy. "She's retiring this June."

Nicole thought she detected a note of sadness in his voice, as if he actually knew the woman he was talking about well enough to carry on a conversation with her. As if he would miss her when she left.

He cleared his throat. The smell of cleansers melding irritated it. "I'm going to have to find someone to take her place."

From early on, Nicole had always liked doing things for herself. If you did them yourself, you weren't indebted to anyone. Housework, however, had never made that list. She would have been perfectly satisfied having someone take care of the mundane chores of cleaning for her, the way Sally had when she was growing up.

Nicole looked at the cleansers piled up on the side ruefully. Maybe she'd skip cleaning the tub this time around. It was getting more and more difficult to bend over these days.

Dusting, however, always needed to be done. She retrieved a dust cloth from the pile. "Let me know if you want to time-share," she quipped absently.

Dennis looked at her over his shoulder. "Are you serious?"

She wished. Nicole sighed. "No, not really." She folded the cloth in half and began rubbing away at the counter top. "I can't afford a luxury like that at the moment." She glanced down at her swollen stomach. "This baby is going to be all the luxury I have in my life for a while."

Squatting on the floor, Dennis sank back on his heels and looked up at her. His expression was innocent. "I don't mean to pry—"

Now there was an opening line. "But you will." She advanced to another surface, rubbing hard, waiting.

He lifted one shoulder and let it drop carelessly. She expected him to say "Aw, shucks" next. "Call it conversation."

Only in the broadest sense. He was reaching. "Euphemism."

She wasn't telling him to mind his own business. There was a crack forming in the wall. Dennis worked at making it larger. He grinned at her engagingly. "That too." Without missing a beat, he began again. "I'm not a racing fan—"

Neither was she anymore. Not for a long, long time. The thrill had dissipated when she realized what the consequences were.

And they had all come to pass.

Nicole looked off into space. "I won't hold that against you—"

Her voice was soft, distant, as if he'd disturbed something. He wondered what it was. "But your husband was pretty well-known in his class."

Craig and class had little to do with one another. Class meant knowing when to quit. And when to hold back. Craig hadn't known when to do either.

Nicole nodded. "Yes." When Dennis hesitated, she filled the words in for him. Placing her cloth down on the kitchen table, she looked down at him. "You're going to ask me why he didn't leave me well-off."

"I wouldn't have been that blunt, but something like that, yes." He didn't expect her to be stringently honest with him, but he was hoping to make a little headway. Expertly masking the curiosity he felt, he looked up at her and listened.

Bitterness twisted her mouth as Nicole remembered how excited Craig had been when the offers had finally begun to come in. Money from endorsements and sponsorships. More money than he had ever known.

And he had lost it all more than once.

Abandoning dusting altogether, Nicole lowered herself into a chair at the kitchen table. "He would have if he hadn't kept running around with men like Standish. Craig liked the thrill of gambling almost as much as he liked defying gravity and racing in that yellow-checkered car of his."

And just about as much as he liked acquiring groupies and making love with them.

She thought of the almost depleted bank account. She worked part-time at the art gallery. That gave her a paycheck and there was still a little left from the money that her grandmother had left her. The largest chunk had gone to buy Craig's first car, but she had husbanded the rest zealously, instinctively knowing that it was her security blanket. The money in the account was all hers. Craig's was all gone, swallowed up by debts and the high life. There had been barely enough to pay for his funeral.

Dennis pretended to be taking all this in slowly. The information he had been given showed that when he died, Craig Logan was in debt to the Syndicate by a good hundred thousand. Even if he had won the last race, he wouldn't have been able to pay it off.

"Even with the endorsements?"

"Even with the endorsements." Irony tinged her voice. She stopped toying with the dust cloth and looked at him suspiciously. "Why all the questions?"

It was time to retreat. Nicole's confidence had to be won slowly. If he pushed too hard, she would close up completely.

Dennis turned his attention back to the disposal. Craning his neck, he felt around for a button at the base of the metal casing. He found it in the center.

"It comes naturally in my line of work." He plugged the disposal in again. Pressing the button, he tried turning the unit on one last time. There was only a faint, feeble buzz in response.

Nicole realized that he hadn't told her what he did for a living. But then, she hadn't asked, either. "You're a gossip columnist?"

Dennis unplugged the disposal as he laughed. "I'm a tax lawyer."

That wouldn't have been her first choice. He didn't look like the shark type. "A lawyer?"

Squatting down again, he looked at her over his shoulder. "You say that as if lawyers were only one step above lepers." He wondered what she called Justice Department investigators.

Watching him fiddle around with the disposal was preferable to dusting. Nicole remained seated. "No. I say that as if lawyers were one step *below* lepers."

She said it vehemently, as if it were personal. "Had a bad run-in with one?"

She thought of the lawyer who had attached himself to Craig during his zenith. Jerome Banks had been a small, piglike man who was one step away from being an ambulance chaser. He'd looked at Craig and seen only a meal ticket. Banks had certainly sucked out his share. All his hangers-on had, she thought.

"Something like that," she answered vaguely. Nicole wanted the focus off her and on something else.

She folded her hands and looked down at him. Dennis was in an awkward position beneath the sink, doing something with his wrench. What, she hadn't the faintest idea.

"So what's a tax lawyer doing fixing a garbage disposal?" Dennis's answer came to her as soon as the question had left her lips. "Wait, don't tell me. You're 'being neighborly.'" She said it the way a children's show host would announce the answer to a group of five-year-olds.

Her barb amused him. He studied the way the disposal had been installed. Damn, whoever put this in had all but welded it into place. And destroyed connections while they were at it. Nothing he tried made the disposal work. He snaked his way into the cabinet.

His voice drifted out to her. "I was about to say that I had a life before I became a lawyer. That life included knowing how to do some things for myself—and my mother."

There was undisguised love in his voice. For a moment,

without knowing any of the circumstances of his life beyond the fact that he had had a mother to bond with, she envied him.

"Only child?"

Rather than crawl out again, Dennis stuck his hand out. "Hand me that screwdriver, will you? I have a sister," he answered.

"Me, too. Older?" Moving to the edge of her chair, Nicole looked down into the toolbox. There were several screwdrivers on the top. Which one was "that" screwdriver?

"Younger. Yours?"

"Older." She saw him wiggle his fingers expectantly. "Which one do you want?"

"The Phillips head."

He might as well have been speaking a foreign language. "And that would be—?"

He tried not to laugh. Moira would have been severely disappointed with Nicole for sounding so hopelessly "female" about tools. Moira knew how to take a car apart and put it back together. And how to hot-wire one as well.

"The one that looks as if it has a starburst on its tip."

So why hadn't he said so in the first place? Pushing a few tools aside, she located it. "The short, stubby one."

"The short, stubby one," he confirmed. His arm was beginning to ache.

Nicole slapped the screwdriver into his hand before he could ask her for it a second time. "My sister just had a baby three weeks ago."

He edged out from beneath the sink. Looking at her, he grinned. It came effortlessly this time. "Must be something in the water."

"Speaking of water, will I have any today?"

Dennis scooted back under the sink. "Patience, Nikk—

Nicole," he amended. "I've only been working on this for a few minutes."

And from what he could see, this job was going to be at least a couple of hours long. It didn't look as if the disposal could be resurrected. Which was good. It gave him the excuse he needed to hang around and work his way into her trust a little more.

She had let her eyes travel up the length of his torso as he laid there on her floor. Even lying down, the man looked as if he were as hard as rock. Not an ounce of fat on him anywhere. Nicole bit her lower lip, then roused herself.

"Seeing as how plumbers all get paid by the hour, I have a feeling that if you were a plumber, I couldn't afford you."

Grasping the base of the disposal, he tried moving it to see how solidly it was inserted and how difficult it would be to remove. Nothing budged.

"Lucky for you I'm a tax lawyer." He kept his voice casual. "Have you figured out what you're going to do about Standish?"

The mention of the man's name had the hairs on the back of her neck standing up. "Yes."

She said the word with finality. He waited, but nothing followed. Working with the screwdriver, he loosened a screw on either side of the disposal. "Well?"

He asked her questions as if he thought he had every right to the answers. She frowned. "Do you interrogate everyone you know?"

Dennis's voice echoed from beneath the sink. "Only women with great legs whose garbage disposals I happen to be working on."

The compliment secretly pleased her. She'd been feeling particularly dumpy this morning. "How can you see them under the sink?"

"I don't have to see them now." His laugh curled around her like a warm scarf tucked around her shoulders on a cold winter night. "Your legs were the first thing I noticed about you."

She found that almost impossible to believe. "Not my stomach?"

"Nope. Your legs. They happen to be a weakness of mine and yours are gorgeous." He said it simply, as if it were a given fact. His answer required no creativity on his part. They *had* been the first thing about her he'd noticed.

It was hard keeping the smile from her lips. She didn't want to encourage him, but at this stage of the game, she was hungry for compliments.

"Thank you."

"Don't mention it." He left the screws where they were. He'd finish unscrewing them when he had another disposal to replace this one. Dennis slipped out again. Sitting up, he let his screwdriver clank into the toolbox.

"So, you were saying—?"

She noticed that he had managed to have the tool face in the same direction as the others. She had a feeling that when his cleaning lady came, she didn't have all that much to clean.

"About what?" she asked innocently.

She didn't like answering questions unless her back was to the wall, he mused. He was going to have to dismantle that wall. "What are you planning to do about your friendly neighborhood shakedown artist?"

Friendly. That word kept coming up in his conversation. She wondered if his life was really as uncomplicated as it sounded.

Nicole shrugged. "Look around the apartment and see if there really is something that might have belonged to him, although I can't imagine what he's looking for."

Nicole exhaled a short, exasperated breath. She wasn't looking forward to going through Craig's things. "I'm surprised he didn't come here asking for money. Craig owed everyone at one time or another.'' He had even tried to borrow money from Marlene, but she had put a stop to it. Craig was her problem, not Marlene's. ''It never seemed to come in fast enough for him.''

Dennis sat looking up at her from the floor. Damn, but she did stir protective feelings within him. He had to keep that in check.

''But if a cleaning lady is a luxury that's out of reach, how do you manage to keep up the apartment—?''

She was tired of questions. And even more tired of the answers she had come up with. They trapped her. ''I'm going to sell my favors on a street corner to weirdos in downtown L.A.''

His light, easy smile defused her temper. ''I'm sure you'd have takers. Sorry, that wasn't any of my business.'' Then his expression grew more serious. Though he was unaware of it, a slight note of concern entered his voice. ''What will you do if you can't find whatever it is?''

''Reason with him.'' There was nothing else she could do. ''He can't get what I don't have.''

But he could try, Dennis thought. And Standish would. ''He didn't look like the type of man who could be reasoned with.''

Nicole sighed, rising to her feet. If she sat too long, she began to feel like a blob. ''I don't want to talk about this anymore.''

He tried one more time before he let go, testing just how much she knew. ''What do you think it was that he thinks your husband had?''

Nicole looked into the toolbox. ''Do you need me to hand you another tool?'' she asked sweetly. Bending, she picked up a torque wrench and held it aloft.

The message was received, loud and clear. Dennis grinned. ''And I've got a clear image of just where you'd like to hand that to me.''

Satisfied that she'd gotten her point across, Nicole let the wrench fall back into the toolbox. "You catch on fast."

He rose, dusting off his hands and then turned to the sink. He tried the rubber drain cover to see if it could be easily removed. It was. "Beatrice Lincoln didn't raise any stupid children."

Nicole supposed that would be his mother. She wasn't in the mood to talk about mothers. She had no stories to offer in trade.

"I'm sure she'd be happy to hear that." She picked up her dust cloth again. The dust wasn't going to get rid of itself. "Well, if you don't need my help, I'll get out of your way."

He turned. His eyes stopped her before he said anything. "Don't."

She looked at him uncertainly. "What?"

"Don't leave." He crouched down again, checking his tools to see if he had everything he needed to properly remove the disposal and install a new one. He was going to have to pick up some plumber's putty. "I like the company. Lately, I haven't had a chance to just talk to anyone if it didn't involve business."

Which was true. It had been a long time since he'd had a conversation that didn't revolve around his job. For a moment, Dennis could pretend that this really wasn't about work.

He paused, attempting to apply his own feelings to the man he was supposed to be. "I've gotten caught up on a treadmill and it almost feels as if I can't step off without getting dragged under."

He was a workaholic. To look at him, Nicole wouldn't have placed him in the same category as her sister, but obviously, looks could be deceiving. "Today's Saturday. Why aren't you out now, doing something interesting?"

Dennis smiled at her. "I am." His eyes teased her as he

held up a wrench and a screwdriver for emphasis. Retiring them to the toolbox, he looked at her seriously. "I'm afraid I have some bad news for you."

His face was so solemn, she had no idea what he was going to say. "What is it?"

"I'm afraid your disposal is terminal." He wiped his hands on the back of his jeans. She took the time to notice that though they were faded and frayed, they adhered to his body like a well-worn second skin. "You're going to need a new one."

She sighed. Was that all? "Isn't this something the management is supposed to take care of?"

"Yes, if you can find them." He gestured elaborately at the telephone. "Want to try?"

He was right, that was futile. If it wasn't one thing, it was another, she thought, annoyed. Nicole left the room, heading toward the bedroom where she kept her purse.

"Never mind. I'll go to the hardware store." She stopped abruptly. She had no idea what she was looking for. Were there different types? Did you have to order them ahead of time? God, she hoped not. "What kind do I need?"

"The kind that works." He saw the annoyed look intensify on her face. "Don't worry, I'll take a run down to the hardware store myself." She opened her mouth, to protest no doubt. "I'll know which kind to buy."

So would she, if he told her. Why was he being so nice to her? She was no one to him. "Are you trying to earn a merit badge?"

He grinned in response. It was the most guileless grin she'd ever seen. But Nicole knew that in reality, there was no such thing as guileless. Still, looking at Dennis, she could almost believe that there was.

"You found me out," he admitted solemnly. "How'm I doing?"

On the outside chance that he really was as nice as he

seemed, Nicole amended the sharp retort that rose to her lips. She glanced at the disconnected disposal. ''Halfway there.''

''I'll be back soon,'' he promised.

Halfway there. It would be interesting, he mused as he left, purely on a theoretical basis, to see what it would take to get the rest of the way there.

If he didn't have a job to do.

Replacing the disposal took him a great deal longer than she knew he had anticipated. According to Dennis, the disposal had turned out to be a real challenge to remove. He told her that whoever had initially installed it had wedged it in at just enough of an angle to defy prying it out easily.

Finished with her dusting, Nicole had hung around the kitchen, feeling as useful as a fly on the wall. Dennis had spent most of the time tugging and grunting, and making conversation. Though she had meant to remain close-mouthed, she found him incredibly easy to talk to.

She still couldn't figure out why he had volunteered to do this in the first place.

Dennis spent the duration hunkered in a position equivalent to early Christian martyrs doing penance. He was on her floor almost longer than Craig had remained in the apartment on any one of his stops as he passed through to yet another race. Another party.

When Dennis finally scooted out from beneath the sink and unfolded his body to stand beside the counter, she looked down into the sink uneasily.

''Is it done?''

He thought it was, but he knew the danger of being overly optimistic. About anything. It always paid to have backup. When he had left for the store, his partner Winston had maintained surveillance on Nicole's apartment in case she left, or someone else came in.

"That remains to be seen." Dennis turned on the water over the sink with the disposal, then switched on the disposal.

A whirling, grinding sound filled the air. The impotent buzz they'd heard in the morning was a thing of the past.

Like Henry Ford gesturing at the very first automobile as it came off the assembly line, Dennis motioned toward the sink.

"Ma'am," he drawled, "I give you your garbage disposal."

Nicole looked down at it. Such a little thing, such a huge inconvenience. She was grateful to him.

She turned her eyes up to Dennis's face. "I feel guilty about this. I've taken up the better part of your Saturday."

He liked her choice of words. "It was only the better part because I spent it with you."

Nicole shook her head. "Like I said, you have a very low threshold of pleasure."

Dennis paused, studying her face for a moment. Her eyes were beautiful, he thought. "Do you really feel guilty?"

She'd said as much, hadn't she? "Yes." Nicole stretched out the word as she wondered where this was leading to.

Had she been wearing that scent all day? Why had he just noticed it now? And why did it feel as if it were filling him? She was frowning thoughtfully, but she made him think of the sun, trying its damnedest to peer out from behind a cloud.

"Okay. Do you want to pay me back?"

Instantly, she braced herself. Here it came. The payoff. What did he expect to get from her? Nicole looked at him warily. "How?"

"Dinner." He stooped down and began to clear away the mess he'd left on the floor. Tools clinked as they joined others in the toolbox. He screwed the lid back on the jar of putty, then tucked the old disposal into the box the new one had been packed in.

Nicole wasn't certain if it was a question or an answer. She took it as a question and met it with one of her own. "I don't understand. If you take me out for dinner, how will that be my paying you back?"

Finished, he rose again. Dennis leaned a hip against the edge of the counter. "I was thinking of you cooking it."

"Oh." Reflexively, she glanced at the refrigerator. She could probably whip up something. "Okay. What would you like?"

The food didn't really matter. What mattered was the opportunity to continue talking to her. And if he found that rather pleasant, well, he couldn't be faulted for liking his work. "Anything that would be easy for you would be fine."

Her eyes shifted to the wall phone. "Picking up the telephone and calling for pizza."

"Whatever. I'm easy."

"Apparently." The thought of cooking for someone suddenly pleased her. It had been a long time since she had. Whenever Craig was around, they would eat out. "All right, you want a home-cooked meal, you'll get a home-cooked meal." She'd kibitzed while he had worked on the disposal, but she didn't want him looking over her shoulder while she cooked. "Now go home and come back at seven."

So far, so good. Dennis crossed to the door. "Best offer I've had all day."

Nicole looked at the defunct disposal now reposing in the open box. "Yeah, right." She remembered the chicken breasts she had in the freezer. "How do you feel about chicken?"

He paused, his hand on the door. "That depends. To eat or as a pet?"

Nicole stared at him. "For a basically simple man, you say the strangest things, Lincoln."

You have no idea. "That's because I'm trying to get you to smile."

Suspicion rubbed elbows with an odd sense of pleasure. "Why?"

He looked down into her face, smiling himself. "Because I think that it looks good on you." Before he could stop himself, he cupped her cheek. "Really good." Dennis felt the muscles in Nicole's face stiffening. He dropped his hand to his side. "Sorry, I'm a toucher. My sister says that if my hands were tied behind my back, I probably couldn't express myself at all." He saw the wariness in her eyes dissipate a little. Maybe he had played this a little too far, but the move had been natural. She had drawn it from him. "Dinner still on?"

"Why not? The chicken's already dead."

He laughed. "Can't have it die for nothing. Seven, right?"

"Seven," she echoed, closing the door behind him.

She turned away just as his voice floated in from the other side of the door. "Flip the lock."

She'd forgotten. It was his fault. He had rattled her, unsettling her common sense.

Nicole flipped the lock in slow motion, deliberately elaborating on the sound. "Okay?"

"Okay."

She could hear the grin in his voice. Odd that it didn't annoy her.

With a shake of her head, Nicole went to see if there was anything creative that she could do with the chicken presently residing in her freezer.

All in all, she had to admit that it wasn't all that bad, having a "neighborly" neighbor—just as long as the line remained drawn there.

She wasn't aware that she had started humming.

But, listening on the other side of her door, Dennis was. The sound seemed to seep into his being. It was oddly soothing. Something vaguely akin to guilt stirred within him.

He ignored it as he went to his own apartment.

Chapter 5

He arrived promptly at seven, holding a slim-necked light green bottle aloft. "I brought wine for the chicken."

"I'm sure the chicken will be very happy with it." She took it from him. It felt cold to the touch. "You chilled it."

She had changed, he noted. She was wearing a soft jade dress that cascaded over her body, almost guarding her secret. Had she been a couple of months less pregnant, he might not have guessed her condition.

"Seemed like the thing to do with wine."

"But I can't drink it," she admonished. "It wouldn't be good for the baby."

He was ahead of her. Leaving Winston's night shift replacement, Dombrowski, on the alert, he had made a quick stop at the store. It had taken some looking on his part. Dennis pointed to the label. "It's nonalcoholic."

She glanced at it. "Oh." Nicole raised her eyes to his. He looked good tonight. Very good. But then, he'd looked very good this morning as well. *Don't start,* she warned herself. "You think of everything."

"I try," he replied glibly. He followed her to the dining room. Nicole set the bottle on the table beside the main course.

The aroma pervading the small apartment smelled tempting. As did she. Except for her very rounded stomach, Nicole looked exactly the way she did in the photograph he had in his file on the case. Sunshine and sex in a short skirt.

It was hard to get that image out of his mind.

Dinner was ready. Anticipating his arrival, she had just set the main course on the table when he had rung the bell. She gestured toward it. "We might as well begin."

Nicole felt a nervous little ripple flutter through her, as if she were entertaining someone other than just a neighbor who'd been stubbornly kind enough to come to her aid.

She dismissed the feeling. The tension that was strumming over her nerves was due to Standish and his ghoulish threat last night, not because of the man who was in her apartment now. So he was sexy in a clean-cut sort of way, so what? She'd had her shots against sexy. And against vulnerable feelings.

Turning around to face him, Nicole laced her fingers together. "You never told me what I owe you for the disposal."

With a practiced eye, Dennis surveyed the table. There was a large, crystal bowl filled with garden salad, another with white rice. In the center was a bowl of a red sauce with chunks of chicken floating in it. The aroma knotted his stomach, reminding him that he really hadn't eaten very much all day.

"No," he agreed, "I never did."

She ran her hand along the back of her chair as she looked at him expectantly. "Well?"

He indicated the dinner. "I'll take the replacement cost to maintenance. As for labor, consider it paid in full. One garbage disposal installation for one dinner." The sauce looked like marinara, but he could be wrong. Dennis raised a brow as he looked down at her. ''So, what was the chicken's ultimate fate?''

''Cacciatore.'' Determined to cook him a meal he'd remember, she had made the sauce from scratch. As she did with everything she put her hand to, Nicole had taken a few liberties with the recipe, adding a generous dose of mozzarella cheese along with a number of spices and seasonings. She liked putting her own stamp on things. ''My own version.''

''Sounds intriguing.'' Dennis helped her with her chair. ''A little like its creator.''

Nicole had grown leery of flattery. She'd learned the hard way that its function was usually to hide the truth from the unsuspecting.

''Augmentor, not creator. And I'm not intriguing,'' she said firmly.

Dennis turned his attention to the wine. Having brought his own corkscrew, he began to work the tip into the cork.

''Intrigue is another word for mystery and I have to drag almost everything out of you. I'd say that makes you intriguing.'' The cork came out of the bottle with a resounding pop.

She offered her goblet up to him. Rosy red liquid flowed into the glass. ''What I'd say was intriguing was why you want to drag everything out of me in the first place.''

He poured a little wine into his own goblet, then tapped the cork back into place. ''Simple, I like knowing answers.''

Well, whether he did or not, she wasn't about to give him any. She didn't like talking about herself. Or the mistakes she'd made.

''Sometimes the answers are disappointing.'' Nicole toyed with the liquid in her glass for a moment, then set it down beside her plate. ''Better to sustain the aura of mystery.''

He moved toward the salad, picking up the tongs. "In this case, I don't think so." Capturing a fair amount of lettuce, tomatoes and cucumbers, Dennis deposited them in her salad bowl.

Nicole took the tongs from him. "You fixed the disposal. This time I'll serve."

"This time," he repeated, rolling the words over on his tongue. "Does that mean that there's going to be a next time?"

She couldn't decide whether he was as innocent as he seemed, or a very clever operator.

"I was referring to the last time. Yesterday." She handed him the bottle of dressing. "You don't look like the pushy type."

Blue cheese poured out of the bottle, slowly covering his serving. "That places the element of surprise in my corner." He passed the bottle to her. "Seriously, I just like knowing things about my friends."

The lie felt heavy on his tongue. She wasn't a friend, she was someone he was investigating, someone he was subtly pumping for information. It was all part of his job. So why did he feel dirty doing it? Just because she had the bluest eyes he'd ever seen, filled with pain and innocence, shouldn't have any bearing on the situation.

But it did.

She paused, her fork suspended above her salad as she slanted a look at him. She'd never had a man as just a friend. Her relationships before Craig had been instantaneous and intense. Labeled wild by her father years before she graduated high school, she had looked for love and acceptance in all the wrong arms. No one had ever just extended a hand in friendship to her before.

"We're friends?"

His smile was easy. "I spent the morning on my back in your kitchen, I'd say that makes us friends." Dennis moved his bowl aside. "You don't do that for just an acquaintance."

Nicole watched as he helped himself to a large serving of rice and then the chicken cacciatore. Either his eyes were larger than his stomach, or he had a tapeworm. If he ate like that regularly, she opted for the tapeworm theory.

"I wouldn't," she agreed. Nicole took a small spoonful of rice herself, then covered it with an equal amount of cacciatore. She'd been gaining too much weight lately, even eating for two. "But I think you would."

"Maybe," he conceded. Dennis felt as if they were shadowboxing. The conversation needed substance. It needed to unfold and he had a hunch that she wouldn't do the honors on her own. "I'll make it easy on you. I'll start."

Like a rabbit surviving the tail end of hunting season when it heard a gunshot, Nicole was instantly alert. "Start what?"

The first mouthful slid down his throat, salvos of flavor announcing its passage. He raised his fork a fraction in acknowledgment. "Good."

She hardly tasted hers. Her taste buds seemed to be scrambled. "Thank you."

"And to answer your question, I'll start the dialogue going."

He savored another forkful before continuing. Dennis noted the pleased look in her eyes as she watched him. Logan probably hadn't stuck around long enough to appreciate her cooking. Or any of her other finer points, either. The man had been an idiot.

"You already know that I have a younger sister. Moira." He smiled as he said his sister's name. "She's kind of a free spirit. Moira teaches English Lit at UCLA and keeps a menagerie on the side." His voice sobered a little as he continued. "My mother, Beatrice, died two years ago." He'd been on assignment and hadn't been able to get back in time. He'd left his mother a frail woman in a hospital bed and returned to see her in her casket. He supposed that was when the job had begun turning sour on him.

"I'm sorry." The words came automatically. The sympathy a step behind.

At least he'd had a mother, one who hadn't walked out on him.

He nodded. As with the death of his father, he'd gotten accustomed to the loss. But never comfortable with it.

"Yeah, me too. I miss her a lot." He thought of Christmas. Though he wasn't sentimental, somehow it was hardest then. "Especially around the holidays." He banished the encroaching mood. How had they turned down this corner, anyway? He saw the look in her eyes and realized that inadvertently, he had managed to take a step further with her touching on his own life. "Basically, Moira and I are the only family we have."

"Father gone?" The question seemed to flow naturally from her lips. It surprised her. She never pried. Questions begat questions. And she didn't want to be on the receiving end.

"Yeah. A long time ago." He'd been a casualty of the gambling sickness, just like her husband had been. Except that his father had killed himself, shamed by the depth to which he had brought his family. Logan's death had been orchestrated by a hand other than his own.

Dennis didn't think she knew that.

He took a sip of wine to clear his palate. Nonalcoholic wine wasn't half bad, he decided. At least it kept his senses clear. He raised his glass toward her. "Your turn."

Like the legendary gopher confronted with its shadow, she instantly retreated. Her attention reverted to her plate. "I never said I'd take a turn."

"You have to," he said simply, as if there were no arguing the point. "You're the only other one here and we've already done my background."

He was a lawyer all right. But she was familiar with badgering that was far more insistent than his. "Not completely. Why a tax lawyer? Why not a fireman? Or some kind of other lawyer?"

Though he seemed soft spoken, something about him made her envision Dennis as a criminal lawyer. She could see him standing up before a jury box, calmly swaying the people seated in it.

Maybe it *was* time to go into details. Fabricated details. It seemed the only way to get her to trust him and open up. At this point, Dennis wasn't sure what it was she was hiding, but there definitely was something.

"That would have to do with my father."

She jumped to the first logical conclusion. "He was a tax lawyer, too?"

That would have certainly simplified matters. For all of them. He thought of the profile he'd written for himself before he'd knocked on her door.

"No, but he could have used one. A good one." Dennis retired his fork and leaned back. "My father had his own software company. Built it up from scratch and imagination. He was one of the ones on the frontier of this whole computer craze."

That sounded better than saying his father was a dreamer. A dreamer who always pursued the next turn of the card, the next toss of the dice, confident that it would change his luck. The quest for Lady Luck had taken him from place to place and had ended in an alleyway, outside a casino in Nevada.

"He was into the creative end of it and not very smart about money." At least, that much was true. Money never managed to remain in his hands for more than a few days at a time. When he won, he wanted to win more. When he lost, he was always sure that he would win again. It was a deadly cycle.

He saw sympathy in her eyes and knew he had struck a good chord.

"It's an old story, really. His partner managed to embezzle most of the company's money before my father knew what was happening. Jack disappeared, leaving my father with a mountain of debts and the IRS breathing down his back, demanding back taxes."

Dennis's mouth curved cynically. It wasn't the IRS but the Syndicate who had wanted payment on the debts his father had run up at the tables. "Suddenly there was a lien on the house and the bank account."

Nicole tried to envision herself in his position. How awful that must have been for him. The underpinnings of his world had been pulled out from under him. Just as hers had for her. Empathy flooded through her.

Dennis shrugged matter-of-factly, reciting the rest of the story. "We downscaled a lot and the debts were paid off. But my father never quite recovered from the shame he felt at failing to provide my mother with the life he had promised her when they got married. He killed himself."

He looked across the table at Nicole and saw the sympathy in her eyes. It touched him and stirred his guilt again. He had no idea why, but at that moment, he knew that she knew nothing about Craig Logan's dealings with the underworld.

He pressed on with his story. "If he'd had a good tax lawyer at his side, maybe things would have gone differently for him."

He loved his father, she thought. She wondered what that felt like. For as long as she could remember, her father was someone she had disliked. There was no warmth, no understanding, no love about James Bailey. Just demanding expectations.

"Your father sounds a great deal different from mine." Again, she envied him. Funny, she thought she had worked through emotions like that. Obviously not. "James T. Bailey didn't suffer embarrassments and qualms of conscience," she said loftily, mimicking a tone her father had used with her during his numerous lectures. "He delegated them to other people and made them suffer instead."

"It doesn't sound like you and your father get along." It didn't take a rocket scientist to figure that one out. Animosity fairly throbbed in her voice.

Now there was the understatement of the century. "We didn't."

"Didn't," Dennis repeated. "You reconciled with him?"

Nicole laughed shortly. "No. He died. We never got the chance to reconcile—not that he would have."

There was never any thought on her father's part that he might have been wrong, or insensitive, or lacking in any way. In his own eyes, she was sure her father thought he was perfect.

"He was a hardworking man who was very good at what he did—advertising. But he should have stuck to his work and never had children."

Nicole took a long sip of her drink and let the flavor settle. "I never understood how he could be so good at honing in on what would entice the public to buy something or avail themselves of some service when he didn't have a clue as to what his own family needed."

She supposed that would be chalked up to one of the mysteries of life, a secret that had been lost when her father had suffered a heart attack and died at his desk.

Gently, he tried to lead her in the direction that was his ultimate goal. Her husband. But he couldn't do it directly. He didn't want to raise her suspicions. "There was just you and your sister?"

She was talking too much. Nicole didn't know what was

the matter with her. She couldn't blame it on the wine. It wasn't making her talk. There was no alcohol in it. But once she'd begun, the words just seemed to be pouring out, like water through a hole in the dam.

"I had an older brother who died when he was twelve. It was a freak accident." She recited the event as if it had happened to another family. She'd been too young to really be affected by Robby's death. Not like Marlene. "Robby fell out of a tree."

Her eyes shifted toward Dennis. There was nothing but sympathy in his eyes. She shouldn't be saying this, she thought. She didn't want sympathy. Sympathy made her feel vulnerable.

"It was while we were on vacation up in the mountains. Marlene was with him when he died. She was the only one." Nicole took a deep breath. "I think it haunted her for a long time." Nicole hadn't realized that until years later.

He noticed that she purposely avoided talking about her own feelings. "And you?" he asked.

Nicole lifted her shoulders and let them fall in a vague motion.

"I missed him, but I was only six at the time. I didn't really know him very well." And it didn't feel the same as when her mother had left. That had devastated her. And, in time, it had made her very angry.

Dennis thought of his father's death and how hard it had been on his mother. She had barely been able to place one foot in front of another for months afterward. How much harder was it to lose a child? "That must have been really hard on your mother."

Muscles tightened in her face. She doubted if her mother even knew that Robby had died. Or, if she did, that she'd care.

"I wouldn't know," Nicole said woodenly. "She was gone by that time."

There was something ominous in her voice, something he couldn't quite put his finger on. Playing his role, he asked the logical question.

"She died?"

Nicole shook her head. "No." She didn't want to talk about this anymore. It was her own fault for opening her big mouth, she thought.

She indicated the depleted bowl of chicken cacciatore. He hadn't taken a second helping, but then, the first had been pretty large.

"Is it spicy enough for you? I didn't want to make it too hot, but I noticed that you really seemed to enjoy the spicy chicken last night."

Dennis could almost hear the gate slam shut. The conversation regarding her mother was over. "The cacciatore is great. Actually, it's better than great, it's terrific." The meal he'd just eaten hadn't been slapped together. There had been subtle tastes in the sauce. She knew her way around a kitchen. "Who taught you how to cook?"

"Sally. Our housekeeper." Her mouth curved fondly. Sally had been a rock for Marlene and for her. "I think she was a former drill sergeant in the marines, but she's dynamite in a kitchen."

There was a great deal left unsaid. He heard the inference in her voice.

Nicole took a last sip of her drink, finishing it. "I guess you could say that she was the most constant part of our lives. Even now." She saw the question in Dennis's eyes. "Sally stayed on with my sister at the house after my father died."

"Do you and your sister get along?"

What an odd question. "Yes." Nicole paused to consider her answer. She and Marlene approached life on different paths, but they complemented one another. And there was the past to bond them. There wasn't anything she wouldn't do for Marlene. "We have our differences, but, yes, we do."

He knew that Marlene Bailey lived in an exclusive neighborhood in Newport Beach in the family home. If she got along with her sister, what was Nicole doing here on her own with a baby coming?

"Wouldn't it be easier for you if you moved in with your sister?"

As if Marlene hadn't already suggested that a hundred times. It was part of almost every conversation they'd had in the last year, intensifying after Craig died. But she wasn't looking for someone else's haven. She wanted to create one of her own.

"Maybe it would be easier, but it's not what I'm about to do. I like finding my own way." Her eyes held his. "I always have."

He didn't doubt it for a minute. Strong willed was a totally inadequate word to describe her, Dennis mused. Time to nudge her along. "When did you meet Craig?"

When did she meet Craig? The question echoed in her head. God, looking back, it seemed like a hundred years ago. "When I was in college."

She stood up rather abruptly. The plastic tabs on the chair legs squeaked in protest. She didn't want to talk about herself anymore.

"I think it's about time for dessert, don't you? I made a banana cream pie." Even saying it felt sinfully caloric. "Oh, I know at my size I shouldn't, but I've gained so much weight, what's another thousand calories or so?"

He laughed at her flippant remark. He had a feeling that after the baby was born, Nicole would shed her pounds with the same determination she seemed to face everything else.

Because she seemed bent on serving, he remained seated as Nicole disappeared into the kitchen. He raised his voice so she could hear him. "What would you turn the conversation to if there wasn't this food?"

She returned, carrying the plates and forks beneath the pie. He took them from her and set one at each place.

"If there wasn't this food, you wouldn't be here and there'd be no conversation to turn." Placing the pie between them, she picked up her knife. "Now, are you game for banana cream pie or not?"

Dessert was a luxury he didn't often indulge in. There were many luxuries he didn't indulge in anymore. Like taking time off from his world to be with a woman. "Does the sun set in the West?"

"Last time I checked." Nicole cut a wide section for Dennis, then one of equal size for herself. The two slices comprised almost half of the entire pie.

Maneuvering her spatula beneath the slice, she eased it out of the pie tin and onto his plate. This looked homemade as well. She was going to make her kid a great mother, he thought.

He raised his eyes to hers. "A quarter of the pie?"

With space to work with, taking the second piece was a lot easier. She placed it on her plate.

"I could cut delicate pieces and then go through the charade of 'just a tiny sliver more,' but why bother?" She sank her fork into the whipped topping. "This is more honest."

The last word hovered between them.

There was just a dab of whipped cream at the corner of her mouth. Dennis had the sudden and intense urge to sample it. He shifted his attention to his own serving. "And you believe in honesty?"

For the first time since he had met her, Nicole grinned. He'd been right. It was an incredible sight. Like the sun coming out after a storm. "Whenever a lie doesn't work."

He laughed, amused with her answer. "You're something else, Nicole."

"Yes, I am." She still wasn't quite sure about him, but she was taking no chances. "And there's no prize if you guess what. Eat."

He didn't have to be told twice. "Yes, ma'am." The pie tasted like a little bit of heaven, served with whipped cream.

The packers at the supermarket called her ma'am. She hated it. "You say that word one more time and you'll be wearing the rest of the pie."

He contemplated the remaining portion. "Not a bad offer." Dennis looked at her. She sounded pretty adamant. "My drawl bother you?"

If pressed, she would have had to admit that she rather liked the way words slipped out of his mouth. It reminded her of honey being poured over pancakes.

"No, the word *ma'am* does." She wasn't the only one. Marlene had mentioned how much the term irritated her. And for the same reason. "It makes me feel like I'm a hundred years old."

She barely looked as if she were old enough to vote. "If you were, in your present condition you'd make the national news." He took another bite. "Besides, 'ma'am' is a term of respect."

Maybe, but it was hard to accept it as such when it made her feel as if she were old and frumpy looking. "You're being deliberately cheerful."

"Sorry." His smile took over his eyes as well. "I'm having a good time."

It wasn't a lie. If he didn't think of this as an assignment, he could honestly say that it was the best time he'd had in a long time. She made it easy to enjoy himself. Too easy.

She shouldn't believe him, but she did. Which was probably a huge mistake. "Shouldn't you be out with someone?"

His eyes held hers for a moment. "I am." He didn't want her on her guard, so he added, "In a manner of speaking.

Just because it's Saturday night and I'm under thirty-five doesn't mean I should be prowling around, looking to score."

That would make him entirely different from the men in the crowd she had hung around with in her late teens. Different, too, from the crowd that had been Craig's main staple of life.

She studied Dennis for a moment. "How much under thirty-five?"

"Two years."

He looked younger, she thought. Or was it that she just felt old? "Nine."

"Are you contradicting, or actually volunteering a piece of information?" He knew she was twenty-six, but as her neighbor, there was no way he could have had that information.

"Volunteering." She supposed it had been another moment of weakness. After all, he hadn't asked. "And don't let it go to your head."

"Too late. It's already there." It was an encouraging sign. He was making headway more quickly than he had anticipated.

With an exaggerated, contented sigh, he placed his fork on his plate and rose.

There was nothing left to serve and perhaps nothing left to say. "Leaving?"

"Clearing. The dishes," he added when she didn't seem to understand.

Craig wouldn't have lifted a dish unless it was stuck to him with Super Glue. She waved a hand at the table. "I can take care of them later."

Dennis was already piling one dish on top of another. "I can take care of them now." Carrying the plates and bowls, he walked into the kitchen.

Just who did he think he was, taking over as if she were some helpless dolt? Nicole followed him into the kitchen.

"You don't have to wash them."

He deposited the pile on the counter beside the sink. "Actually, I was thinking of stacking them in the dishwasher."

Maybe she was overreacting. She supposed that there was no harm in letting him do that. Nicole relaxed. "Your mother and sister certainly trained you right."

He pulled out the dish rack and began stacking dishes. "No, actually, that restaurant where I worked during college trained me well. I started out as a dishwasher, worked my way up through busboy to waiter." He put in the detergent and closed the door.

"And then you became a lawyer." She set the dial and started the machine. Whirling noises began to emit from behind the door.

"And then I became a lawyer," he echoed. For about two minutes before he had gone to work for the Justice Department. But that was something she wasn't going to know until this was all over.

She was trying very hard not to feel comfortable around him. Being comfortable always clouded her judgment and led to mistakes.

But it was becoming increasingly more difficult.

It was time to go, he thought. To push too much would be overplaying his hand. The evening had passed rapidly and pleasantly. After they'd stacked up the dishes, they'd gone to the living room and talked for a little while longer, with the muted sounds of instrumentals playing in the CD player.

They'd skirted past backgrounds and discovered several things they had in common, and some they did not, including opinions on a recent book that had climbed the bestseller charts. He'd hated it, she'd loved it.

It was late and she was beginning to look tired. With a trace of reluctance he didn't have to feign, Dennis got up from the sofa.

Nicole rose beside him, surprised that he was leaving without being urged to. Surprised that she didn't want him to leave.

"I guess I'd better be going. It was a great dinner, Nicole, thanks for having me."

She walked him to the door. "Thanks for fixing the disposal. Did this satisfy your damsel in distress fantasy?"

He laughed. "Not quite, but it came close. We're missing a dragon, among other things."

His laugh was infectious. It was difficult not to join in. "What other things?"

Her eyes seemed incredibly blue, so blue he could have waded in them from the hips on down.

"In my fantasy, the damsel, who's very grateful, always kissed the knight."

It was an entirely crazy impulse and she didn't know what came over her. Nicole rose on her toes and brushed her lips against his cheek. As she did, she felt something tingle within her. The baby must have moved and pressed against a vital organ.

"Okay?"

"Almost."

Maybe there was something in the air, or maybe it was the look in her eyes. Whatever the explanation for the sensation, the soft touch of her lips ignited a reaction within him.

Cupping her cheek, Dennis lowered his mouth to hers.

Chapter 6

Looking back, Dennis had no idea what had possessed him. When he did look back, he knew that that moment was the beginning of everything.

He'd only meant to brush his lips against Nicole's, touching them as lightly as she had glided hers against his cheek.

How the kiss had evolved, flowering into an entity that was much larger than the sum of its parts, was something that he wasn't quite sure of, and would remain unsure of no matter how many times he reexamined the moment.

It seemed that one minute he was bidding her good-night at her door, the next he was threading his fingers through her hair, tilting her head back so that he could deepen the kiss.

He deepened it so much that he fell in.

It was his personal theory that a woman with legs that could weaken a man's knees would know how to kiss the socks off that same man. He wasn't disappointed. Overwhelmed perhaps, stunned even, but definitely not disappointed.

This, he realized, was something poets wistfully referred to as chemistry.

God, what was she doing?

She could feel every fiber of her being shaking. Wobbly, she was definitely wobbly. Trying to deny it, Nicole grasped the front of Dennis's shirt to steady herself.

This wasn't supposed to be happening. And she had no one to blame for it but herself. If she hadn't kissed his cheek, he would have gone home, leaving her in peace. She had instigated this in a moment of unprecedented weakness.

In a moment of need.

It had sprung out of the fact that it had been so long since she'd felt like a woman, so long since she'd felt that anyone cared. Something had just erupted within her, galvanizing itself to the very real attraction that she felt.

Nicole couldn't remember the last time she'd actually *felt* anything.

Even the baby hadn't been conceived in a moment of love. It had been conceived in a hurricane of violence.

Following the circuit had brought Craig home for a week. He'd returned, roaring drunk, from a party celebrating his latest trophy-winning race. She had vainly attempted to put him to bed. He'd responded by pushing her away, then suddenly yanking her to him by her hair, demanding to have what belonged to him. No amount of reasoning or protest could dissuade him or make him stop and she had been too proud to plead.

The bruises had remained with her for days. What he had done, the way he had taken her, had remained with her forever.

From that day forward Nicole had been certain that she had lost the ability to respond to anyone.

She was responding to Dennis now.

Melting. She felt as if her body were melting, turning into

vapor. She couldn't allow this to be happening. She was pregnant, for God's sake, what was she thinking of?

What was *he* thinking of?

But her thoughts kept vanishing, like misty prints on a foggy window. She couldn't carry out a complete sentence in her mind. Dennis was numbing it with his gentleness. Nicole had to struggle to think. The sensations dancing through her veins were wonderful, but she knew she had to pull free of them, of their drugging effect. All drugs ultimately brought you to destruction, and she had already been to hers.

Nicole wedged her hands between them and pushed Dennis away. It only registered belatedly that she didn't have to push hard. He stepped back at the first sign of protest.

Craig wouldn't have done that. Craig *hadn't* done that.

She could hardly focus on Dennis's face, or on the anger she knew she should be feeling. "That wasn't included in the meal."

He felt as if he'd just taken a dive off a cliff and his bungee cord had snapped. For such a little thing, and pregnant at that, she packed a hell of a wallop. "If it was, you'd make a fortune with a franchise."

Though he hated to admit it, it took Dennis a moment to gather himself together. He looked down into her face and couldn't read a damn thing. Had the electricity he felt just been one-sided? He didn't think so.

Damn it, what did he think he was doing? There wasn't supposed to be electricity of any kind.

But there had been and he was going to have to work with it. He couldn't just pretend it hadn't taken place. Dennis struggled to keep things from getting any more complicated.

"I won't say that I'm sorry, Nicole, because I'm not. That's probably the nicest thing that's happened to me in a long, long time." He had an urge to run his thumb along her lower lip, but that would just be compounding his mistake. "But I don't want it interfering with our friendship." And certainly not with the real reason he was here.

That, he thought, was going to be a hell of a good trick.

He'd shaken her down to her very toes and he was still peddling that angle? "Friends don't kiss."

His smile was slow, seductive, even while it was boyishly innocent. "Sure they do."

Nicole frowned, wishing she didn't feel as if she'd just taken a long, terminal ride in a blender. "Not like that."

There she had him. "No, not unless they're very lucky." He took a deep breath. This was going to take a great deal of sorting out. "Sweet dreams, Nicole." He paused, then added, "I know I'll have them." She began to close the door, probably eager to get him out of her apartment. He couldn't blame her. "Do you still have my number?"

Wariness filled her. "I'm not about to use it anymore now than I was last night."

She was going to take patience, that much he knew. He hoped he hadn't blown things just then. "That's because Standish didn't come back last night. If he does—"

She shrugged, cutting him off. "If he does, I'll call."

I'd call 911 before I'd call you. At least I know what I'm getting with them.

He knew she wouldn't. Dennis crossed to the kitchen table and took out a napkin. "Here, let me—"

She stopped him from writing his phone number down again by reciting it to him.

He looked at her in surprise. "You didn't throw it away."

"Yes, I did," she contradicted. "But I have total recall." She thought of something Craig had once said to her about her and her "damn memory." She recalled every time he'd ever strayed. It was part of the reason she'd stopped traveling with him. She knew he wouldn't stop, but at least she didn't have to be around to see it. "Something that used to annoy my husband no end."

He had no doubt. Logan probably thought she was going to use all the dates and facts and hit him up for a divorce and huge alimony payments. "I think it's kind of nice, actually. Saves paper and cuts down on clutter."

Nicole held the door wide open, issuing Dennis a blatant hint. She shook her head at his comment. "Are you *always* this annoyingly cheerful, or are you saving all this just for me?"

He crossed the threshold and stood outside her apartment. "I'd like to say that you bring it out of me, but the truth is that I've never seen the point in looking at the downside." It caught up with you fast enough as it was, he added silently.

"I don't know about that. At least that way you're never disappointed." She murmured the words more to herself than to him. Aware that she had said something aloud that she'd meant to keep to herself, Nicole firmly closed the door. "Good night, Lincoln."

"Good night, Nicole," he called. "Don't forget to lock your door."

She let out an exasperated sigh. Did he think he was her keeper? That she couldn't think for herself? "I'm locking it, I'm locking it." Shaking her head, she flipped the lock above the knob.

Her body still tingled.

She had trouble falling asleep that night. Restlessness pervaded her. She told herself it was because the baby was moving around, making her uncomfortable. But it wasn't just that. Her mind was restless for an entirely different reason.

And the reason had a name and a face.

Dennis's.

She couldn't find a position that was comfortable. And

every time Nicole closed her eyes, she saw his face and relived the scene at the door.

Body tense, she stared up into the darkness. She was being adolescent. A pregnant woman shouldn't feel this way. And *she* didn't feel at all. Not anymore.

Thoroughly drained, she finally drifted off to sleep a little after midnight.

The doorbell rang, chiming like church bells on a Victorian Christmas morning. Rousing herself, Nicole hurried to the door. When she opened it, Dennis was standing there, a bouquet of white poinsettias in his hand, desire in his eyes.

And she was as slender as a reed, as light as the very air.

As hungry as an uncontained forest fire, consuming everything in its path.

Anticipation filled her, tensing her body and spilling through it like port wine, slowly, thickly.

Dennis whispered something in her ear, but she wasn't certain what, only that his breath warmed her. Words didn't matter. He was here, with her, and that was all that *did* matter.

Turning, her pulse racing, Nicole placed the flowers in a crystal vase that seemed to materialize before her out of nowhere. She recognized it suddenly, distantly. It had been her mother's vase. Her mother's favorite. The last time she had seen it, there had been a single scrawny dandelion in it. She had picked it for her mother and her mother had made a huge fuss over it. It had pleased her, making her feel special and so very grown-up.

How the vase had suddenly appeared in her apartment, she didn't know, but it was there, filled with water and waiting for her flowers.

As she slipped the poinsettias into the vase, Nicole felt Dennis's hands softly glide along her bare arms. Her body seemed to vibrate at his very touch.

His hands were gentle, worshipful. They made her ache to be touched intimately, to be wanted. Cherished. She wanted Dennis to make her feel the way she never had felt before. In her heart, she knew he could, that out of a world full of men, he was the one she'd always been looking for.

Nicole didn't just want to have sex with Dennis, she wanted to make love with him.

Sex with Craig had been hot, passionate, wild. It had taken her breath away. But at bottom, it had always been just sex. Nothing more. It was like opening up a beautifully wrapped Christmas present to find nothing inside.

More than anything else, Nicole wanted to feel as if she were loved before she was ignited.

As if he had read her mind, Dennis's very manner made her feel loved. Made her feel safe. She'd never felt safe before.

With every kiss that whispered along her face, every kiss that fluttered along her throat, every caress that swept along her body, Nicole felt loved. More, she felt protected. The world outside the circle of his arms couldn't hurt her as long as he was here.

The feeling was almost a tangible thing that she could wrap around herself.

Nicole moaned as Dennis's skillful hands slipped along her body, playing her as if she were a Stradivarius and he the only one with a bow.

She wanted more, needed more, and she wanted it quickly.

But Dennis went slowly, so very slowly. Her body throbbed and ached, but his pace remained relentlessly rhythmic.

Even so, or maybe because it was so, the fire flared in her loins, her breasts, her belly, now so flat. It poured like molten lava through her veins. Her clothes felt as if they weighed a ton.

She began to struggle out of them herself, but he stopped her hands.

"Slowly," he whispered. The word skimmed along her skin. "We have forever."

And she believed him. Handed lines all her life, she believed him. Because she knew in her heart that he wouldn't lie to her.

Nicole clenched her hands in his hair, holding tightly as his mouth took hers. Over and over again he kissed her. Sounds rushed in her ears. Jets taking off. The tide pounding along the beach. Freedom soaring through the imprisoned.

Passion leaped up higher as she felt his strong, capable hands cupping her breasts, molding them. She arched against his palms. Against him, her body imploring him for more.

Nicole could feel his desire hardening him. And still he went slowly.

It was all the more powerful for its steadily increasing pace.

When Dennis began to unbutton her blouse, a cranberry silk blouse she knew she hadn't worn in years, Nicole could feel her heart pounding in her chest, vibrating in her body, throbbing in her head.

The cadence seemed to whisper his name over and over again. It was almost more than she could stand.

Smiling into her eyes, Dennis toyed with the flowered clasp at the front of her bra. He was teasing her and it excited her beyond belief.

Then, with a light flick of his thumb and forefinger, Dennis opened the clasp. The cups slid from her damp skin. His hands replaced the material that had slipped away, rubbing slowly, gliding along the surface, hardening the nipples beneath his palms until they ached.

Her own hands trembling, just as her body had trembled at her door when he had first kissed her, Nicole began to unbutton his shirt. But midway through, his shirt turned into a blue pullover, the same one he had worn when he had come over that morning.

Impatient to be rid of it, she tugged the pullover up over his head and then down his arms. Heart racing, she tossed the shirt aside. It fell on her blouse, tangling with it just as she wanted to tangle with him.

And then, in a blink of an eye, she was standing nude before him, with no memory of when or how the rest of her clothes had been removed.

It was almost as if she had wished them gone and they were.

Nudity had always embarrassed her. Divested of her clothing, Nicole had always felt like something a little less than human, to be enjoyed by Craig and then forgotten. Like a drink or a cigarette, except less so.

The first tinge of embarrassment that fluttered through her instantly faded into mist as she looked up into Dennis's eyes and saw herself mirrored there.

Saw herself adored there.

Dennis held her hands apart and though he didn't say a word, she knew he had asked to just look at her for a moment.

She felt like a queen. She felt beautiful.

And then he brought her to him, his body molding to hers. The jeans he was wearing melted away as if they had never been there to begin with. Nicole felt the hot press of his body against hers. Sealing itself to her. Fitting into the curves as if she were half of a puzzle and he the missing half.

The desire that urgently shot through her was uncontrollable.

They were suddenly transported out of the living room. Walls melted away and they were in her bedroom, on her bed. She knew it was hers even though she couldn't recognize the covers. They were blue satin, like the sheets beneath them, and felt cool against her skin.

As cool as he felt hot.

He was making love to her the way she had always wanted to be made love to. Gently, lovingly, passionately, with a reverence that was beyond description.

His mouth was everywhere at once, raining kisses on every inch of her skin. She withered and twisted beneath his hot, plundering mouth wanting to prolong this ecstasy, stunned that it had gone on for so long.

When she felt his mouth and tongue dip down between her thighs, she caught her lower lip between her teeth to keep from crying out. She felt hot, moist and still so achy that she could cry.

She peaked.

Once, twice, and still there was more.

Climax after climax flowed into one another, pealing through her body like rolls of thunder.

And then he was over her, his hard, muscular body as agile as a gymnast. His eyes made love to her before he ever lowered himself to her, before his body took what was already his.

Nicole felt that he had been holding himself back. Holding himself back for her. Nothing was said, but in her soul, she knew.

She felt tears forming at the corner of her eyes.

When they slid down her cheeks, Dennis kissed them both away before finding her mouth once more. He framed her face with his arms, burying his hands in her hair.

This time the kiss was all raw passion. Elated, she rushed to meet it. To be one with it. To be one with him. As it was meant to be.

Their bodies, primed, ready, glistening, tangled as they rolled along the bed, scrambling the covers. Scrambling their desires.

And then he entered her.

His eyes were intent on hers as he sheathed himself in her, telling her things she'd never seen in anyone's eyes before.

She'd never felt this beautiful. This desired.

His eyes never left hers. Very slowly, the rhythm began, increasing in tempo only as she willed it. It was impossibly wondrous.

His fingers spread and threaded through hers. Joined in every possible way, he took her to the highest peak and kept her there.

Nicole cried when it was over. Cried because it was so beautiful, cried because it had been just the way she'd always wanted it to be. Cried because it was over.

He whispered to her that it would happen again, whenever she was ready.

He kept his word.

They made love again and again, each time more exhilarating than the last. She was in the center of a kaleidoscope as emotions, as sensations burst upon her, claiming her. Making her numb.

Making her soar.

Nicole woke with a start, her heart almost hammering out of her chest. There was a pool of sweat on the pillow beneath her head even though the apartment was cold now. She'd turned down the heat before going to bed. There was no reason to feel this hot.

No reason except for the dream.

It hadn't been a dream, it had been an entire experience, wrapped up in sleep. Even now it seemed real to her.

Too hot to endure them, Nicole threw off the covers. She waited for the chilly night air to play over her body, cooling it.

In the darkness, Nicole brought her fingertips to her lips

and lightly touched them. As soon as she did, she relived the kiss at her door. By Craig's standards, it had been almost chaste. The first time he had kissed her, he had all but sucked out her soul.

But there was a latent promise in Dennis's kiss that was hopelessly sexy.

Her breathing was still ragged. Nicole lay there for a moment, trying to cool off. Trying to cool down.

Her thoughts were scattered, eluding her like tiny grasshoppers springing to freedom out of an overturned jar.

She waited for her pulse to steady and her breathing to become regular again. It was as if she'd been visited in the night, she thought, actually plucked out of her bed to a netherworld where she experienced a night of gentle, erotic lovemaking.

Gentle-erotic. That was a complete contradiction in terms, she thought, raising herself up on her elbow to get a better look at the clock.

The ice blue digital numbers glowed back at her. It was only five. No light filtered through her thin curtains. The world around her was still sitting inside an inkwell. There were no stars. Even the moon had hidden its face.

Probably in embarrassment, she thought, a whimsical smile lifting her lips.

Nicole pulled her elbows to her sides and fell back against the bed. She felt completely drained and exhausted but she knew that there was no getting back to sleep for her. The dream had left her wound up as well as tired.

With effort, Nicole lay there, her hand over her stomach, vainly attempting to calm her frayed nerves.

It was a dream, she told herself, just a dream. There was nothing to it except wishful thinking.

Dennis's image flashed through her mind and she pushed it back. This hadn't been about him, she thought, not really. It could have been about anyone.

But it *had* been about him, a small voice whispered in her mind.

She clenched her hands, refusing to give in. She had experienced a mild attraction to him, sure. He was good looking, but that wasn't the point. What her dream had symbolized was that she had always wanted someone to love her for herself, not for who she was or how she could prove useful.

Her father hadn't loved her. All James Bailey required from his daughter, from all his children, was perfection—and that they not embarrass him.

So, of course, she did. At every opportunity. It was to teach him a lesson for treating her like a lifeless figurine. It didn't matter. He had never learned the lesson.

There had been a number of men she had turned to in her youth, men Nicole had secretly hoped would make up for the incredible lack she felt. All they had wanted was a good time.

And then Craig had come along, providing his own good time. But all Craig had really wanted was her money, not her. She'd found that out several months into the marriage.

But she had made her bed and to leave it would have been tantamount to telling her father that he had been right. That Craig was a loser. So she had struggled to turn Craig into a winner. She had funded his dream and he became a winner.

Craig had liked the feeling so much, he did everything he could to perpetuate it. To remain a winner. At least, on the track.

And off the track he had reaped whatever benefits that kind of life offered him. He'd thought there were no price tags to pay, but there were. Big price tags. And she had paid them all.

She felt cold now.

Nicole drew the covers back up over herself and watched

the shadows on the ceiling slowly melt away as dawn approached.

"So what are you telling me?" Marlene handed Nicole a cup of eggnog.

Marlene nodded absently at a familiar face she recognized from one of her numerous visits to Dr. Pollack's office while she was carrying Robby. The doctor, in the spirit of generosity and Christmas, had invited all of her patients to a Christmas party at a restaurant owned by her uncle. It was a nice way to mark Christmas Eve.

Even nicer was actually being taken into her sister's confidence. As a rule, Nicole kept to herself about matters that concerned her. She'd had to learn from the pages of a society column just what a womanizer her late brother-in-law had been. Nicole had never said a word.

Nicole frowned as she sipped her drink. The eggnog was delicious, but it didn't help. Nothing helped chase away this restless feeling she'd had ever since that vivid dream had captured her two days ago. It was still holding her prisoner.

"I don't know what I'm telling you." Nicole sighed impatiently. "There's a man living next door to me who I'm having erotic dreams about."

And she didn't look happy about it. Nicole had never been this unsettled about a man. This was something new, Marlene thought. "What's he like?"

Nicole shrugged, feeling helpless. How did she begin to describe Dennis? "He fixed my garbage disposal for me."

Marlene struggled to piece together what her younger sister was saying. "He's a plumber?"

This was coming out all wrong. Nicole shook her head. "He's a tax lawyer."

Marlene felt as if she were stumbling around in the dark. She'd been doing a great deal of that lately, ever since Sullivan had entered her life. But the dark could be a very nice place, she thought, when you were there with the right person.

She looked at her sister, bemused. "But he fixes garbage disposals as a hobby."

Nicole let out an exasperated breath. "He messes with my mind as a hobby."

Marlene threaded her arm around Nicole and hugged her. "And he seems to have done a very good job of it, too." She studied her sister for a moment. Nicole had always been the wild one, the one who met life head-on and got up after every bruise. Even so, she felt very protective of her sister. "Do you like him?"

Nicole wanted to say no, but couldn't. The truth was, she didn't know. "If my dream is any indication, I guess I must."

"That's not what I asked." But Marlene had gotten her answer. If it had been no, Nicole would have said so straight away. The last thing she wanted was for Nicole to be hurt again. Though she had never actually complained about it, Marlene knew that Craig had done a job on her sister's heart. "Go slow, Nic, okay?"

Nicole laughed shortly. "I don't intend to go anywhere, Marlene." With her free hand, she patted her stomach. "Except to the hospital to have this baby."

A plate materialized between them, attached to a very dainty hand. "Well, before you do, you have to try this cake. It's to die for," Erin Collins declared behind them.

The redhead maneuvered between the two women. She knew Nicole from the time they had spent in the doctor's waiting room. She had just been introduced to Marlene earlier.

She had three slices of chocolate fudge cake on a festive looking paper plate and offered one to each of them. "I think the doctor is just filling us up with food so that she can lecture us about moderation during the next weigh-in."

Marlene glanced over toward Sheila Pollack. The statuesque blond physician was standing in the middle of a circle of patients, most of whom were pregnant. "I think she's too pleased with her Baby of the Month Club to issue any lectures."

"Baby of the Month Club," Erin echoed. "Is that what she calls us?"

"Anywhere you look here, you could gather twelve women and come up with a continuous calendar." Nicole nodded toward her sister. "Marlene gave birth a little over three weeks ago and I'm due in January."

Erin playfully raised her hand. "I've got dibs on February and I know Mallory is due in March." She pointed toward a bubbly, dark-haired woman by the brick fireplace. She was carrying on an animated conversation with two other guests.

"Wonder who's got April?" Nicole murmured as she looked around the large room.

"Brady." The answer slipped out before Erin could think better of it.

"Brady?" Marlene raised her brow. It seemed an odd name for a woman.

Erin flushed, her light complexion growing almost crimson. "That's the name of the bum who walked out on me." She tried to sound flippant, but even as she said it, her eyes clouded over with the sheen of unshed tears.

You'd think by now, they'd be all gone.

Nicole slipped her arm through Erin's. Compassion filled her. Erin had shared the story with her last month. She knew what it was like to be abandoned.

Nicole explained for Marlene's benefit. "He stepped out on her almost what, five months ago?" she asked Erin.

It felt a great deal longer than that when she counted it in sleepless nights. "Almost. I haven't heard a word from him. No one has." It was as if Brady had decided to disappear off the face of the earth rather than to deal with the issue between them.

That sounded rather odd to Marlene. "Have you filed a missing person's report on him?"

Erin nodded. "So far there's been no response. It's as if Brady doesn't want to be found—" she shrugged helplessly. "We had a fight."

It must have been some fight to have lasted this long without a resolution. Marlene thought of the recent battles in her own life, the misunderstandings that had been straightened out. There were always solutions as long as you had the courage to look for them.

"Have you thought of taking out an ad in the personals to get in contact with him?" she asked Erin.

Erin looked at her. "A what?"

"A personal ad," Marlene repeated.

"Marlene's in advertising," Nicole explained affectionately. "She thinks everything can be solved with an ad."

Erin looked at the other women thoughtfully. An ad, she thought, turning the idea over in her mind.

Just maybe...

Chapter 7

Nicole spent the night before Christmas at home. Dennis debated going over to see her, then decided against it. He still needed some time to sort out what had happened between them. In the last few days he had made it a point to maintain his distance. He pretended to leave each morning and to return after six each evening.

His attraction to her bothered him. This was a case, nothing more. No different than the ones that had come before, no different than the ones that would follow. He could say it, he just couldn't make himself really believe it.

He felt edgy. There was no doubt in his mind that either Standish or someone like him would show up again. Word at the department had it that Standish was spending the holidays with his family at Lake Tahoe. Dennis knew better than to relax.

On Christmas Day Nicole left her apartment early. Through his monitor, he saw that she hesitated before his door, then obviously thought better of what she was about to do. Turning abruptly, she hurried away to her car.

Dennis picked up his transmitter. "She's on her way out."

"I see her," Winston answered a beat later. "Merry Christmas."

"Yeah, Merry Christmas." For them, the holiday would come later, when the job was done.

Holding the transmitter in one hand, Dennis grabbed his jacket from the sofa where he had thrown it the day before. He tucked it under his arm and opened the refrigerator. He quickly tossed a few things into a paper bag. He had a hunch this might be a lengthy ordeal.

"I'm following."

"Why don't I get to follow once in a while?" Winston complained.

"The van's too big and I'm better at this," Dennis answered. He knew Winston would take no offense. They'd been partners almost from the first and had worked out an amiable camaraderie and a verbal shorthand that made working together easy and comfortable.

"That's because you get all the practice," Winston grumbled in reply. "Well, get your tail out here or you'll lose her, homing device or no homing device."

"On my way."

Dennis followed Nicole at a discreet distance. The homing device he had attached to the underside of her car made keeping track of her simple. When she turned onto MacArthur, heading south, he knew she was on her way to her sister's house.

Dennis called the information in to Winston. "Looks like she's spending the day at Marlene's."

"Wish I was spending the day at Marlene's instead of in a van."

"Make yourself at home in the apartment while I'm gone," Dennis suggested. "Just don't forget which monitor you're supposed to be watching." He knew that Winston had a weakness for football games.

"You do your job, Lincoln, I'll do mine." Winston broke the connection.

Dennis retracted the antenna on his portable telephone and settled back in his seat, making himself as comfortable as possible. He was parked behind the structural skeleton of a custom-made house that was only partially completed. Located near the top of the hill, it was the perfect cover, allowing him to see without being observed by anyone else.

Around noon, having depleted half a bag of the cookies he had brought with him, he called Moira to wish her Merry Christmas.

"And Merry Christmas to you, too. Why don't you drop by and bring that sorry partner of yours with you? I'm having a few people over, but there's plenty to go around. There's a present under the tree with your name on it," she coaxed when he didn't answer.

There was a dog barking in the background. Knowing Moira, he was surprised it was only one. "Can't, I'm working."

"But it's Christmas."

"The bad guys don't know that."

She sighed. "Which is what makes them bad guys. Okay, come when you can. And I don't have to tell you—"

"Be careful," he finished for her. "Always am."

"Yeah, right."

He knew she was thinking of the time he had been shot. The doctors hadn't held out much hope. But he had gone on to confound them all. "Stop worrying."

"Can't. I love you even though you're ugly and stupid."

"Same goes," he answered. He heard a doorbell ring and the dog barking again. "I think you're being paged."

"'Bye."

He flipped the phone closed and went on waiting. He

entertained himself by playing solitaire until he ran out of light.

It was nine o'clock and Nicole was still at Marlene's. It looked as if she was going to spend the night. He crossed his arms before him and closed his eyes, confident that the signal from her car would wake him up if she turned on the ignition.

He'd spent worse Christmases.

Dennis was awake long before Nicole left Marlene's house at eight the following morning. He glanced at his depleted food supply and sighed. Breakfast would have to wait until he was in the apartment again. If that was where she was going.

He tailed her car, keeping a good city block between them. He was just pulling his Mustang into the carport when he heard Nicole scream. This time he knew the difference between annoyance and anguish. This wasn't a garbage disposal acting up. His car door was still hanging open as he ran for her apartment.

"Nicole!" He pounded on the door. "Open the door, it's Dennis." What the hell could have gone wrong? Winston was supposed to be monitoring her apartment from the van.

She was pale when she opened the door. Pale and shaking. He grabbed her by the shoulders, afraid that she was going to faint.

"What is it? Is it the baby? Is it coming?"

For a moment, she couldn't speak. She felt so violated, so angry and so completely impotent all at the same time. It almost paralyzed her. Finally, she shook her head, struggling to get control over herself.

"Look," she said in a hoarse whisper. "Look." Nicole repeated the word, her voice growing stronger. She wrenched free of his grasp and turned to gesture around behind her. "Look at what they've done!"

For the first time, he saw. The apartment had been completely torn apart. The sofa had been almost dismantled, cushions were knifed, their insides savagely dragged out and slashed. Paintings that she had hung on the wall were either dangling on their sides or ripped off, lying on the ground, with their frames broken. In the kitchen, the cabinets had all been emptied, their contents thrown on the ground. A shattered jar of sauce congealed in the strewn contents of a cereal box. Glasses that had previously lined a shelf had been swept to one side and had fallen on the floor, shattered.

There wasn't a single place that had been left untouched.

The dazed look in her eyes gave way to horror. "Omigod, the nursery."

Before he could stop her, Nicole ran into the spare bedroom. The room she had worked over so diligently to transform into her baby's nursery. Dennis hurried after her.

Chaos had entered here as well. Everything had been overturned and emptied. Savage, plundering hands had been everywhere.

Nicole stood in the center of the room without saying a word.

Dennis began to place his arm around her, wanting to comfort her. He was at a loss as to what to say. Anger choked him.

She shook him off. When she spun around to face him, the fear in her eyes had been replaced by fury. She didn't have to be told who had done this.

"Who does he think he is?" she demanded hotly. "Who the hell does that bastard think he is, coming in here and tearing apart my things?" Tears stung her eyes and she blinked, keeping them back.

She ran her hand along the railing of the crib she had spent hours assembling. The crib had been broken like so much kindling, shattered purely out of spite.

Nicole's anguish was almost palpable. This shouldn't

have happened, Dennis fumed. "I'll tell you who. The number two man in a very powerful gambling syndicate."

She looked at him, stunned. She had thought the man was just one of the sleazy people Craig had kept in his inner circle the last couple of years. She had no idea Standish was anyone of notoriety. "How would you know that?"

He shrugged carelessly, making his knowledge seem nothing out of the ordinary. If he still thought she was knowingly involved, this clinched it for him. "You hear things and get to know the underbelly of society when you're a lawyer."

She wouldn't have thought that he knew anyone like that. Nicole let out a shaky breath as she looked around the room.

Nicole jumped when she felt the hand on her shoulder.

He hated the fear that had leaped into her eyes. He knew it would take her a long time to get over it. "Want to sit down?"

She shook her head. "No, I want to kill him with my bare hands."

He laughed shortly, but there was no smile on his face. "You and probably a lot of other people."

She didn't doubt that for a moment. She hated the man and the power he had over her life, the power to make her afraid.

"I was wondering when he was going to contact me." There was irony in her voice as she mocked herself. "I thought he'd call."

"He did, just not the way you expected him to." Dennis wanted to get her out of here; he didn't care what his superiors had to say about his interference. "You can't stay here."

"Why not?" It was going to be all right. Standish had been here and gone. Why would he come back a third time? "He saw that I didn't have whatever it is he's looking for."

That wasn't a foregone conclusion. "Maybe he thinks you hid it."

Nicole turned from the wreckage and looked at him incredulously. Her eyes were wide with disbelief. "He'll be back?"

He hated doing this to her, but better this than having her hurt. "Maybe."

That wasn't good enough. How long was she expected to stay away? A day, a week, a month?

"I'm not running based on a 'maybe.' This is my home," she insisted heatedly. "Mine."

He knew how she felt, but that didn't alter the facts. "A dead bolt isn't going to keep him out."

Nicole set her mouth stubbornly. Frustration filled him. His hands were tied. He couldn't make her leave if she didn't want to, and he couldn't tell her who he was without surrendering his cover. He couldn't afford to do that. Even if he did risk it, she might not believe him. Or believe anything he told her after that.

There had to be another way.

"But a dog might." It was thin, but it was better than nothing.

She looked over to the window. A piece of the lamp Marlene had given her was sticking up. A lamp that matched the one in Robby's room. She picked it up.

"I don't have a dog," she said dully.

"But Moira does." She looked at him, confused and he hurried to explain. "My sister loves animals and trains dogs as a hobby. She's always picking up strays, bringing them home and training them."

His words weren't making any sense to her. "I don't see how—"

She was in shock, he thought. She just didn't know enough to realize it. He took the fragments of the lamp out of her hands.

"You need some sort of protection. We've already seen what they can do with locks. If you have a Doberman or a German shepherd in the apartment—temporarily," he added, "it can protect you."

She'd never had a dog. Her father hadn't allowed it. The idea of a large dog looming around didn't make her feel better. "What'll protect me from the Doberman?"

He smiled, wanting to reassure her. "All of Moira's animals are good-natured and well trained."

She had her doubts. "So they'll lick intruders to death."

"Something like that." He was already crossing the threshold. Moira was home. He knew she'd have no objections to helping out. "Let me make a call—" Dennis stopped. Nicole, despite her anger, was still very pale. "You'll be all right alone?"

"Sure."

He wasn't convinced, but there was something he had to see to first. Dennis righted the overturned rocking chair for her and checked it over quickly. The runners weren't broken.

Gently, he coaxed her over to it. "Sit down and wait for me." She seemed to collapse into it, as if her legs wouldn't have been able to support her a minute longer. "I'll be right back," he promised. "I'll help you clean up this mess."

"I—"

He wasn't about to let her push him away. "Don't argue."

Nicole swallowed. There was a huge lump in her throat, but she refused to cry. "I wasn't going to argue. I was going to say thank you."

He nodded, not knowing how to respond. He was better quipped to counter her arguments than deal with her gratitude.

"Sit there," he ordered.

He strode out of the apartment. But it wasn't to call

Moira. Dennis glanced to make sure Nicole hadn't gone to the window, then took an indirect route to where Winston was parked in the van.

Containing his anger, Dennis rapped lightly once. The door was unlocked and he let himself in.

The interior of the van was outfitted with state-of-the-art surveillance equipment. Had Winston McNally been as tall as his partner, there wouldn't have been enough room for both of them.

If there had been three times as much room, the anger in Dennis's eyes would have been impossible to miss. "Her apartment looks like the site of World War Three. Where the hell were you while all this was happening?"

"Right here. They just left. There were two of them." Winston raised his hand before Dennis could say anything. "Hey, don't get me wrong. I feel bad, but it's my job to observe and record, not to interfere."

Dennis thought of the look of devastation on Nicole's face. As if something precious had been robbed from her. "This isn't some prime directive on 'Star Trek,' Winston."

"No, it's not," Winston agreed. "It's real."

He spoke patiently, as if he were instructing a class full of rookies. Dennis knew he was behaving like one and he didn't like it. He liked knowing that he would also have had to stand by and allow the break-in to happen even less, but it went with the job. You didn't always feel good about yourself.

"Interfering would have blown our cover and jeopardized months of the department's work. We need to know where the disk is as much as they do," Winston reminded Dennis. He moved a container of stale coffee. "Now, she might be involved and she might not—"

Dennis cut him short. "She's not."

He said that with too much feeling. Winston raised a skeptical brow. "And you would know that because...?"

Dennis knew that look and he didn't care for it being directed at him. "It's a gut feeling."

"A gut feeling," Winston repeated. "And you're turning your gut over to Sherwood as hard evidence?"

Dennis sighed, dragging his hands through his hair. Maybe he had come on too strong. "Who broke in?"

"It wasn't Goldilocks, looking for porridge." Winston hit one of the recorders and cued it up. As Dennis watched, he saw two average looking men let themselves into Nicole's apartment. Winston gestured to the monitor. "A couple of ugly looking goons, even uglier looking than my brothers-in-law. They were in and out in less than twenty minutes. And they didn't appear to be very happy when they left." Winston had watched, waiting for them to find the disk. If they had, he would have had backup at the complex within minutes. "They didn't find what they were looking for."

Dennis hit the play button. The men on the monitor began taking the living room apart. He clenched his fists, rage battering at his chest. "That's because she doesn't have it."

"Gut feeling again?"

An angry retort rose to his lips, but he let it go. "You had to be there."

A smile curled along Winston's thin lips. "I almost was."

Dennis looked at his partner, not following him.

Winston pointed to another monitor, the one corresponding to the camera positioned in her kitchen. "You kissed her. It's all there on tape." Winston shook his head. "Don't get involved."

Dennis shrugged. "I'm not."

"Look me in the eye and say that."

Dennis reached for the door handle. "You know I don't like to look at anything ugly."

"Yeah? Then how do you shave in the morning?" Winston waved at the door. "You'd better get back, or she'll wonder where you went."

Dennis looked at the monitor. Nicole wasn't sitting where he had left her. Instead, she was on her knees, folding baby clothing and placing them into one of the drawers that had been yanked out of the overturned bureau.

Nicole was crying. He felt something twist inside his chest.

Swearing, he left the van without saying anything further. He wanted to go to her, but he had to call Moira first. There was still the matter of the dog.

The door had barely closed behind him as he tapped out his sister's phone number on the keypad. He filled her in quickly.

"Sure, I have just the sort of dog you want." Moira said. "He's great with kids, a real puppy dog. And very protective. I was going to name him after you, but I decided that it might be a little confusing. It'd be hard to tell the two of you apart."

Normally, he didn't mind her teasing. But his nerves were on a short leash. He wanted to get back to Nicole. "Thanks. When can I pick him up?"

"He's yours anytime you want him. Just give me a call."

He was about to thank her and hang up, when he realized that Nicole might want to know a little more about the dog. "What kind of a dog is he?"

"A Labrador. But don't tell him. He thinks he's people."

Dennis laughed. "You really should get out more, Moira."

"I could say the same thing about you, big brother." Moira's tone was curious, although she heard something different in his voice. "Is this for a case or is there something more involved?"

He didn't want to get into it with her. He'd put up with enough from Winston. "Just a case, Moira. I'll give you a call later."

"I'll be here."

Dennis hung up and hurried to Nicole's apartment. The door was unlocked, not that locks mattered, he thought darkly.

He walked into the nursery. Nicole was struggling to pick up the bureau, still devoid of drawers.

Damn, but she was stubborn. Dennis crossed to her, moving Nicole aside. "You were supposed to stay put, not move furniture."

She gasped, startled, her hand flying to her mouth. She felt embarrassed and angry over her reaction. Her heart pounded hard in her chest and felt as if it were repositioning itself in her throat.

"I didn't hear you come in." She took a deep breath, trying to steady her frayed nerves. "Couldn't you have knocked or something?"

"Sorry." She looked so frail, as if she were going to break at any moment. Instincts took over and he took her into his arms. "I didn't mean to startle you."

She shrugged, accepting the apology. Her temper cooled. "I think I'm going to be startled by any noise I hear for a long time."

He knew she was. Unable to help himself, he ran the back of his hand along her cheek. "My sister has a dog we can use."

She tried not to think how comforting his presence was. She knew the danger of depending on someone. "We?" she echoed.

"You," he corrected. He knew she was pigheaded, but she also knew she was afraid. "If it makes you feel any better, I can stay here tonight," he suggested softly.

Her reaction was instant. "No, I have to face this on my…" Nicole faltered. What if Standish did return? "Well, maybe just for one night." She'd feel better about this in the morning she promised herself. "If you don't mind."

He held her close to him, wishing there was a way he

could have spared her this. "It was my suggestion, wasn't it?"

It was, but it wasn't fair to put him out like this. This was her problem, not his. "You don't have to do this for me."

"Yes, I do." He was beginning to chafe under the image she had of him. Under the image he had created. "Call it my way of keeping America safe."

She laughed at the way he worded it. The man was unbelievably sweet. And he'd accomplished the impossible. He'd made her feel better. "Does the American flag come down and unfurl now?"

"Complete with the rendition of 'The Star Spangled Banner'— sung in the right key."

She laughed but the laugh ended in tears. Embarrassment colored her cheeks and she buried her face in his chest. It took all he had not to stroke her hair. More than he had. Murmuring words of endearment, he gently threaded his fingers through her hair. He felt her crying against him.

"I'm being an idiot." She certainly felt like one.

"No, you're not." Knowing that Winston was monitoring them, it was a little easier to refrain from kissing her. A little, but not much. "You'd be an idiot if you weren't afraid."

She looked up, trying to smile. "Then you don't mind if I get your shirt wet?"

"It's washable."

Her sigh was ragged as she fought for composure. "It's just that I was trying so hard to get my life back together again." She shut her eyes, squeezing out the tears. She refused to allow any more to form. Tears were useless. "Craig and I weren't close anymore, but his death really devastated me. It wasn't easy, but I was finally pulling myself up when—when—" She gestured around, afraid that she was going to cry again.

He cupped her face in his hands and brushed her tears away with his thumbs. "Everything's going to be all right."

She forced a smile to her lips. "You sound as if you're making me a promise."

"Maybe I am."

The sigh that escaped seemed to shimmer in the air. She sniffed as she looked around the room. "I guess I'd better get busy."

"We'd better get busy," he corrected her.

It felt good, she thought, having someone to turn to.

"What's his name?" Nicole asked as she warily eyed the big black dog standing in the middle of her living room.

They had spent five hours getting the worst of the mess cleared away and the apartment back together. Then Dennis had left her to pick up the dog. She had waited tensely for his return, but now, seeing the animal, she began to have second thoughts. He looked awfully large.

"Romeo." Dennis thought that it was a stupid name for a dog, but then Moira had always done things in her own unique way.

"Romeo," Nicole repeated. The dog's ears pricked up at the sound of his name. Nicole smiled. "Romeo," she called to the dog. He trotted over to her. After a moment of apparent indecision, he licked her hand.

Dennis looked very pleased with himself. "I think he just adopted you."

Nicole petted the stately head. Maybe this wouldn't be so bad after all. "What do I feed him?"

His sister had covered all the bases. "Moira sent over a twenty-pound bag of his food and a few of his things so that he wouldn't have too much trouble adjusting." Romeo was nuzzling against Nicole. Dennis grinned. "My guess is that she shouldn't have bothered. He looks right at home now."

Nicole looked up at Dennis. "I don't know how to thank you."

"There isn't any need to thank me." It would only make him feel worse in the long run, when everything came out in the open.

"Where are you going?" she called after him.

"To get Romeo's food before he decides to lick your hand off."

She felt like a child asking, but it was the woman who was afraid. A child could seek refuge in make-believe, a woman could not. "Are you still going to stay here tonight?"

"If you want me to." He paused, waiting.

Outside the kitchen window, a car rumbled to life. The sudden noise sent a shiver down her spine. Nicole pressed her lips together. "I want you to."

Chapter 8

There was a warm sensation traveling along his face. Something moist and wet.

Instantly awake, Dennis bolted upright on the sofa. Moira's dog yelped and stumbled backward, his long tongue lolling to one side.

"Dumb mutt," Dennis muttered, wiping residue dog slobber from his cheek.

He heard Nicole laughing behind him. Twisting around, he saw her standing in the tiny hallway that connected the two bedrooms. The dog had retreated beside her.

"I'm sorry," she apologized, though it didn't stop her from laughing again. "It's just that you looked so funny. You were smiling when he licked you." She wondered what he had been dreaming about. Nicole stroked the dog's head. "I think he's really taken with you."

"The feeling isn't exactly mutual." He looked at her. Nicole was wearing fawn-colored calf-length boots and a mint green, long-sleeved dress. There was a shawl draped over one arm. Dennis glanced at his wristwatch. It wasn't even seven o'clock. Where was she going at this hour? "How long have you been standing there?"

"Not long at all." Just long enough to observe him. He'd seemed so natural, sleeping there, his blond hair falling into his face. Seeing him like that had tugged at her heart, as if a little voice were whispering to her that this is the way it should be.

But it wasn't and she couldn't allow herself to be carried away by daydreams of what might have been or should be. Not again. This time she didn't have just herself to think of.

He knew the art gallery didn't open until ten. Did she have an early day?

"Going to work?"

She instinctively hesitated. Yet, after yesterday, Dennis was entitled to ask a few questions.

Nicole shook her head. "No, things are kind of slow there. I've arranged to take the next few days off." She tried to divorce herself from her words. "I told Lawrence what happened."

Dennis raised a brow. "Lawrence?"

"My boss. Lawrence Patterson. He owns the art gallery where I work." Lawrence had been very sympathetic and told her to take all the time she needed to pull herself together. Her job would be waiting for her when she got back. Well-off, the gallery was more of a hobby for him than a way to make a living.

Nicole's eyes slid over Dennis's chest. The blanket she had thrown over him during the night had slid to the floor. She'd stood watching his bare chest rise and fall for a few minutes before the dog had decided to anoint him.

Dennis leaned over and reached for his shirt on the coffee table. He shrugged into it. "So, where are you going?"

Lowering her eyes from his torso, Nicole checked her purse for her wallet. It was on the top of her checkbook. "I have an appointment at the hospital. Dr. Pollack wants to make sure that there's only one occupant in here." She rubbed her stomach and sighed. "I seem to be too large to be carrying just one baby."

That sounded a little haphazard to him. "Shouldn't he have done that before?"

"She," Nicole corrected. "And she did, but she wants to do another test to double-check the results."

The doctor had cornered her at the Christmas party and suggested having a second test. Now she was almost sorry she had agreed. Just something more to worry about until she knew the results. She'd know if she was having twins, wouldn't she? Nicole thought a little desperately. She just couldn't be carrying more than one.

"Dr. Pollack says sometimes one baby hides behind the other and the sonogram only shows one."

He heard the concern in her voice. Dennis got up. Romeo jumped to his feet, ready to play. He gave the dog the command to stay the way Moira had shown him. "Give me a couple of minutes and I'll drive you."

But Nicole was already crossing to the door. "No, don't bother. You've done more than enough for me already." She paused as she realized what time it was. "Besides, don't you have to go to work?"

It took him only a minute to come up with an excuse. "I have a lot of vacation time coming to me. It was a case of use it or lose it so I took the week between Christmas and New Year's off." That would buy him a little time, he thought.

She nodded. That would explain why he was here yesterday during the day. "Well, I don't want you wasting it on me."

She wasn't being coy, but she was no longer dismissive, either. His eyes touched her face. "I don't consider it wasted."

The way he looked at her made the very air catch in her lungs. Just like in her dream. Except that this was real. A little too real.

Back off, Nicole, you don't need any more complications in your life.

She cleared her throat and nodded toward the kitchen. "There're frozen waffles in the freezer and a couple of boxes of cereal in the pantry. Help yourself to breakfast."

She barely had her hand on the doorknob when a loud bark stopped her in her tracks. She'd forgotten about the dog.

Nicole turned around and looked at Dennis. "Do I feed him breakfast?"

"He's an adult dog. He only eats once a day." Dennis buttoned his shirt and tucked it into his jeans. He noticed that the dog was sniffing around the corners of the kitchen. "And all the food he can scrounge up," he added with a grin.

"The way I keep house, he'll get fat while he's here." She looked toward Dennis, indecisive. She shouldn't even ask. "I'll see you later?"

He nodded. "I'll be here." Despite her condition and the makeup she had skillfully applied, she looked like a waif. He didn't like the idea of her leaving alone. "Sure you don't want me to—?"

She cut him off. "I'm sure. I like being independent."

Nicole opened the door. Her car was standing just where she had left it yesterday. She hesitated in the doorway.

Dennis came up behind her. Instinctively protective, he placed his hands on her shoulders. "What?"

She felt like an idiot, but fear was hard to shake off once it got a good hold. "I know this is stupid..."

"But?"

The words rushed out. "But I saw this movie once where

this man's car was wired with a bomb..." Her voice trailed off as she bit her lower lip.

He wished he had been here instead of Winston during the break-in. Cover or no cover, he would have found a way to stop them. "Standish just wanted to scare you, Nicole. If he thinks you have something that belongs to him, he's not going to kill you. That would be self-defeating. Standish isn't dumb."

She nodded, trying hard to hang on to what he was telling her. "Makes sense."

He turned her around to face him. "If you're afraid, we can always take my car."

No, he was right. She couldn't succumb to fear. Nicole shook her head. "I'm just seeing ghosts where there aren't any." She smiled at him. "Thanks for being so logical." Standing on her toes, she kissed him lightly, then took a step back. The moment seemed to freeze in time.

His eyes on hers, Dennis threaded his fingers through her hair. Lowering his head, he kissed her again. Kissed her with feeling. The dog barked sharply, obviously feeling left out and wanting attention. He ignored Romeo. Ignored everything except the dizzying effect she was having on him.

Damn, but a man could get used to being knocked senseless like this.

His lips worked over hers slowly, savoring every movement, every sensation. She tasted faintly of raspberry jam and desire.

Nicole wound her arms around his neck. This was crazy, she shouldn't be letting this happen. And yet she couldn't *not* let it happen. It felt like the one ray of sunshine in a world that was filled with rain.

The dog barked louder and nosed them apart. She laughed, slipping her arms from his neck. "I think he's jealous."

"I could ask Moira for another dog," he suggested half seriously.

Nicole shook her head. "Just as well. That wasn't a very logical thing to do."

Logic certainly had nothing to do with what he was feeling right now. "Why?"

"Well for starters, I'm pregnant and there's a really nasty character out to get me."

He worded it very carefully. "They're out to get something they think you have, not you. And besides, complications are what make life more interesting." Not that he needed any, he reminded himself.

She didn't have time to discuss this with him. If she didn't leave now, she was going to be late for her appointment.

Nicole hurried out. "I'll see you later."

"Count on it." He remained in the doorway, watching until he couldn't see her car any longer.

She was right, he thought as he closed the door again. This wasn't logical. But for now, he was stuck with it.

Less than five minutes later, the door opened again. Dennis turned, thinking that perhaps she had forgotten something.

But instead of Nicole, he saw Winston's four-by-four body entering as the latter walked toward him.

Winston jerked a thumb behind him at the door. "I thought I'd let myself in." He looked at the black Labrador that was shadowing every move Dennis made. "Bonding with the dog?"

Dennis threw a stuffed, well-chewed fuzzy toy over to the corner of the room. Romeo chased after it and then settled down with the toy between his paws.

"I have an affinity for dumb animals." Dennis turned to look at his partner. "Speaking of which, what are you doing out of your cage?"

Free of the van's confinement, Winston stretched his legs and went directly to the refrigerator. He'd heard Nicole's instructions to Dennis regarding breakfast and extended them to include himself. He poured himself a bowl of cereal, and then went for the milk.

"I've been thinking. If you believe she doesn't have anything to do with the Syndicate, and they obviously didn't find the disk, why do we tell Sherwood we're still hanging around here?"

Dennis watched as Winston made short work of the cereal. "Because somehow, she's the connection." He'd worked this out for himself earlier. "Logan had that disk. He wouldn't have destroyed it." Dennis was certain of that. "He would have hidden it somewhere safe, thinking it was his insurance policy against the Syndicate."

Finished, Winston rinsed out the bowl and placed it on the rack. "Boy, was he wrong."

"Yeah, but that disk is still around somewhere. My guess is that she doesn't know she knows."

Winston turned his attention to the bananas in the fruit bowl. He broke off one banana from the bunch, offering the rest to Dennis. Dennis placed them back in the bowl.

Inhaling the banana, Winston tossed the peel into the garbage. "So what are you going to do, hypnotize her?"

He let the wisecrack pass. "I'm going to invest a little more time and see if I can figure out where Logan hid it. Something I say might trigger her memory."

Winston raised his eyes toward the miniature camera. "Just be careful you don't wind up triggering other things."

Dennis put his hand on the doorknob. "Your van's calling to you."

But Winston remained where he was. He nodded toward the Labrador. "What did you say the pooch's name was?"

"Romeo."

Winston called out, "Sic 'im, Romeo."

Romeo looked from one man to the other and continued chewing on the stuffed toy. It was shaped to look like a man and Dennis couldn't help wondering what the dog thought as he methodically worked on the toy's leg.

Winston shook his head. "Doesn't respond to commands very well, does he?"

"I told him to stay."

Winston sighed. "Figures." He looked out the window. Craning his neck, he could see the converted Volkswagen bus. "Lucky thing I'm not claustrophobic."

"You make up for it by being a chronic complainer," Dennis deadpanned.

Winston muttered something under his breath about applying for a transfer as he left.

Nicole drove home from the hospital in a daze. She wasn't even certain how she got into the car, or how the car had found its way to the freeway.

She didn't need this.

The words echoed over and over again in her mind. This wasn't the kind of surprise she was free to welcome now. Under other circumstances, she might have even been overjoyed, a little stunned, maybe, but definitely happy. But not now. In her present situation, with ghouls hiding in the shadows, waiting to upend her life, or worse, she just wasn't equipped to handle this latest piece of news.

Automatically, she eased down on the brake as she came to a stop sign at the end of the freeway exit. As the car stopped, she looked down at her stomach in wonder.

Twins. She was going to have twins. Two babies. Two mouths to feed, two bottoms to change. Two tiny human beings depending on her to show them the right path. Nicole pressed her lips together, sealing in a moan.

Oh, God.

The numbness increased instead of abated as she approached her apartment complex. She pulled into her designated spot in the carport and then just sat there, too overwhelmed to get out.

It felt like the straw that ultimately broke the camel's back.

Dennis looked out the front window and wondered why Nicole was just sitting there. Since she hadn't wanted him to take her, Dennis had requested that another agent follow her to the hospital while he remained in her apartment. There was an outside chance that Standish's men might return, and he wanted to be there if they did. He had remained in her apartment the entire time she'd been gone, sifting through things, looking for anything that might give him a clue where the disk was hidden. He'd come up with nothing.

Shirley, an agent he sometimes worked with, had called in half an hour ago, saying nothing eventful had taken place and that Nicole was on her way home. Yet something must have happened. Even from where he was standing, Nicole looked as white as a sheet.

He wondered if the shock of having her apartment ransacked had hit her belatedly. When she still didn't get out, Dennis hurried out to the car.

"Are you all right?"

Nicole looked to her left. The window was rolled down and Dennis was crouching beside her. Still in a mental fog, she hadn't heard him approach. She shook her head slowly. "No. I may never be all right again."

He couldn't begin to guess what was wrong. Nicole didn't look any different than when she had left, except that the color had drained out of her face.

"What—?"

She stared down at her swollen abdomen as if it didn't belong to her. "I'm having twins."

Everything was all right. She hadn't been approached by

Standish's men. Relief nudged aside the concern that had been mushrooming within him.

He wasn't supposed to be concerned. Not to this extent. There had always been a small section of himself that he'd held in reserve. He did it consciously. It allowed him to step back and view situations impartially. That was a necessary part of the job.

It was also, he supposed, a survival mechanism. Remaining uninvolved allowed him to maintain an overview that always showed him the way out.

But right now, he couldn't find that line, that boundary limit that he refrained from crossing over. Without that boundary, he felt himself slipping into Nicole's world. It was the look on her face that had done it. Or perhaps her obstinacy not to accept any help when she obviously needed it.

She made him feel protective.

"Twins?" He stood up again. "Is that all? That's great."

The look on her face told him that she didn't think it was so great.

He opened the door for her and took her elbow to help her out. Nicole went through the motions of pulling away, but it was halfhearted at best.

"It's all right, I can walk." Her words sounded wooden, hollow. She made him think of a foreign movie in which the character's lips were out of sync with the sound track.

Dennis closed the car door behind her, locking it. He took her arm again. "Humor me, you've obviously had a shock."

"It's not a shock," Nicole protested, the words springing to her lips reflexively. It was a mistake, the sonogram was wrong. She wasn't having twins. She couldn't be. "It's a..." Her voice trailed off as helplessness fought for control of her. "A shock," she conceded ruefully.

He was leading her to her door. She moved in a trance, barely aware of her surroundings.

"God, what am I going to do? Twins." She looked at Dennis, her eyes wide. "Double the work, double the expense."

How in God's name was she supposed to manage all this? Craig hadn't left any insurance policy to cover expenses in case he died. He had planned on living forever. She shook her head, attempting to clear it. He hadn't left anything except debts and trouble.

Dennis pushed the door open now and gently urged Nicole toward the threshold. "Look at it from the positive side," he suggested.

Nicole blinked and looked at him as if suddenly realizing where she was. She looked up. The air was brisker now. And the sky so blue it made her long to be somewhere else. As someone else. It was the kind of day you sat on a bench, your hands thrust deep into your pockets, talking to someone you were in love with. It wasn't meant to be spent in a tailspin. Which was exactly the way she felt.

She walked inside the apartment. "Such as?"

Romeo came bounding over, waiting to be petted. Dennis quickly shut the door and obliged the animal. His eyes never left Nicole's.

"Double the fun. Double the love." It was what he felt she needed to hear.

Her expression was incredulous. He was the kind of man she pictured with a baby on each knee. He'd be good at it, not her.

"Doesn't your plane ever land? I'm going to need two of everything." God, but she felt overwhelmed. "Like two sets of hands to start with." She blew out a breath, suddenly feeling cheated. Worrying took away the joy. "I was really looking forward to this baby."

That shouldn't have changed. "You still can." He slanted a look at her face. "Twice as much."

Was he trying to be funny? And what did he care, anyway? It wasn't his problem. None of this was. She looked at him petulantly. "Do you realize that for the rest of my life, I'm going to be outnumbered?"

She looked so serious, Dennis laughed in response. He couldn't help himself. Annoyed at first, Nicole suddenly joined in. The laughter helped clear away some of the stress she felt.

"Well, I will be," she insisted, gasping for breath.

He urged her toward the kitchen chair, then opened the refrigerator. He poured a glass of orange juice and set it in front of her.

"Don't think of it as 'them' and 'you,'" Dennis told her. "Think of it as an 'us.' Besides, the twins will have built-in playmates. You won't have to worry about them getting lonely."

He was right, but she didn't feel like conceding that to him. Not right away. Not until she got over being mad at the world.

"What makes you such an expert?"

"I got along really well with my sister, except for occasionally burying her Barbie doll." He ran his long fingers along Romeo's head. The dog was sitting beside the table, his tail thumping on the ground. "We're still pretty close."

Nicole took a sip of her juice. He had a point. She and Marlene got along well, although there had been a period of time that they didn't. But that rift had been caused by their father, not because of any real animosity between them. She had regarded Marlene as her father's puppet and had urged her to break free. In turn, Marlene had tried to make her conform to acceptable behavior. They might have spared themselves the trouble. Except when he criticized them, their father had ignored them both.

"This could be a good thing," she murmured, more to herself than to him. "At least for the baby. Babies," she amended.

This, she thought, was going to take a hell of a lot of getting used to.

Dennis knew she was right about one thing. She was going to need twice as many things. He thought of Rick Abrahams. He'd helped to recover the man's kidnapped son. Grateful beyond words, Abrahams had offered him his life's savings as a reward. Dennis had demurred, not even settling for dinner. Maybe Nicole could purchase a few items of furniture from him at wholesale prices.

"You know," he began slowly, "one of my clients is Tiny Tots Furnishings. Why don't I take you around to the factory today and we'll see what kind of a deal we can arrange?"

Resistance didn't leap up the way it normally might. She needed help and she knew it. Accepting it from him wasn't difficult. "You're being nice again."

For the sake of the role he was playing, Dennis grinned at her easily. They were making progress. She was beginning to trust him. He wished it didn't make him feel so guilty.

"Sorry, I'm trying to dispel the bad publicity lawyers get."

She felt herself smiling. God, for a few minutes back there, she was certain that she would never be able to smile again. "Single-handedly?"

He lifted a shoulder, then let it drop. "It has to start somewhere."

Even if yesterday hadn't happened, she would have still needed more than she had. Another crib, another high chair. Twice as many clothes as she had now.

Nicole set down the empty glass and shook her head as Dennis began to refill it. "You really know a baby furniture manufacturer?"

Dennis nodded. "I saved his factory for him two years ago." He substituted the word *factory* for *son.* "The owner told me to come around if I ever needed to furnish my nursery."

"You don't," she noted.

He didn't know which he disliked more. When she was being wary, or when she looked devastated.

"Semantics. You do. And favors make the world go around."

How well she knew that. You never really got something for nothing. There was always a payment due in the end. Her expression sobered as she looked at Dennis. "And what sort of favor will you expect for this?"

She sounded as if she expected him to exact some sort of horrible payment from her. "Who did this to you, Nicole?"

His voice was so kind, so gentle. So damn understanding. Resistance wasn't easy, but she managed. "Who did what?"

He saw the guarded look in her eyes. It was something he should have heeded. But didn't. "Who made you so suspicious?"

She wasn't going to answer him. She really wasn't. But there was that same understanding look in his eyes. She found herself trusting it. Just for a moment.

Nicole began petting the dog. Romeo accepted it as his due and laid his head on her lap. Nicole knew that if she looked at Dennis, if she saw pity on his face, she wouldn't be able to stand it.

"I've made some really bad choices in my life. I picked the wrong people to care about, the wrong people to trust."

Images of her father, of Craig and of her mother flashed through her mind. Each had abandoned her in their own way. And taught her a lifelong lesson she intended never to forget. A lesson that told her not to place her faith in anyone.

But the man beside her was making it very hard to remember.

It wasn't all that simple. "Sometimes these things are out

of our hands.'' He raised her chin until her eyes were level with his. ''Sometimes we don't have any say in who we care about.''

An edgy panic filled her. She didn't want to slide down that hole again. ''Oh, yes, we do. And I am never going to care about anyone again.''

''Does that go for the baby?'' he asked quietly. ''Or the babies,'' he amended.

She shrugged carelessly, annoyed that he was so quick to point out inconsistencies. Of course it didn't apply to her babies. It didn't apply to Marlene, either. But that was different. Marlene had been there for her since the very beginning. She would always trust Marlene. But no one else.

''It's too late there,'' she answered grudgingly. ''But that's the exception that proves the rule.'' She knew she wasn't making sense, but she didn't care. ''Besides, it'll be years before the babies can walk out on me.''

The pain in her eyes was almost palpable. ''Is that it?'' It was a rhetorical question. ''Did Craig walk out on you?''

She looked down at her hands. Why had she started this? She was normally so closemouthed, so adept at keeping her own counsel. What was it about him that made her babble like some damn proverbial brook?

''In a manner of speaking,'' she said quietly. ''But it wasn't just Craig.''

He knew the basic facts surrounding Logan, but he wasn't interested in Logan now. He was interested in her. ''Who else walked out on you, Nicole?''

She rose. He wanted to take her into his arms, to comfort her, but she didn't need comfort at this moment. She needed to talk, he thought, to get this out of her system.

''Come on, Nicole,'' he coaxed softly. ''You can tell me.''

Her mouth hardened. ''Nobody.''

She'd already said far more than she was comfortable

with, far more than she'd told anyone. Right now, she just wanted to crawl into bed and pull the covers over her head. Later, she'd find a way to deal with all this. With the idea of having twins and Standish and the restructuring of her whole world.

Right now, she was just bone tired.

Dennis let it go. Instead, he left the kitchen and went into the nursery. The dog trotted after him. After a moment, curious, ashamed of her behavior, Nicole followed. She stopped in the doorway. He had repaired the bureau. Nicole felt tears gathering in her eyes.

He felt her presence. After a moment, he closed his toolbox and rose to face her. "Twins run in your family?" he asked mildly.

His tone defused the situation. "Discord ran in my family." She roused herself. "Sorry. No, no twins. At least, not in mine."

He drew the only logical conclusion he could from her words. "Were there twins in your husband's family?"

"I don't know."

She hated to admit that. She didn't know. She didn't know anything about Craig. Everything she had thought she'd known about Craig had turned out to be a lie, fed to her for effect. Craig Logan had laid a trap for a rich brat. As it turned out, it had sprung on both of them. She hadn't gotten the husband she had thought she was getting, and he hadn't gotten the money he was expecting. Her grandmother's legacy was nowhere near the amount Craig had thought went along with the wedding vows.

Nicole knotted her hands in front of her. She'd been every bit the fool her father had accused her of being and it cost her to admit it, even to herself.

She saw Dennis looking at her. "Craig didn't talk much about his family."

"Estranged?" Dennis guessed.

"Yes." It was as good a description as any, especially since she didn't know if Craig even had any family members who were still alive. No one had crawled out of the woodwork to claim filial ties when he started becoming famous on the racing circuit. "There was a lot of that going around."

He knew she was referring to her own family. "You're going to need help with the twins."

"Yes, I know."

Nicole scrubbed her hands over her face. This placed an entirely different perspective on things. She could be stubbornly independent where her own welfare was concerned. And maybe, feeling that she could make it, she could even remain steadfast about not accepting help where a single child was involved. But two children? Lines had to be drawn somewhere. Or rather, she amended, erased.

Much as she hated doing it, she was going to have to talk to Marlene about her trust fund. She came into it at thirty. She needed it now. How ironic. Only last week, when Marlene had asked her when she was going to forgive her father and accept the money, she'd answered maybe someday.

Someday had arrived quickly. She knew Marlene was ready and willing to advance her money against the fund. Up until now, she had refused.

But up until this morning, she had only been having one baby. No matter how she figured it, she fell painfully short. There was no way out but to take the money she had vehemently sworn she'd never touch.

She could almost hear her father saying, "I knew you would come around."

She still looked dazed. Dennis felt helpless. Maybe the furniture would take her mind off everything for a while. "Would you like to go shopping for the furniture now? All I have to do is make a call."

He'd fixed her disposal, brought her a dog, slept on her

sofa to allay her fears. And she'd done nothing but snap at him. "I wish you weren't being as nice as you are."

"I'll rough you up later." A look leaped into her eyes that he recognized as apprehension. Things were becoming clearer. The bastard. "That was a joke, Nicole. Did Craig—?"

She'd tripped herself up enough for one day. "I'm not answering any more questions without a lawyer."

"I am a lawyer," he reminded her.

"Yes, but you're not mine." She sighed and smiled ruefully. "If you're really on the level, I suppose I shouldn't keep pushing you away." But if something was too good to be true, the odds were that it wasn't true. Craig had taught her that, too. "You'll forgive me, but it's just that I keep waiting for you to tell me what you want in exchange for all this."

He knew he could look very guileless when he wanted to. But part of the answer was true. "Friendship."

That couldn't be all. "And?"

Dennis blew out a breath. He took the wariness in her eyes personally, even though at bottom he knew he deserved it. "Your firstborn if you can't spin straw into gold by sunrise."

Nicole laughed, the tension easing away again. "Funny, you don't look like Rumpelstiltskin."

"I'm not."

I'm something worse, he thought. *A liar and a fraud.*

Chapter 9

Nicole picked her way through the nursery holding a cold can of soda. Maneuvering in the small room was not easy. She handed the can to Dennis.

He shoved the screwdriver he was using into his back pocket as he accepted the soda. "Thanks."

It should be she who was thanking him. Over and over, Nicole thought.

She looked around the crowded nursery. "It looks as if today was Christmas."

The bedroom was crammed with several large, flat cardboard boxes. Two were now empty. Four more still housed baby furniture waiting to be assembled. The bounty was the result of two trips to the Tiny Tots Furnishings factory. From the moment they had entered, they were in the care of the owner, Rick Abrahams. Exuding gratitude, the man couldn't seem to do enough for Dennis.

She was beginning to understand the feeling. Dennis had been at it since late this morning, assembling first a bassinet and now one of the new cribs. She had absolutely no idea how to thank him. Not that he wanted any thanks. He seemed to just enjoy being helpful. That made him a pretty special man in her book.

He looked around for somewhere to rest the can. Nicole took it from him and placed it on top of the newly repaired bureau.

"I still can't believe he gave this all to us at cost." And even that had been under protest. The man had wanted to give it for free. "Just how much of a savings did you get from Mr. Abrahams?"

There'd been a moment in the factory when he had been afraid Abrahams was going to slip and tell Nicole the agony he had gone through, not knowing whether his son was alive or dead. When he had called ahead for an appointment, Dennis had cautioned the man not to say anything. Abrahams had been more than happy to go along with any story Dennis wanted to tell. But lying always became complicated.

The screw that had been included to attach the metal frame to the wooden rails was too large. Dennis strained, forcing it into the small hole in the wood.

"You're confusing tax lawyer with tax accountant," he told her matter-of-factly. "He had a very creative bookkeeper who never filed returns, just pocketed the tax money himself. He left the country, leaving Mr. Abrahams woefully in arrears with the IRS."

She tried not to stare at his biceps as they tensed while he worked the screwdriver. "Did you ever find the bookkeeper?"

There, in. He began working on the next screw. This one matched the hole. "Nope."

She thought of the man Dennis had introduced her to. Pity filled her. "I guess that justice only prevails on the movie of the week."

"Sometimes," he agreed. He liked to think that once in

a while, he made a difference. "Sometimes it holds its own."

She was beginning to realize that he was modest to a fault when it came to his own merits. "Tell me."

He stopped and looked at her over his shoulder. She had said the words the way a little girl asking for a bedtime story might. "Tell you what?"

She felt tired. She had felt tired all day and wanted to sit down. But it didn't seem right, not when he was working so hard to assemble her funiture. She remained on her feet, hoping to help somehow.

"About your cases."

"Why?" He laughed shortly. "Do you want to take a nap?"

He was being modest again. She had a feeling he wasn't the type of man who did mundane things. Things became special in his hands, she thought. This time, she was sure she was right. It wasn't the way it had been with Craig. Dennis just looked too honest to be anything but the man he professed to be: simple, kind and yet exciting.

"They can't be that dull."

He didn't feel like inventing stories. He'd lied enough to her as it was.

"Yes, they can." He tested the side of the crib. It felt sturdy. "This is my vacation, the last thing I want to do is talk shop."

She watched him as he picked up the headboard and leaned it against the railing. "I would think that the last thing you'd want to do is spend your vacation with a pregnant woman, helping her assemble baby furniture."

He was going to need help with this, he decided. "Maybe I like baby furniture." Dennis leaned the railing against the wall for a moment, resting the headboard next to it. He looked at her. Her brow was a little puckered and there was a slight bead of perspiration along her hairline. Swollen stomach and all, she was the most beautiful thing he'd ever seen. "Or maybe I just like the pregnant woman."

Very gently, he tilted her chin up until her eyes met his. When they did, he brushed his lips lightly over hers. It was all he would allow himself. Anything more and his mind wouldn't be on his work any longer.

He grinned, withdrawing his hand. "Yup, that must be it." His eyes teased hers.

She felt like a kid, she thought. Pregnant twice over, the target of some hoodlums, and she still felt like giggling. He did this to her, she thought. He did that *for* her. "What?"

Dennis turned back to his work. "I like assembling baby furniture."

Nicole laughed and shook her head. All of her reservations had fallen by the wayside in the last few days, sliding away like the cocoon surrounding a butterfly in the summer. She trusted him. It felt wonderful not to be suspicious, not to be wary. It was as if a weight had been removed from her shoulders. He'd pitched in and helped her get the apartment back together again, even salvaging some of the Christmas decorations, carefully packing them away. He had been attentive, helpful and at times he seemed to second guess her, knowing what she wanted before she said a word. At night, they stayed in and watched videos or just talked. She couldn't remember when she had been happier.

She had almost forgotten about the break-in. Dennis made her feel safe, protected. Though she had initially resisted her feelings, it was no use. She could feel her heart being drawn toward him.

He was one in a million.

And he deserved to know it, she thought. Especially after the way she had originally treated him, like a pariah when all he wanted to do was "be neighborly."

Her mouth twisted in a smile as she watched him. He was hunkered down, fiddling with a screw at the bottom of the railing. She moved closer to him, talking to the top of his head.

"I don't know what I've done to deserve you, but I want you to know that I am grateful."

Her words cut through him like a knife. He didn't want her gratitude. He didn't deserve it. "Don't."

He had almost snapped the warning at her. Why? "What?"

Dennis rose without facing her. He unconsciously pressed his lips together, suppressing the urge to tell her the truth: that he was a Justice Department agent investigating her husband's connection to an organized crime syndicate. He wasn't free to tell her any of that, which only made what she said worse.

"Don't be grateful, Nicole."

Was it so hard for him to accept her thanks? "You make that sound ominous."

He kept his back to her. "No, gratitude tends to color the way you see things." He reached for a smaller screwdriver with a wider head. "You should always keep your eyes open."

Dennis sounded as if he didn't want her gratitude. That did make him one in a million. "Now there's a first, a man warning me away from him." The ones she had known would have used her feelings to take advantage of her. "All my life, I've had men trying to talk me out of my clothes and into bed on the slightest excuse and here you are, pushing me away."

He turned around to face her. "I'm not pushing you away. I'm moralizing." This was getting too serious. He grinned. "Lawyers like to do that once in a while. You know, all those unused ethics floating around."

Uncomfortable with the look in her eyes, with the feeling flowing through his own veins, Dennis shifted his attention back to the crib.

Like a photographer arranging a pose, he placed her hands on top of the railing. "Here, hold on to this for me, will you?"

This was the first time he'd asked her to do anything. Every time she volunteered, he'd told her to sit down and watch. When she protested, he had said she'd only get in the way.

Amusement curved her mouth. "Sure that's not too technical for me?"

He couldn't help himself. Cupping the back of her head, he kissed her again. He had to stop doing that, he thought. A man could get accustomed to a habit like that. Too accustomed.

"Maybe." He winked at her. "But I think you're up to it."

"Thanks for the vote of confidence." She clenched her teeth to keep from wincing as a strange twinge zipped through her. She slanted a look to see if Dennis had noticed. To her relief, he hadn't. If Dennis thought she was in pain, Nicole knew that he wouldn't let her do anything.

Dennis quickly attached the other two sides to the ones that Nicole was keeping upright. Dropping the springs onto the iron rungs, he made sure that they held. When they seemed secure, he snaked his way under the bed.

"Can I let go now?" The backs of her legs were beginning to ache. The pain she felt had shot up into her spine.

"Complain, complain. Almost," he answered. "I'm almost finished." Carefully, he tightened one screw, then another in each of the four corners.

Bored, Romeo followed Dennis under the crib. Looking for attention, the animal began to lick his arm.

Surprised, Dennis almost dropped the screwdriver as he hit his head against the springs. "Hey!"

Nicole suppressed a laugh. "I think he feels left out."

"He's too damn spoiled." Dennis moved Romeo back

with the point of his elbow. "Moira lets these dogs run her life." He let out an exasperated breath as the dog whined. Romeo was clearly put out because he was prevented from licking Dennis's face. "Call him or something."

"Come here, Romeo." The dog gave no indication that he heard. She laughed. "Boy, some guard dog you brought me."

"You probably have to scream when you call him." Finished, Dennis slid out from under the crib springs and sat up. He realized she was still holding the railing. "You can let go now."

Romeo scooted out, scrambling to his oversize feet beside Dennis. The dog began to whine again, this time tugging on Dennis's shirt.

Maybe getting her the dog *had* been a bad idea. Dennis pulled his shirt out of the dog's mouth. "What is it, boy? Did Timmy fall down the well again?"

Nicole was beginning to identify the different noises the dog made. "No, but I think that Lassie may need to be walked."

Nicole was probably right. Dennis stood up, wiping his hands on the back of his jeans. He tossed the screwdriver into the open toolbox. As he began to cross to the door, the dog eagerly pranced ahead of him.

"Okay, I'll be back in a few minutes," he told Nicole. "Don't—"

She rolled her eyes, but the annoyance she would have felt only a week ago wasn't there. It was nice to have someone care about her. "—Open the door to anyone, yes I know." Her smile was affectionate. "I think I have that part down."

"See that you do." How had she managed to get under his skin so fast when he had tried so hard to keep her out? The dog whined again. "All right, all right, I'm coming, dog."

Grabbing the leash from the kitchen table where he had dropped it last, Dennis attached it to the dog's collar. When he opened the door, Romeo yanked him across the threshold. Dennis just managed to slam the door in his wake before he was off and running behind the dog.

Romeo was eighty-five pounds of sheer energy and urgency.

They took a path along the perimeter of the complex. It had become incredibly familiar in the last few days. Funny how quickly routines took hold, Dennis thought. It felt as if he'd been involved in this one for a long time instead of less than a week.

He wondered how much longer it would be before he was on another assignment and Nicole was continuing on with her life—without him. More than that he wondered what she would say if she knew that the man she was obviously growing to trust was not who he pretended to be. What would she say if she knew that Dennis Lincoln, tax lawyer, did not exist?

Dennis shook off the thought. That didn't matter. The only thing that mattered was finding the disk. What he had told Winston last week was true. He firmly believed that somehow, Nicole knew without knowing she knew. Nicole was the link.

Sherwood obviously believed it as well, or else he and Winston wouldn't still be here. It had taken very little persuasion on his part to get his superior to agree and extend their undercover work here.

Romeo saw a cat lounging in an apartment window, absorbing the afternoon sun. Barking loudly, he strained at his leash. Dennis gave it a quick tug. "Sorry, no appetizers."

Subdued, the dog returned to examining the patch of grass beneath his paws.

Dennis hadn't lost sight of the fact that this was, after all, a personal matter for him. There was no question that Paul

Trask was involved in this up to his slimy neck. Paul Trask, the man responsible for his father's suicide. His father had been found in the alley behind Trask's casino, a note to his wife in his pocket. It had begged for her forgiveness. Dennis would have liked nothing better than to find a way to bring Trask up on charges that would stick. He was certain that the disk that Craig Logan had stolen would accomplish that.

If they could find it.

Dennis continued walking, absorbing everything within his surroundings and cataloging it out of habit. It looked like another normal day in paradise, he thought cryptically.

Helping Nicole assemble the furniture gave him further opportunity to look around the apartment. Despite the fact that Standish's men had done a good job of tearing the place apart, there might have been something they missed. Something out in plain sight. After all, the disk had to be somewhere. But where? Where would Logan have hidden it where it couldn't be found unless he wanted it to be found?

Offhand, the only thing Dennis could think of was that Logan had hidden it somewhere in his racer. But the car had been destroyed in the crash. It had ignited when the brakes had failed and the car had careened into the wall. There was nothing left of it but ashes and rubble.

That meant that the disk had to be somewhere else. Standish and his people wouldn't have gone through all the trouble of looking for it if they were confident that it had been destroyed along with Craig.

Romeo finally relieved himself. He began to urgently sniff around the base of a eucalyptus tree. A low growl drifted through the air. Obviously another dog had marked the area.

Dennis pulled on the leash, urging Romeo on his way. "C'mon, dog, I don't want to stand here all day—"

The tiny beeper he wore clipped to the side of his jeans

went off. Dennis shut it off automatically. Winston was trying to reach him.

With a snap of his wrist, he turned the dog around and quickly hurried back to the complex. As he approached the area where Winston had parked his van, he saw the stocky man in the driver's seat. Winston waved him urgently on to Nicole's apartment.

Dennis ran to the apartment. Damn, had they returned? No, Winston wouldn't have allowed anything to happen to Nicole. He must have seen something else in the monitor. But what?

Not knowing what to expect, Dennis knocked on the door. There was no answer. He tried the doorknob. She'd locked it, just as he had told her to.

"Nicole?" he called. He thought he heard a moan in response. "Nicole?" he called again, this time louder. He laid his ear to the door. Dennis was certain he heard her. She was moaning, calling his name.

Dennis swore under his breath. He should have never left her. Threading the leash over his wrist, he took out his skeleton keys. His fingers felt particularly thick as he worked the lock. Romeo barked repeatedly, as if he could sense that something was wrong.

It felt as if it were taking forever, but Dennis was in the apartment in under a minute.

"Nicole?" Dropping the leash, he rushed inside.

She wasn't in the kitchen or the living room. He tried the bedroom.

"Here," he heard her call weakly. "I'm in the nursery."

Pivoting, Dennis changed direction. Nicole was lying on the floor. Anticipating the worst, he dropped to his knees beside her.

As gently as he could, he gathered Nicole in his arms. "What happened?"

She felt like an idiot, an angry, embarrassed idiot. It was

a stupid thing to have done. "I was trying to move that box out of the way."

She pointed to the one containing the high chair. There was a small storage closet on the side of the tiny patio. Nicole was trying to pull the box out of the nursery toward the patio when the horrible pain had come crashing over her, sapping her breath and strength away like a tsunami.

Dennis slid his hands under her arms. When would she learn? "This is the nineties, Nicole. You don't have to be superwoman anymore."

As he began to lift her up, his hand brushed against the edge of her smock. It was wet. Very wet. Dennis looked down and saw the small streaks of blood darkening the pink fabric. This definitely didn't look like a good sign.

He raised his eyes to hers. "Nicole?"

Instinctively, she looked down. When she saw the blood, she froze. No wonder it had felt as if a mule had kicked her. Her water had broken.

Oh, boy.

"I see it," she whispered, unable to look away.

With his body braced against her back to hold her steady, Dennis reached for the large white embroidered comforter Abrahams had insisted they take along with the baby furniture.

"Take it as a gift from a grateful man," he had urged them.

Nicole had fallen in love with it on sight. Tiny blue lambs chased after pink pigs on a field of white. She looked in horror as Dennis pulled the comforter over to her.

"No, don't," she cried. "It's for the babies. I don't want to ruin it." There was more blood on the floor than she would have expected. A chill passed over her. Was something wrong?

No, it couldn't be. She'd just been to the doctor for an

examination. Dr. Pollack hadn't said that she was ready to give birth. She was as healthy as a horse.

This wasn't the time to worry about possessions. He wanted her to be as comfortable as possible. "I'll get you another one."

Easing his hand out from beneath her, he rose to his feet. Romeo trotted into the room. The dog went straight for Nicole.

"Lick her and you're dead, dog," Dennis said sharply. The dog lay down immediately. Dennis looked at Nicole. "Don't move anything," he ordered, leaving the room. "Including yourself."

Nicole bit her lower lip as fresh pain began to pulsate through her. She didn't want to be alone. She could stand the pain if he remained with her.

"What are you doing?" she called after him.

"Ordering pizza," he yelled back. What did she think he was doing at a time like this? "I'm calling 911 to get an ambulance."

Ambulance. People grabbing at her. People staring. She wished that it were already over with. "I'd rather have the pizza."

"Later," he promised. The dispatcher came on the line. Dennis quickly gave her all the necessary details. Hanging up, he hurried back to Nicole.

Romeo had laid down beside her. The dog raised his head as Dennis approached. There was a protective glint in his dark brown eyes.

"Easy, boy, I'm worried about her, too," Dennis said to the dog as he sank on his heels beside Nicole. His expression softened as he looked at her. "They're on their way."

Maybe there was some mistake. Maybe they were just jumping the gun. It was too soon. "I'm not due until the middle of January."

It almost sounded like a plea, he thought. Nicole was in

denial. "That's only two weeks away. Didn't you say that your sister delivered early? And didn't the doctor mention that twins usually arrive before their due date?"

At least she wasn't giving birth in an elevator, like Marlene had. Still, Nicole had thought that she'd have time to mentally prepare herself.

"Yes, but—"

There wasn't any room for "but." "Looks like you're making it a family tradition."

She laughed shortly. Traditions? Not her family. "We don't have any."

Nicole looked awfully pale, he thought. God, he felt incredibly helpless. He could assemble and dismantle twelve different kinds of weapons in record time, but he didn't know the first thing about childbirth. "Maybe this will start one."

She raised her hand to wave away the suggestion. He took it into his. Her fingers felt as if they'd been dunked in ice water. Enveloping her hand between both of his, he began rubbing it.

Nicole licked her lips, trying not to give in to the panic that was beginning to rise. This didn't feel right. "I'm scared, Dennis."

"There's nothing to be afraid of, Nicole." At least he fervently hoped there wasn't.

His voice was soothing, gentle. But it didn't help calm her. Pain knotted, hard and demanding, in her loins, then ebbed away after two beats. It was just flexing its muscles.

She turned her head toward him. "Easy for you to say, you're a man."

He smiled, stroking her damp forehead. "Thank you for noticing."

"I noticed." The words rode out on short breaths. "I noticed a lot." Her eyes skimmed over his face and she smiled distantly, floating in and out. She was vaguely aware that she was admitting too much. "I don't know how, in this condition, but I did."

He didn't want Nicole saying things she'd regret once she knew the truth. "Shh, you want to save your strength."

"No, I want someone else to have this baby," she gasped. "These babies," she corrected after a moment. "God, that's so hard to remember. I'm having two, not one." Her eyes widened suddenly with new fear. "You don't think she made a mistake, do you? You don't think that there's more than two in here."

It was a possibility, but not one she looked up to exploring at the moment. "No," he told her firmly, "I'd say two's your limit."

She was grateful for the assurance. Right now, she needed anything she could get to hang on to. "Oh!"

His hand tightened on hers, wishing he could absorb some of the pain. "Are you having contractions?"

"I don't know. I've never had any before." She supposed that's what the pain was. Hoped that was what the pain was. She had come so far, she didn't want to lose these babies. *Please God, don't let anything happen to my babies.* "You have to call the doctor. I want her there with me."

He didn't want to leave her, but she was right. The doctor had to be notified. "What's her number?"

Nicole screwed up her face as another wave went over her. "Use the phone in the kitchen. She's number three on my speed dial."

He was out of the room with lightning speed. When he returned, Nicole had rolled herself up into a ball as much as possible. She was gasping.

"Hang on, Nicole, hang on." The only thing he could do was comfort her. Dennis took her hand again. "You can't be having the babies already."

"Says who?" Nicole let out a long, shaky breath. That

had been a particularly bad one. "Marlene had hers in less than half an hour."

He felt her begin to squeeze his hand harder again. Here came another one, he thought. "You don't believe in traditions, remember?"

She rolled her head from side to side. She couldn't elude it. The pain followed. "I don't remember anything. Hold my hand, Dennis. Please hold my hand."

He tightened his hold on her. "I am."

She had to look to realize that he was. "Harder. I don't feel it. I don't feel anything except this awful pain."

If she could have, Nicole would have rocked to and fro to try to hold the pain back. But she was almost paralyzed with the searing sensation that was slicing her in half.

Finally, it receded. She waited in fear for it to return. "It figures."

She was babbling, he thought. "What does?"

"The baby—babies—were conceived in pain." Sweat was flowing out of every pore, mingling with the blood. Drenching her. "I guess they'll be born in pain, too."

Dennis wanted to keep her talking. It might help distract her. "What do you mean?" Where the hell was the ambulance, he wondered irritably.

"He raped me. Craig raped me." That night returned to her in vivid shades of shame. "Said he was paying for me, he might as well get to use the facilities once in a while." She bit her lower lip so hard it bled, but she didn't feel it. All she could feel was the pain of that night. It blended with the present. "So he did."

"Oh, God." It explained a lot, he thought. The wariness in her eyes when he kissed her, her distrust of men. It explained a hell of a lot. Logan had been a worthless bastard.

She didn't hear him. She heard nothing but the sound of water rushing in her ears. "I'm glad he's out of my life. I didn't want him dead, but I didn't want him part of this, either. He hated the baby, hated me. Hated everything but winning."

She was delirious, she thought, floating above her body, above the pain.

It was a pattern. The pattern of her life. She cared about the wrong people. "My father hated everything but working. Money did it for my mother."

"Money?"

"Yeah." Her throat felt dry, so dry. But the words wanted to come out. She couldn't stop them. "She traded it for me and Marlene. Robby, too. My brother."

Her voice was growing faint. Dennis had to lean over to hear. "I don't understand."

"Neither do I. How could a mother just walk out on her kids without even saying goodbye?" She could see herself as a four-year-old running into her mother's room. The room where her mother slept apart from her father. It was empty. *Mommy? Mommy, where are you? Mommy, I need you.* "One morning she was just gone," Nicole whispered. "My father said he paid her to leave and she did. A hundred thousand dollars. That made it thirty-three and a third for each of us."

Tears were gathering in her eyes, tears she wasn't aware of. They trickled out of the corners of her eyes, down the slope of her cheeks.

"I want her here now. Isn't that stupid? All these years, and I still want her. Stupid, stupid, stupid."

"It's not stupid," he said softly. "It's very, very normal."

The sound of Dennis's voice brought her back. She opened her eyes and tried to focus on his face. It swam in front of her. "I don't think this can hurt any worse. I feel like I'm dying."

"You're not dying, Nicole." It was an order. He stroked her hair, her face. "You're not dying."

"Yes, I am."

It was the last thing she said before she passed out. Somewhere in the distance, someone was calling her name, but she was too weak to answer.

Chapter 10

Nicole surfaced by degrees. She was vaguely aware of a rocking motion encompassing her just beyond the perimeter of her wakefulness. As she grasped on to consciousness, pain cut through the disorientation that was swimming around her.

She didn't remember opening her eyes, but when she came to, she was looking up at Dennis's face. Concern was etched into his kind features.

Even enveloped in a sea of pain, it touched her. He cared. He really cared.

There was something attached to her. She was having difficulty focusing. Nicole blinked several times before it became clear that what she felt was a tube feeding clear liquid into her arm.

"Am I dead?"

Dennis tightened his arms around her. He hadn't let go ever since he had gotten into the ambulance. She'd had him worried for a while. "Do I look like an angel to you?"

Nicole smiled weakly, or attempted to. "Yes."

She wouldn't think that if she knew the truth. "You're not dead." Suddenly, Nicole gasped, arching on the gurney. If she hadn't been strapped onto it, the sudden motion would have made her fall. She was having a contraction, he thought helplessly. "You may just want to be for a while."

There had to be a better way than this to have a baby.

She was vaguely aware that there was someone behind Dennis. "Where am I?"

"In an ambulance. We're going to the hospital." Just as he told her, the vehicle came to a rather sudden stop. The driver turned the ambulance expertly around, bringing the rear up to the emergency entrance. "Actually, it looks like we're here."

She had been unconscious the entire trip to the hospital. She didn't even remember the paramedics arriving. The last thing she recalled was Dennis hovering over her in the nursery.

Dennis saw the urgency in her eyes when she looked up at him. He leaned forward to hear her as the ambulance came to a full stop. "What?"

"Don't...don't leave me," she whispered.

It wasn't that long ago that she couldn't wait to get rid of him. Guilt bit into him with pointy teeth.

"Not a chance."

The next moment, the doors flew open. A team of nurses, orderlies and an emergency room physician surrounded the gurney as they pulled it from inside the ambulance.

Dennis jumped down after it, melding with the team as they hurried through the emergency entrance's open electronic doors.

A nurse wearing her years of experience with grace looked at him as Dennis ran alongside the gurney. "You the father?"

There was no hesitation in his answer. "Yes."

Out of the corner of his eye, Dennis saw the ambulance driver give him a quizzical look. When he had opened the door for the paramedics earlier, Dennis had told them that he was Nicole's neighbor. He waited for the man to say something, but the driver merely gave the physician the pertinent details of the pickup.

Another lie to add to the others, Dennis thought. But some hospitals had a strict policy about visitors. He might not be allowed to remain with Nicole if he didn't have some direct connection to her. There was no way he was going to leave her. Saying he was her husband seemed to be the simplest way to go.

Working his way around the IV, the doctor was checking Nicole's vital signs. The nurse placed a hand on Dennis's shoulder, drawing him gently aside. "We're going to need you to fill out some forms."

The words penetrated Nicole's haze. "I'm preregistered," she murmured.

Dennis looked at her. Her expression gave no indication that she'd heard him tell the nurse that he was her husband.

The nurse looked at Nicole compassionately. "That's what I like to hear," she said soothingly, "Everybody sticking to a nice, orderly procedure." With a maternal smile, she patted Nicole's arm as the physician removed the blood pressure cuff. "We'll have this baby in your arms before you know it."

"Two," she corrected with a tight whisper. Every muscle in her body tensed as another wave of pain swept from her toes, up her legs and through the rest of her. "I'm having two babies, not one."

The nurse took the IV bag from the paramedic and held it aloft. With her other hand, she held on to the tube to keep it from getting tangled.

"Save your strength, honey, you're going to need it." With well-practiced steps, she moved with the team as they quickly transferred Nicole from the ambulance gurney to one of their own.

The paramedics receded into the background as the hospital team hurried down the corridor toward the elevators.

Satisfied that she was stable, the physician detached himself from the circle. ''Your wife'll be fine,'' he assured Dennis.

The nurse, still holding the IV aloft beside the gurney, took charge. ''This one's going all the way to the fifth floor, gentlemen,'' she told the orderlies. They reached the bank of elevators and the nurse turned to Dennis. ''Did you call her doctor?''

''Yes.'' He had reached Dr. Pollack's answering service, and they promised to page her immediately with the information.

A smile crinkled the generous mouth, its warmth softening the spidery wrinkles. The elevator arrived. The orderlies moved the gurney onto the empty car.

''You've got yourself a good one, honey,'' she told Nicole.

Dennis heard Nicole murmur, ''Finally.'' The single word rubbed against his conscience like new shoes against a blister.

''Shh,'' he chided Nicole, taking her hand again. ''The nurse said to save your strength.''

Nicole stared at the large, black-framed clock on the wall opposite her bed. It was ten minutes to midnight. She had been in the hospital over seven hours. Seven hours spent in excruciating pain. She felt as if there were nothing left inside her to give.

And still they didn't emerge.

The minutes dragged by, outlined in flames. Her babies remained where they were, clinging to life within the womb as if they knew that the world outside was far colder, far harder than what they were accustomed to.

As she had done every half hour since she arrived, Sheila Pollack came into the room to check on Nicole. Inside her locker outside the delivery room hung a short, silver dress she'd worn at the New Year's Eve party she'd been attending when her service had called to tell her that Nicole had gone into labor.

It wouldn't be long before she couldn't fit into that dress anymore, she mused as she gave Nicole a reassuring smile. Within a few months, she was going to be as large as her patient.

Well, almost as large, she amended. She was only carrying one child. But until she began to show, Sheila intended to keep the matter a secret.

She supposed it was a matter of pride. She didn't want her patients to feel uneasy, knowing their doctor might be unavailable because she'd gone into labor.

Sheila slid onto the stool that was positioned at the foot of Nicole's bed. She moved back the sheet to see how far Nicole had dilated. "So, how are we doing?" she asked cheerfully.

"Awful," Nicole complained.

"She's in a lot of pain, Doctor," Dennis told her.

She sympathized and empathized with what Nicole was going through. "I know, but it shouldn't be too long now." She drew the sheet back into position as she rose to her feet.

"Well?" Nicole asked anxiously.

Sheila shook her head. "Not yet." Disappointment moved across Nicole's face like a dark rain cloud. Sheila placed her hand over her patient's and gave her a compassionate squeeze. "If you're not fully dilated within the next half hour, I'm going to perform a C-section."

"No."

The vehemence in the word surprised Dennis. He thought

that Nicole would have welcomed the end of the ordeal. He noticed that the doctor looked unfazed.

Sheila continued speaking in a soothing cadence. The last thing Nicole needed right now was an argument. "I would have thought you'd want to have this over with, Nicole."

More than anything in the world. "I do, but not like that. I—"

Was she afraid? Sheila wondered. When she had first come to her, Nicole had said that she hadn't been to a doctor in years. "There's nothing to it."

Nicole turned her head and watched the blips on the fetal monitor. They were strong, steady. "I don't want a scar."

So that was it. Sheila smiled. Vanity at a time like this. Who would have ever thought it? "The incision is a lot smaller now than it used to be."

Nicole's gaze shifted toward Dennis. When the time came, she wanted to come to him whole, unmarred. She moved her head from side to side. "No."

Sheila thought she understood. "We'll see."

As much as possible, she acquiesced to her patients' wishes. But she drew the line when she thought it interfered with their safety. So far, there was no sign of fetal distress, but it would be inhumane to allow Nicole to suffer much longer.

Sheila glanced at the clock. It was almost midnight. She thought of the party she had left. It was better for her to be here tonight, working. It helped her not to think.

She wondered where he was and what he was doing before she could lock away the thought.

She forced a smile to her lips. "Looks like you're not going to have a tax deduction for this year after all."

Sheila looked at Dennis. The nurse had referred to him as Nicole's husband. She knew he wasn't, but whoever he was, he was helping Nicole through this and that was all that really counted.

"I'll be down the hall for a few minutes if you need me." There was a candy bar in the vending machine with her name on it.

Dennis nodded, then stepped in to take the doctor's place beside the bed. He waited until the woman left the room. He wondered why Nicole was so adamantly against the procedure. What did a little scar matter when she was obviously suffering?

He leaned over the bed. Nicole looked so flushed. "Maybe you should let her perform the C-section."

Nicole looked at the IV tubes in her arm. They were there to replenish the blood she had lost and to guard against infection. There was a monitor strapped to her stomach and one snaking into her womb to monitor the fetal heartbeats. She watched them whenever the pain didn't seize her, taking comfort in the fact that the heartbeats were steady, strong. If it was a matter of the babies' survival, she would have agreed to the cesarean, but if it was just to curtail her own agony, she would hang on for as long as possible. Somehow, she would find the strength.

"It's going to be all right." Each word was framed in exhaustion. She couldn't tell him why she didn't want the cesarean, so she turned to backup reasons. "I don't want to be put under. I want to have my babies naturally."

It was a noble thought, but made before reality arrived. She just couldn't go on like this indefinitely. "It's not natural to have this much pain."

She didn't have the strength to argue with him. Another contraction was coming, harder, faster than the last.

Dennis saw the contraction's approach on the monitor before it had a chance to take hold. He tightened his hand on hers. "Breathe, Nicole, breathe."

Her lungs felt as if they were shaking as she panted. When the contraction left, she sank deeper into her pillow. She smiled weakly at Dennis, so grateful that he was here.

"I guess I didn't keep up with the family tradition after all. This is a hell of a lot longer than the half hour Marlene took to have Robby." She closed her eyes and for a moment, Dennis thought she had fainted again. But then she opened them, searching his face. "Did you call her?"

He said yes, he had, just the way he had told her twice before when she'd asked.

He had called Marlene as soon as the nurses had taken Nicole into the labor room. They'd asked him to remain outside while they prepared her. He had used the time to make telephone calls in the lounge.

"I'll be right down," Marlene had said as soon as he told her about Nicole. "But Sally's gone to visit a friend, so I'll have to get someone to stay with Robby."

He heard a baby crying in the background and remembered that she was a new mother herself. "There's no need to hurry. It looks like it might take a while. Why don't I call you when she's delivered?"

He could almost hear the hesitancy. "You're Dennis, aren't you?"

"Yes."

"Nic told me about you. I'm grateful for what you're doing. This was a very tough time for her." But he probably already knew that.

More gratitude to mingle in with the guilt. "I haven't done anything special."

"Yes, you have." Marlene paused, weighing her words. She made it a policy not to interfere, but this was Nicole. Just this once, she had a right. "Don't hurt her, Dennis. She's very fragile."

He chafed at the warning. "I have no intentions of hurting Nicole." No intentions, but it would happen, he thought. There was no way out.

She certainly hoped he meant what he said. Nicole had been through enough. "Call me as soon as they're born."

"I will." He hung up. It took him a minute to shake the heavy pall that had fallen over him.

The next call had gone to Winston.

Winston had listened as Dennis quickly filled him in. He'd had a hunch Nicole was in labor when Dennis didn't return to the apartment.

"Then she's okay?"

He thought of what Marlene had said. "For now."

Winston relaxed. Though he'd had no personal contact with Nicole, he'd grown fond of her during the time he had been monitoring the apartment.

"Boy, there's no end to the excitement on this job, is there?" Winston's tone was deadpan, but Dennis was certain he had detected a note of envy in his partner's voice. Winston didn't relish being cooped up in the van. He couldn't say that he blamed him.

Dennis watched the entrance to the room down the hall, but no one had come out looking for him so far. He shifted the telephone against his other ear and lowered his voice. "I want you to see if you can find Laura Bailey."

The monitors remained blank in the van. No one had attempted to enter the apartment while Nicole was gone. He was going stir-crazy and welcomed any diversion. "Who's Laura Bailey?"

"Nicole's mother."

"Why?"

The scene in the apartment flashed through Dennis's mind. Nicole's voice echoed in his head. "She wants to see her mother."

Winston's voice was quizzical but agreeable. "You have a number?"

"It's not that simple. The woman walked out on the family about twenty years ago. According to Nicole, she was paid off by her husband to leave the kids alone."

"Doesn't sound like a family that would be any competition to the Waltons." Dennis heard the faint clicking of the computer keys, and knew Winston had accepted the challenge. "Boy, you don't ask for much, do you?"

Dennis knew Winston was grinning. "Not from you. You're the best."

Winston laughed. It had almost a sinister sound. "You're only saying that because you know I was going to ask Sherwood to stick you in the van on the next assignment."

That would never happen. Though he complained otherwise, Dennis knew Winston was far more at home with his electronic gadgets than he was interacting with people. Dennis saw a nurse emerge from the room. The woman looked up and down the hall, then seeing him, she beckoned.

They were ready for him. "See what you can find, okay?"

"What do I tell Sherwood? What are you going to be doing while I hunt for the mother of the year?"

Dennis was impatient to get off. "I'm going to stay with Nicole."

"I don't think Standish is going to try anything while she's surrounded by nurses."

"It's not Standish I'm thinking of." They'd been partners too long for Winston not to have figured that out for himself, Dennis thought.

"Sure you're thinking?"

Probably not. This just got him deeper into a situation he had no business being in in the first place. Not in this capacity. But it was to late to be logical. She needed him.

"Just see what you can find, all right?"

Winston sighed. "Will do."

Dennis looked down at Nicole now, wondering how he was ever going to tell her the truth. There didn't seem to be a right moment to confess that everything he'd been telling her was a lie. A lie he was hoping would continue to go on for a little while longer.

A contraction started, following on the heels of the one that had just ebbed away. Dennis kept talking about anything that popped into his head, trying to get Nicole's mind off the pain that was turning her inside out. This one seemed to last forever. When it was finally over, she tugged on his hand urgently.

"Call her." Nicole panted, trying to gather enough energy to continue talking. "Call the doctor. I'm ready."

This had to be hell for her. "But she just examined you," Dennis told her gently.

She shook her head. The pillow beneath it was soaked with her perspiration.

"I don't care, call her. I'm ready. I can feel it." There was an urgency in her face he hadn't seen before. "I have to push, Dennis!"

"Okay, I'll call her."

He reached the doorway in a few strides, his eyes remaining trained on Nicole. He was afraid that if another contraction started, she was going to pull free of one of the host of tethers she had along her body.

"Dr. Pollack!"

Sheila came hurrying down the hall instantly. From the other direction, a nurse rushed to join her. "What's wrong?" Sheila asked Dennis.

"She says she's ready." He saw the skeptical look on the doctor's face.

Nicole didn't want to wait for a debate on the subject. She was going to have her babies here and now. There was no question about what signals her body was giving her.

"I am," Nicole cried out. She gripped the handrails on either side. "I am."

Sheila knew better than to argue. By the book, it should have taken Nicole a full half hour to dilate to the next stage. But babies waiting to be born rarely read textbooks.

It took Sheila only a moment to ascertain what Nicole already was aware of.

"You're right, it's time. You're fully dilated." In what seemed to be record time, she thought. Sheila let the sheet drop back into place and looked at Nicole with a smile. "Nicole, you're about to become a mother."

From somewhere, Nicole mustered enough energy to smile in response. "And here I thought all along that it was just indigestion."

Sheila laughed. The nurse began to untether Nicole from the fetal monitor. Sheila turned to Dennis as she pressed the button for another nurse. "We're going to have to get you into surgical clothes."

It was time to own up to at least a fraction of the truth. "I'm not her husband."

A small smile graced Sheila's lips. "I know. The point is, she wants you there." She looked at Nicole. "Right?"

There was no question in her mind. "Right," Nicole whispered weakly, her eyes on Dennis.

Sheila paused. "So, are you coming or not?"

His immediate response would have been, no, that he didn't belong in the delivery room. But if Nicole wanted him there, that took the decision out of his hands. He had come all this way, he wasn't about to leave her now.

That would probably come later, he thought, when she found out the truth. When Nicole wanted him out of her life for lying to her the way he knew that everyone else had.

Another nurse entered the room. Sheila turned toward her. "Barbara, show him where he can change."

It wasn't the way he would have imagined it, he thought. The delivery room was small. Along its walls were machines that stood like silent sentries, ready to be deployed at the slightest sign of need.

A hell of a lot of things could go wrong in this room, he thought.

Sheila watched his expression as he walked into the delivery room. He was a tall, strapping man, but right now, his complexion had a green tinge to it that rivaled the surgical livery he wore. She hoped he wasn't the type to pass out.

She gestured to the delivery table. "You have your choice of positions," she told him.

He moved close to Nicole, taking her hand in his. "I'll take here." He'd sooner face down the barrel of a Magnum than stand where the doctor was at the moment.

Good choice, Sheila thought.

"Good, then get behind her and lift her shoulders up. She's going to need support." She looked at Dennis to see if he understood her meaning.

He nodded and did as instructed. Dennis slipped his hands beneath the sheet and against Nicole's shoulders.

Sheila turned her attention to center stage. "Nicole, I don't want you to push until I tell you to. Is that clear?"

It was asking for almost more than she was capable of. Nicole licked her lips. They were so incredibly dry while the rest of her was so damp. She wished she had another ice chip.

"I really feel—"

Sheila cut her short. "I know, Nicole, I know. Just listen to me and we'll have your babies cleaned up and ready for college before you know it." She brought the stool to the foot of the table and sat down. She glanced up quickly and nodded at Dennis. "All right, Nicole. I want you to bear down and push. Now."

Nicole squeezed her eyes tight as every fiber of her body concentrated on that one command.

Sheila counted off the seconds in her head. "Okay, stop."

It took Nicole several moments before she could protest. "But they're not here yet."

"Soon," Dennis promised her. "Soon. Breathe." From the corner of his eye, he saw the look of approval on the doctor's face. But all that mattered was getting Nicole through this.

After a beat, Sheila reissued the command. "All right. Push."

Dennis lifted Nicole up again. He could feel the tension running along her spine, her shoulders. Nicole was absolutely rigid as she worked to bring her babies into the world. He held his breath along with Nicole as she bore down and pushed.

"All right, stop," Sheila ordered.

Nicole could have cried if she had the energy. She fell back against Dennis's hands, exhausted. They cradled her. Distantly, she was aware that she was a mass of perspiration. A nurse mopped her forehead. Or was that Dennis? She tried to focus. Everything was swimming and she felt so lightheaded.

"Once more," Sheila told her. She smiled in response to the moan. "We're almost there, Nicole. I see the head."

Nicole had no idea where the strength came from. She could have sworn that there was none left. With Dennis's help, she raised herself up again and bore down with every shred of her being. Her hands were clenched so hard, her nails bit through the skin on her palms.

"And behind door number one we have—a baby!" Sheila cried out with unmistakable pleasure. Quickly, she handed the infant to a waiting nurse. "You have a daughter, Nicole. A beautiful baby girl."

"A girl. I have a girl," Nicole panted. Joy mingled with exhaustion. Her eyes felt as if they were rimmed with sweat as she looked up at Dennis. "A girl."

He wiped the perspiration from her brow as he smiled. "I heard."

It wasn't over yet. Sheila prepared to catch the second one. "You also have another occupant to evict, Nicole. You've done this before. This one'll be a piece of cake," Sheila coaxed. "All right, push."

Nicole didn't think she could anymore. "Can't you just pull this one out?" she pleaded.

Sheila laughed as she shook her head. "Afraid not. Push, Nicole. Now!"

Nicole thought she was going to pass out as she did as she was told. It took her two tries instead of three, but the second twin, almost a carbon copy of its sibling, came out with a lusty wail of protest.

I don't blame you, Tiger. You're going to have to do things on your own from now on, Dennis thought. He leaned forward to see what sex the infant was.

The doctor announced it for him. "It's a boy." Sheila looked up at the clock overhead. Nine minutes past twelve. She'd missed New Year's. Sheila looked down at the infant in her hands. Well, maybe not.

Another nurse took the second infant. Sheila rose from the stool and came forward.

"Happy New Year, Nicole. You have two fine, healthy babies." She looked at Dennis. "You did very well."

He had done nothing except be there. "All I did was hold her up."

Sheila knew what it was like, facing a pregnancy alone. "Yes," she said significantly. "You did."

"Can I hold them?" Nicole asked. Now that it was over, she wanted nothing more than to touch her children, to see for herself that they were all right.

Sheila beckoned to the nurses. "Just for a minute. We have to see about getting all three of you cleaned up."

Nicole hardly heard her. Nurses on either side of the bed

were carefully tucking her children into her arms. Nicole let out a deep, heartfelt sigh.

It had been worth it.

Dennis was positive that he would remember the way she looked at that moment until his dying day.

Chapter 11

One hand on the dead bolt, Nicole raised herself on her toes to look through the peephole. She already knew that it was Dennis who was knocking. But she did it anyway because he would lecture her if she didn't. He'd left for the grocery store an hour and ten minutes ago and she could set her watch by his return. In the last week and a half since she'd been home from the hospital, Dennis had insisted on pitching in and helping her with her newly acquired handful. Or handfuls. Erika and Ethan demanded lots of attention.

He was a hell of a lot more helpful than Craig would have ever been, Nicole thought. She couldn't help wondering if, after all these years, she'd finally gotten lucky. It certainly looked that way from where she was standing.

She stepped back, opening the door wide. Dennis walked in, the handles of four plastic bags slung over each wrist. There were two more bags in his hands.

"Sure you're carrying enough?" she asked, grinning as she closed the door behind him.

"I hate making multiple trips." Dennis maneuvered the bags onto the kitchen table.

He'd managed to get all the groceries into the house in one trip without dropping anything, he thought with satisfaction. Funny how that pleased him. He'd gotten so involved with his work, he'd forgotten what it felt like to lead a normal, day-to-day life.

Like the one he was leading with Nicole.

Pretending to lead, he corrected himself. Only pretending.

"I got everything on your list," he said as he began to unpack one of the bags.

She didn't have to check to know he had. Craig hadn't even known what the inside of a grocery store looked like. In all the years they were married, he'd never offered to help her with the shopping even once, much less do it himself. Dennis didn't wait to be asked; he volunteered.

The twins were both asleep, providing her with what was becoming a rare moment without one or two babies in her arms. She took advantage of the luxury and began putting away the groceries he unpacked.

He looked so at home here, she thought. And she was getting very used to having Dennis around.

"Now, I don't want you to take this the wrong way," Nicole began slowly.

He noticed she was chewing on her lip, a habit she had whenever there was something on her mind. Because there was so much he had to hide, Dennis immediately felt uneasy.

He managed to sound casual as he asked. "But?"

By her count, he'd been away from his job as long as she had from hers. Over two and a half weeks. She was on maternity leave. What was he on? She knew he'd said that he was taking vacation time for the week between Christmas and New Year's, but this was already nearly two weeks into the new year.

She hoped she didn't offend him by inquiring. "Don't you have a life to get back to, people to defend?"

He was wondering when she'd get around to asking him about that. "I told the head of the firm I had a personal emergency situation arise. I gave my caseload to one of the junior partners at the firm, Winston. He's taking over things for me until I get back."

He wondered how Winston would feel being used as part of an alibi. Everything that was said in the kitchen, the living room and the nursery reached Winston's ears as it went on tape to be cataloged and later debriefed as the situation called for.

Nicole stacked the large cans of formula on the bottom shelf in her pantry. Like Marlene, she'd discovered that she was unable to nurse. Though she missed the idea of bonding on that level, she had to admit that, in a way, it was a relief. She'd envisioned herself permanently attached to one hungry baby or the other for the next six months.

She looked at Dennis over her shoulder, surprised by his explanation. Did he consider her a personal emergency? That meant she was important to him. She rather liked the sound of that. "You can do that?"

"Sure." He emptied out the last bag onto the table. "I've covered for him plenty of times. Besides, I do still have vacation time to take if I want to." He looked at her as he gathered the empty bags together, depositing them into one main one. "And I want to."

When he looked into her eyes like that, she felt giddy, like a young girl. Like the young girl she had once been.

"It's not that I don't appreciate your being here, I do," Nicole paused. Maybe she was going a little too fast for him. But then, he'd been the one who pushed his way into her life in the first place. She grinned at him as she made space for a bag of chocolate chip cookies. "It's like having my own built-in nanny." He'd remained with her last night and not for the first time. It was all purely altruistic. He'd stayed so that she could get some sleep. He'd gotten up for the feedings. She doubted if there was another man like him in the world. "You don't sleep much, do you?"

He shrugged. "I've learned to make do on very little."

When there wasn't a party to attend or a race to prepare for, Craig could sleep until noon. Every way she measured him, Dennis was so different from Craig. So incredibly, wonderfully different. The only similarity was the attraction she felt, and even that was different if she examined it. She didn't think she'd ever felt this rush when Craig just touched her hand. She did with Dennis.

"Why?"

He put the bags away where she kept them, in the drawer next to the sink. "So I could pull all-nighters and still be fresh enough to take the exam in the morning."

That sounded like him. She tucked away two dry cereal boxes, angling for space in an already crowded pantry. Nicole closed the doors behind her and turned to face him.

"Well, I don't know why you want to put yourself out and pull all-nighters for me, but you've certainly turned into my guardian angel."

He placed two containers of milk into the refrigerator. "There's that word again."

"What word?"

"*Angel.*" Dennis had felt uncomfortable when she'd referred to him as one in the ambulance, but she had been barely conscious then. He felt twice as bad now because she knew what she was saying. Or thought she did.

Add modest to the growing list of attributes. Something else Craig hadn't been. Nicole smiled at him. "Well, you are."

The refrigerator door handle slid from his fingers. Dennis turned to look at her. He couldn't let this go on this way.

She'd hate him even more once she knew. "Nicole, I'm no angel."

He looked so serious that for a moment, she was afraid that he was going to tell her something terrible about himself. But she sincerely doubted that there was anything terrible enough to negate the good he'd done for her.

She moved closer, her hands lightly resting on his arms. "I'm not exactly proud about some of the things in my past, either. Whatever you've done, Dennis, it doesn't matter."

He knew all about her past. And she knew nothing of his. Dennis shook his head as he took her hands in his. "You don't know anything about me."

He was wrong there. Dead wrong. "I know all I need to know. I know that you're good, and kind." The smile on her lips was mirrored in her eyes. Eyes, he noted, that were no longer wary. "And neighborly." She slipped her hands from his and continued putting things away. "I wish I could have met your mother."

The remark, coming out of the blue, took him by surprise. Winston was still trying to track down Laura Bailey's whereabouts. What did his mother have to do with anything?

"Why?"

"Because she must have been a very special lady." Nicole leaned into the refrigerator, pushing aside an army of small baby bottles on the top shelf to make room for a couple of loaves of bread. "She had to have been, to have turned out someone like you,"

"Yeah." It made him restless to talk about himself. He was beginning to worry that his conscience was going to get the better of him.

A tiny wail wafted through the air out of the nursery. Saved by the baby. Dennis began to back out of the kitchen. "I think one of the twins needs attention."

She put the last item away and hurried to join him in the nursery.

Four tiny legs were kicking the air. Both twins were fussing now. Dennis looked in her direction.

"I think they need changing," he guessed. He was starting to distinguish between the different kinds of cries. He had no idea that he'd become so good at it this quickly. But then he'd always liked children.

Nicole felt the perimeter of Erika's diaper. "Give the man a cigar," she murmured.

They each changed one baby. By then, it was time to feed them again. It seemed like an endless merry-go-round to Nicole. She knew she would have gotten dizzy on it, no matter how much she loved them, if it hadn't been for Dennis. The extra two hands were a godsend.

He was a godsend.

Changed, fed and burped, the babies began to settle down again. It wasn't soon enough for Nicole. She leaned against the doorjamb, looking at them. The windup mobiles that Dennis had bought were slowly moving above the two cribs, lulling the babies back to sleep.

She sighed, tired and grateful. "They lied."

Slowly, Dennis backed out of the room, afraid that any misstep might bring about fresh wails.

"Who did?" he whispered as he turned his face toward her.

She felt his breath along her cheek and struggled not to give in to the shiver that slipped along her spine. "Teachers. They told me that one and one is two. It's not." She looked at her babies. "It's an army."

Dennis laughed softly as he slipped his arm around her shoulders. "Feeling a little overwhelmed?"

"No, I'm feeling a lot overwhelmed," she corrected as she closed the door behind them. With any luck, they had bought themselves an hour of peace and quiet. Her hand in his, Nicole followed Dennis to the living room. "I really don't know what I would have done these last few days without you. These last few weeks without you," she amended.

Nicole sat down on the sofa. As he sat down beside her, she had a feeling that everything was going to be perfect from here on in.

"Funny how you came into my world just when I'd given up on life in general." Which made Dennis her own private miracle, she thought.

Oh God, if it weren't for the fact that Winston was monitoring all this, he would have made a clean breast of it now. There was no way she was involved in her husband's dealings. Through records and informants, he and Winston had established her innocence. And even if they hadn't, he would have known she was blameless. Yesterday, he had helped her pack the last of Craig's clothes to send off to charity. He'd watched her go through all the pockets before folding the garments up. No sign of a disk anywhere.

If it weren't for the fact that he had a gut feeling Standish would return, Dennis would have left her life as quickly as he had entered it.

The hell he would have, he thought, touching her cheek. Somehow or other, he would have found an excuse to stick around a few more days.

"Never give up, Nicole." His eyes held hers. How long before she looked at him with loathing? "No matter what happens. Never give up."

Nicole reached up and stroked the furrow between his brows. "You sound like you're warning me."

"Maybe I am," he said quietly.

She frowned. He was scaring her. "This isn't like you."

No, he thought, it wasn't. He was always the one who could look at things from a distance. Not from close up. "I'm just a little tired."

That she could readily believe. She rose to her feet, drawing him up with her. ''Go home, Dennis. Go back to your apartment and your bed and sleep in until tomorrow. God knows you deserve it.''

He shook off the feeling that was seeping through him, infiltrating his very soul. This was still a job and he still owed her the best protection he could render, even if she wasn't aware of the reasons behind it. He would just have to make the most of the time he had left.

''What, and give up the glamour of motherhood?'' He shook his head. ''Not a chance. I'm just getting my second wind. You're the one who should sleep in.''

Nicole felt relief whispering through her. He had her worried for a moment, but this was more like it. More like him. He was spoiling her, and she had to admit that she liked it.

''If I sleep any more, I'm going to turn into Rip Van Winkle.''

He tugged lightly on her chin. ''More like Sleeping Beauty.''

The comparison pleased her. After spending months as a blimp, she was hungry for compliments. ''You think I'm pretty?''

''No,'' he answered seriously. ''I think you're beautiful.''

Nicole looked down at the cutoffs she was wearing and the kelly green maternity T-shirt which now hung around her body like a vacated tent. Beautiful was really stretching the word.

''Yeah, right.'' She laughed. ''I'm right up there with Cleopatra and Helen of Troy.''

''No.'' Surveillance camera or no surveillance camera, he couldn't help himself. Very subtly, he turned his body so that it hid her from the camera's eye. Dennis took her into his arms. ''You're not up there with them. You're in a class all by yourself.''

God, but he could turn her head and leave her breathless,

panting for more. Very slowly, she brought her mouth closer to his.

"It's lonely being in a class all by myself. Couldn't I have, say just one more occupant there with me?"

He wasn't aware of bringing her body closer to his. He just knew that it was. Heat radiated between them, tempting him. His voice was low, seductive. "Who would you want?"

Her eyes grew soft, dreamy, as she wound her arms around his neck. "You, Dennis. Just you."

Why hadn't he just bumped into her at the supermarket? Or sat next to her in class, years ago? Why did he have to meet Nicole on a covert operation where security forbade him to tell her who he really was? A man sent to spy on her.

"I'm not beautiful, Nicole."

Yes, he was. Inside and out, she thought. Inside and out. "That's your opinion."

He didn't want to hold her. He didn't want to breathe in the fragrance that seemed to be hers alone. It only clouded his mind. Sunshine and sex, that's what he had thought when he had first looked at her photograph. That's what he thought now. And the impact was more powerful each time he encountered it.

Her hips fit against his, as if they were both two halves of a puzzle.

But they weren't. He had to remember that.

"Men aren't beautiful, Nicole. They're cute, they're good-looking, they're handsome. But they are not beautiful."

He looked so serious, she almost laughed. But she managed to bite her lip and keep the sound bubbling within her from surfacing.

"Okay, have it your way," she said.

She reminded him of a pixie, a wicked pixie, with her

eyes sparkling and her mouth so damn tempting it was burning away his resolve.

"So, which am I?" he finally asked. "Cute, good-looking or handsome?"

Her mouth was now just inches away from his. He realized it was because he'd inclined his head, meeting her halfway.

And then he met her all the way as his mouth took hers. He kissed her hard and quickly, knowing that to do anything more would be challenging his own resolve. And giving Winston a show he hadn't bargained for.

Dazed, Nicole took a deep breath as his lips left hers. Singed—she was sure they were singed. She tested them before speaking. "All of the above."

"What?"

"The answer to your question," she breathed. "You're all of the above."

He laughed and kissed her quickly again, then released her. A man could test himself only so much. "You would have made a good lawyer."

Too soon, she thought sadly. It was too soon. Her body needed a little longer to recuperate, but once it had, she wasn't going to let him talk his way out of what she knew they both wanted.

Each other.

Right now, she told herself, she could do with a cup of coffee. Nicole walked into the kitchen. "What I want to be right now is a good mother." *And to have my body stop humming.*

He followed her. "You will be." There was nothing he'd seen to doubt that she was a capable mother already. "You are."

Nicole laughed shortly as she rinsed out the coffeepot. "I don't know about that. I feel as if I'm flying by the seat of my pants."

Dennis took the used filter out of the coffeemaker and threw it out for her. "I hear all good parents feel that way."

It was incredible how in tune they were to one another, she mused, watching Dennis take out the coffee can from the top shelf in the refrigerator. Whether it was taking care of the twins or preparing coffee, they worked so well together.

"Really?"

"Really." But he shouldn't be the one giving her assurances. He was just a bachelor. "If you feel uncertain, why don't you call your sister?"

Nicole didn't see where that would do much good. Taking the can from him, she measured out enough to make five cups. "She's only been a mother a month longer than I have."

That was exactly his point. It was all still fresh for Marlene as well. "Then she's a month ahead of you in her uncertainties."

He was right. As usual. She replaced the coffee can and shut the refrigerator. "Brilliant deduction, counselor. Maybe I will call her."

A small white truck with a blue-and-red insignia drove by, heading out of the complex. The mail had arrived. "Where's your mail key?" he asked. "I just saw the truck go by."

She took it off the hook on the rack beside the calendar. "What service. I think I need a pedicure later."

He grinned as he took the key from her. Dennis looked at her legs. For a short woman, she appeared to be all legs. As far as he was concerned, that was a very good thing.

Dennis forced himself to look at her face. "I'll see what I can do about it."

Nicole sighed as he went out the door, then looked up toward the ceiling. "I don't know what I've finally done right, God, but thank you."

Dennis squared his shoulders as he closed the door behind him.

The section of mailboxes designated to their cluster of apartments was located just beyond the carport. As he began to insert the key into her mailbox, he saw that there was mail in his own. A piece of an envelope was sticking out on the side, as if it were too crowded for it to remain within the metal confines.

Who could be sending him mail? After all, he really didn't live here. Without meaning to, he glanced toward Nicole's apartment. At least, not for long, anyway.

When he opened the door to his mailbox, a profusion of letters, flyers and catalogs came bursting out, the result of weeks of accumulation. Dennis scanned everything quickly. Every last item was addressed to "Occupant" or was a piece of junk mail with his name affixed to it. Talk about waste. Dennis tossed the pile into the receptacle beside the mailboxes.

Opening Nicole's mailbox, he saw several envelopes that looked like bills. Stuffed behind them were a few flyers aimed at new mothers.

Word got around fast, he mused, locking the mailbox again.

"Anything?" Nicole called to him as he walked back into the apartment.

Instead of a cup of coffee, she was holding one of the twins in her arms. Erika. He could tell by the baby's bald head. Her brother Ethan had been born with a full head of hair. The boy had enough hair for both of them. Dennis sincerely hoped for Erika's sake her hair would grow in quickly, although he had to admit that at this stage, he thought she looked rather cute.

"Just the usual." He placed the stack on the kitchen table. He pointed to the top envelope. "Someone wants to sell you an encyclopedia for the kids."

"First they have to learn how to read," she murmured, pushing one envelope after another aside to look at them. Nothing but bills. "And sleep for more than five minutes at a time."

Erika whimpered and Nicole instinctively began to rock without even thinking about it.

At least she didn't have to worry about those anymore, she thought. Dreading bills was a thing of the past. She'd swallowed her pride and spoken to Marlene about the trust fund as soon as she had returned from the hospital. Overjoyed that Nicole had finally "come to her senses," Marlene quickly arranged for their lawyer to begin the paperwork that would allow Nicole earlier access to her own money.

Until that came about, Marlene was extending a loan to help tide her over. Marlene had wanted to give the money to her, but Nicole had remained steadfast on that point. She wasn't taking charity, even from her sister.

"It's not charity, you twit," Marlene had insisted heatedly. "It would have been your money if you hadn't argued with Father every time either of you opened your mouths."

"But I did argue," Nicole had reminded her, "and it was worth every penny." She fixed her sister with a stubborn look that Marlene recognized from their childhood. "Now, we do it my way, or we don't do it at at all."

Marlene had shaken her head. "You're cutting off your nose to spite your face, Nic."

Nicole had raised her chin. "Maybe, but it's my nose."

Marlene surrendered. "Yes, it is. I'll call Monty right away and have him start the paperwork." The trust fund was worded so that Nicole would get the money when she turned thirty. It had been James Bailey's fervent hope that by then, his son-in-law would have been a thing of the past, one way or another, "Every clause has a way around it."

And if anyone could find it, Marlene could, Nicole had

thought. Tenacity and stubbornness were two traits they shared, in their own fashion.

Nicole stopped pushing envelopes around on the table and frowned as she read the return address on the one beneath her fingertips.

Dennis looked down, reading the words on the envelope even though it was upside down. It hadn't attracted his attention when he had gone through her mail. Had he missed something?

"What is it?"

"I don't know. Probably nothing."

Nicole shifted the baby against her and tore open the envelope. It was from a local bank. A bank she knew she had no dealings with. As far as she knew, Craig had never had an account there. He hardly ever hung on to money long enough to open an account. When he did, it was soon closed again for lack of funds.

Inside the envelope was an annual invoice for a safety deposit box. She shrugged and slipped all the bills into a letter organizer she had on the wall. She knew for a fact that Craig hadn't had a will or an insurance policy, so what did he want with a safety deposit box? She had absolutely no idea and right now, she didn't care. Craig was in her past. Dennis was in her present and with all her heart, she hoped he was in her future.

"Anything interesting?" Dennis pressed. Maybe he *had* overlooked something important.

"Just another bill Craig ran up," she answered carelessly.

The coffeemaker finished brewing. She could almost taste the coffee and right about now, she needed another shot of caffeine badly.

"Would you mind holding the baby?" she asked. "I want to have a cup of—"

He had just taken the baby from her when the doorbell rang. Nicole noticed Dennis tense. It was a small, almost imperceptible movement, but she could have sworn his jaw hardened. Did he think Standish was back? She hadn't heard anything from the man and had assumed that he had decided to leave her alone. Now she wondered if she was being foolishly optimistic.

As she went to answer the door, Dennis stepped in front of her, handing the baby back to her.

"I'll get the door."

"Chauffeur, nanny, handyman, butler." She took Erika into her arms. "There seems to be no end to your talents."

"That's me, a regular Renaissance man," Dennis quipped.

His beeper remained silent. Winston would have signaled him if Standish or anyone unfamiliar was approaching.

Unless something had happened to Winston.

Dennis looked cautiously through the peephole. It wasn't Standish or anyone associated with the Syndicate.

Dennis let out a breath quietly as he opened the door. Marlene was standing there, holding her son in her arms. A short, somber looking older woman was beside her.

Marlene had already met Dennis the first day Nicole was home from the hospital. "Hi." She smiled at him, then saw her sister behind him. "How are you doing, Nicole?" she asked cheerfully.

Nicole kissed her sister, delighted by the visit. "Marlene, what are you doing here?" Marlene usually called ahead if she was coming.

"Impulse," Marlene confessed. "I thought it was about time Robby met his cousins." She nodded at the woman behind her as she walked into the apartment. "And I would have had to tie Sally up to keep her from coming with me."

"I'm too fast for her." Sally quickly embraced Nicole, then backed away to give Dennis a very thorough once-over. Dennis had endured lesser scrutiny when he had undergone a series of interviews to join the Department. The woman's eyes were fathomless. "And this is?"

Nicole moved next to Dennis. "Dennis Lincoln," she answered.

Sally looked very unimpressed. "Doesn't he have a tongue?"

He supposed this was what the poets had meant by the term *Tartar.*

"Yes," Dennis answered, "but I seem to have swallowed it under scrutiny."

If it was meant to get a smile from her, it didn't succeed. Sally took a few steps around him. "You a racer?"

"No." Dennis struggled to maintain a straight face.

"He's a tax lawyer, Sally." Nicole led the way into the living room. "And I'll thank you to stop interrogating the man."

"Somebody has to look after you."

Nicole turned to look at Dennis behind her. "Somebody is."

Sally's small, deep-set black eyes shifted from the woman she had raised from an infant back to Dennis, her expression never changing.

"So, it's like that, is it?"

Nicole had put up with enough embarrassment. Sally didn't seem to know when to quit. "Sally, you keep this up and I'm going to have you wait in the car," Marlene warned.

Dennis crossed his arms before him, more amused than anything. "She's just looking out for Nicole."

"You trying to butter me up?'

Dennis shook his head. "I'm just trying to get through this interview with my skin intact."

"Interview?" Sally repeated, then she smiled slowly. Her wrinkled face became almost pretty. "Maybe it is at that."

Nicole flushed. "Sally, why don't you come and see the babies?"

Not waiting for a response, she took the woman's hand and all but dragged her to the nursery.

"That's why I came." Sally gave Dennis one last sharp, backward glance, showing she wasn't about to accept him easily. He and Marlene followed the others into the nursery.

Marlene looked at Nicole apologetically. "I'm sorry, Nic, I really couldn't keep her away." Turning toward the crib where the other baby lay, Marlene looked down at the infant in her own arms. "See, Robby, that's your cousin Ethan." She shifted her son so that he had a clear view of the other twin. "And the one squirming in your Aunt Nicole's arms is Erika."

Moving the blanket aside, Sally looked at the little girl. "She looks like quite a handful."

"She is," Nicole admitted.

Sally smiled knowingly. "Then she's a Bailey all right."

Dennis hung back in the small hallway, feeling as if he were intruding.

Chapter 12

Less than an hour after Dennis brought Nicole home from her two-week exam at the obstetrician, there was a light knock on the door. "Expecting anyone?"

She shook her head. "I've reserved this afternoon for cleaning." Nicole gestured around the apartment. "It could definitely use it."

"Oh, I don't know." Dennis went to answer the door. "I can still see out the windows."

"Wise guy," she shot back.

Dennis looked through the peephole, then stepped back to open the door. The last person in the world he would have expected to be standing there was Winston.

"What are you doing here?" he demanded, lowering his voice.

"Who is it, Dennis?" Nicole called. Before Dennis had an opportunity to frame an answer, she came up behind him.

The affable man on her doorstep looked like a misshapen teddy bear. His casual clothes were a little too tight for his plump body. He resembled what she would have guessed to be his favorite food staple, a doughnut.

Nicole had no idea who he was. "Hello? Can I help you?"

Winston felt uneasy. He had hoped to take Dennis aside before she came out. This needed to be said to his partner face-to-face, not over the phone.

"I'm here to see him." For emphasis, he pointed toward his partner. "Dennis."

The request surprised her, as did the fact that the man looked somewhat ill at ease. Nicole smiled a greeting and took a step back into her apartment, allowing him the additional space he needed to enter.

"Won't you come in?" She glanced at Dennis. He saw the curiosity in her eyes. "How did you know Dennis was here?"

"Um, he wasn't at his own apartment and he mentioned that, um, that is, you..."

Winston and Nicole together. That was the last thing he wanted, Dennis thought.

Dennis took his arm. "Winston won't be staying. He's just here to pick up something I have for him in my apartment." He began to hustle the other man out when Nicole laid a hand on his arm.

"Winston," she repeated, looking at him. "Then you're his law partner."

He certainly didn't look like their family lawyer, Monty. Dennis's partner looked as if he would have been more at home in a bowling alley than a courtroom, but she supposed that was unfair. He probably had a brilliant legal mind.

"Partner?" Winston echoed, looking at Dennis for help.

"Yes," Nicole said. Why did the man look as if he had just swallowed a red-hot poker? "From the law firm."

Had she gotten the relationship confused? She looked at Dennis. She could have sworn he had told her that someone named Winston, a junior partner at the law firm, was handling his cases for him.

"Oh, yes. Yes I am." The words came out slowly, as if it were all news to him. Nicole looked dubiously at Dennis, but said nothing.

He had to get Winston out of here. "I'll only be a few minutes," Dennis promised her.

One hand on Winston's arm, Dennis ushered the man out of Nicole's apartment and into his own as quickly as he could.

"Are you crazy?" he hissed, closing the door behind them. He turned to face Winston. "What do you think you're doing here?"

"Your beeper's not working."

Dennis looked at the device and tapped it with his finger. "Great," he muttered.

He had to get this over quickly, Winston thought. The equipment had to be back by four. Sherwood had another surveillance lined up.

"Okay, two things." Winston dug into his back pocket and took out a folded piece of paper. "First, I wanted to give you this."

"'This?'" Dennis repeated as he took the paper from him. "What is 'this?'"

Winston tapped the paper. "Laura Bailey's address and telephone number." Dennis looked at him, surprised and pleased. "It wasn't easy. The lady covered her trail pretty well." Winston laughed shortly. "But then, I guess I could, too, if my ex had paid me off to do it."

From the bits and pieces he'd managed to get out of Nicole, Dennis had a feeling that there was more to Laura Bailey's story than was generally known. "A hundred thousand's not that much money."

"Maybe not for some people," Winston acknowledged. "But it was twenty years ago. And some people are frugal.

She probably made it last." He let the subject drift to a close as he shrugged his broad shoulders.

"Thanks," Dennis said with feeling. He pocketed the information until he could do something about it. Since the day in her nursery when he had found her on the floor, he couldn't get Nicole's words out of his mind. Nicole needed to be reunited with her mother. "I really appreciate this, Winston."

Winston looked down at his shoes. "Yeah, well, you've done some stuff for me. One hand washes the other and all that trite stuff."

Something was wrong. Winston looked uncomfortable. Dennis knew the man wouldn't have knocked on Nicole's door if it was just a matter of giving him the information. Winston would have found a way to slip it to him at some other time. He paused, waiting, but Winston said nothing.

"What's the other thing?" Dennis pressed.

"Sherwood's pulling Dombrowski and me off the surveillance." Winston paused. He looked at Dennis. "You, too."

That made no sense to him. "Why?"

Winston put it as delicately as he could. "Well, he thinks this is a dead end. Standish or his henchmen haven't been back." He gestured toward the other apartment. "She doesn't seem to know anything. What are we still doing here?"

Dennis would have thought that was self-evident. "Protecting her."

"From what, the smog? No, I think this time, you're not thinking with your head, Lincoln." Winston sighed. "This time, you're letting other parts of you make the decisions."

He saw the anger pass over Dennis's face, knew it was settling into his bones. If he wanted to, Dennis could have lashed out at him. Winston was certainly no match for the man. Instead, he heard Dennis answer in a low, steely voice. "I still think we can find the disk."

Winston couldn't refrain from saying what he believed. What Sherwood believed. They were just wasting their time and miles of videotape staying here.

"Well you're in the minority. Sherwood wants us to pursue another angle. He wanted me to tell you that you've got twenty-four hours to tie up any loose ends and then be out of the apartment."

Dennis slipped his hands into his front pockets. Silence prowled around the room with him as he moved. Finally, he turned and looked at his partner.

"No."

"Dennis, Sherwood's stretching it as it is because he likes you."

Dennis didn't want favors from Sherwood. He wanted to catch the men who had torn apart Nicole's apartment, the men who encouraged others to put everything on the turn of a card. And then gleefully collected the money when they lost.

"No," he repeated with finality. "I'm not leaving." He did some quick calculations. "I've got some time coming, I'll take it now."

"And when it's up?"

Dennis shrugged. "Maybe by then, I'll find the disk."

"What if you don't?"

Dennis didn't want to talk about it now. He hadn't thought anything through yet. "Let me worry about that, okay?"

"This is a mistake, Dennis." The concern in Winston's voice was clear.

There Winston was wrong. So was Sherwood. "I don't think so." He touched his partner's arm, asking for indulgence. And faith. "I told you, I've got a gut feeling about this."

The expression on Winston's round face was skeptical. "Sure it's your gut and not something else?" Dennis opened his mouth to contradict him, but for once, Winston was quicker. "Don't forget, I'm the one who's been sitting at those monitors, getting blisters on my cheeks watching you play Mister Perfect while you're making saucer eyes at her."

The expression broke the tension, making Dennis laugh. "You've got a law degree from Stanford, Winston. Can't you do any better than 'saucer eyes?'"

Winston waved a dismissive hand at the criticism. "I didn't major in English. I majored in common sense, something you seem to have abandoned." Winston paused. "What do you want me to tell Sherwood?"

Dennis knew he was right about this, even if Winston had his doubts. "Just that something came up and I'm taking vacation time."

"Right. Vacation time. In the middle of an investigation. He's really going to buy that."

Right now, what Sherwood thought didn't matter to him. "I don't care if he does or not," Dennis said. "I'm doing what I think is right." He couldn't just walk away from her now. For more than one reason. "She's vulnerable. The minute we all pull out, I know things'll go down."

Winston shook his head. Dennis was asking for trouble. But they had been partners almost from the beginning of their careers. He owed Dennis in more ways than he could enumerate. "What do you want me to do?"

Dennis nodded. When it came down to the wire, he knew he could always count on Winston. One arm around his shoulders, he ushered Winston toward the door. "Keep me informed if something else *does* come up." Dennis turned the doorknob and looked at the man beside him. "And Winston?"

"Yeah?

"Thanks."

Winston shrugged without answering. What was between them went without saying.

"Problem?" Nicole asked when Dennis let himself into her apartment.

Her phraseology caught him off guard. He turned away from her as he closed the door. "With what?"

She felt as if she'd hit a sour note. He hadn't wanted to talk about his work the one time she'd asked him about it. He was always so open about everything else. Was there something wrong?

"Your partner. Winston," she elaborated when he didn't say anything. "Is there a problem at work?" She thought of the worst case scenario, at least as far as she was concerned. "Are you going to have to go back right away?"

Keep it simple and close to the truth, he reminded himself.

"Not right away." Suddenly, his throat felt really dry. He opened the refrigerator and took out a can of soda. "But soon." When he popped the top, a slight spray covered the top of the can. He took a long sip. It didn't help.

Nicole nodded, then took the can from him, taking a sip herself. She'd just put the twins down and was looking forward to spending the next hour alone with Dennis. When Winston showed up, she was afraid that Dennis was going to have to leave with him.

She handed the can back to him. Her hand brushed against his. "I'll miss you."

It was as if she were giving voice to his thoughts. He looked at her in surprise. "What?"

"When you go back to work," she explained. "I'll miss you." Nicole began sorting the laundry out on the sofa. There were so many tiny things to fold. It amazed her that babies went through so many clothes each day. She smiled at him. "I guess I've gotten accustomed to having you around all the time."

He picked up a crib sheet and folded it in quarters. "You mean having me underfoot."

She shook her head. "I didn't say that."

No, she hadn't. And her eyes were saying a great many things to him now that they shouldn't. "You would have when we first met," he reminded her.

That was true enough, but there was a reason for that. "When we first met, I thought you were like all the others. Crafty, deceitful—"

And you were right.

Dennis folded another crib sheet. "Because I wanted you to let the deliverymen in?"

She laughed. That seemed so long ago now. "I thought it was a ploy." She'd heard a lot better, and a lot worse. Nicole knew that she had put Dennis through a great deal when they had first met. And all he had wanted was her friendship.

She placed her hand on his arm. "I'm sorry. It's just after you've had your feelings used as a soccer ball so many times, you get a little wary." She looked into his eyes. "But I know better now."

He sorted out the tiny shirts. Erika wore the yellow flowered ones, Ethan the blue ducks. He had been able to look into the eyes of a terrorist and lie without flinching, but he couldn't look into her eyes. "Well, there's something to be said for being on your guard."

There was that practical side of his. It was almost as if he was trying to warn her away from him. Not a chance. She took the shirts he was holding out of his hand and let them drop onto the pile on the sofa.

"Yes, but not so much that it almost ruins something wonderful for you."

Her body was so close to his, he couldn't think of anything else. "You're making this very difficult to resist."

She raised her eyes to his. There was an unspoken invitation in them. "Then don't." Because he hesitated, she stood on her toes, her hands on his arms for balance, and kissed him.

The kiss, softer than a summer breeze, went directly to his gut like a sucker punch. He took hold of her wrists. "Nicole, I'm only human."

Very deliberately, she maneuvered out of his restraint. Twining her arms around his neck, she kissed him again, this time she lingered a tiny bit longer, heating his blood, heating hers. "I'm glad to hear that."

He wasn't free to do what every inch of his body begged him to do. "You've just had twins."

"Human and observant." Each word was punctuated with a kiss, feathered along his jawline. "What more can I ask for?"

He framed her face with his hands. It seemed the only way to stop her. "You know what I mean. You can't—"

"Yes, I can." He could feel the grin spreading from her lips to his hands. "Dr. Pollack said that she was amazed at how quickly and completely I bounced back, especially considering the way I went into labor." Her body leaned seductively into his. "I asked her if it was all right to have relations."

The smile that rose to his lips seemed to have arrived there on its own. He felt it filtering through his entire body. "And why would you have done that?"

Her eyes teased him as her hands rested on his chest. "Because I want to have them. Relations," she breathed against his neck.

He wondered if she could feel his heart beneath her hands, and if she realized that she owned it. "With anyone in particular?"

The smile on her lips deepened until it was ingrained in every fiber of her being. "Yes, with someone very particular."

He covered her hands with his and then removed them from his chest. "Nicole, you might regret doing this."

It was as close as he could come to refusing her. Because he didn't want to refuse her. More than anything in this world, he wanted her, wanted to make love with her until every inch of his body was exhausted beyond hope of ever recovering.

One in a million, she thought. No other man would have tried to talk her out of it once she had come this far. Slowly, she moved her head from side to side, her eyes on his.

"Uh-uh. There are a lot of things in my life that I regret, but this will never be one of them."

Lord, but he ached for her, ached to feel her body sliding along his, ached to just hold her in the wee hours of the morning and know that she was his. "You don't know that."

"I know that," she contradicted him. As she drew herself up again, her body whispered along his. Her mouth was inches away from his lips and her breath enticed him as she spoke. "I know that this was meant to happen. From the very first, this was meant to happen." She looked into his eyes, searching for answers. "Now, are you going to make me humiliate myself by—"

Dennis laid a finger to her lips. He didn't want her to ask. At least he could spare her that. "Shh. Anyone ever tell you that you talk too much?"

She lifted her chin proudly. "Not anyone who's still breathing."

He grinned. "I didn't think so." He sampled her lips, lips that made him think of wine, delicately aged and incredibly sweet.

Nicole surrendered to the feelings that were rushing

through her. She fell headlong into the kiss she had initiated, letting it make her head swim.

Dennis felt the moan vibrate along her throat as he pressed his lips to the long, slim column. He couldn't believe the way that excited him. He filled his hands with her hair, feeling drunk just being with her. His very brain was scrambled.

His heart was racing in his chest, in his ears, in every pulse point of his body. This was wrong, wrong to take her when she was being deceived, and yet, he couldn't help himself, couldn't stop himself. He would have never taken the first step, but she had, and she had taken him with her.

He had no will of his own. That seemed to have disintegrated the moment her lips had touched his.

Her fingertips feathered along his chest as she worked at opening the buttons on his shirt.

"You know," she told him, trying to maintain a straight face, "I've never had to throw myself at a man before. They were always there, ready to take me if I so much as nodded in their direction." She had been very willing to party then, to place herself on display as she searched for love and acceptance. "This is a whole new experience for me."

The smile slid from her lips. She looked at him seriously. "I like it." Her lips fluttered along his. "I really like it."

His palms itched. Dennis was eager to touch her, to familiarize himself with every inch of her. But he couldn't take her here. What if Winston hadn't turned off the camera? He couldn't let her be captured on film this way.

Nicole undid the last button and slowly slid her fingertips along his chest between the parted sides of his shirt. Dennis shrugged out of it.

The next moment, he swept her into his arms and carried her toward her bedroom. There was no camera there.

Her eyes widened in surprise, then filled with pleasure. "Ooh, I could really get to like this," Nicole laughed.

"We're like Scarlett and Rhett." The next moment, she reconsidered, her lower lip adorably pouty. "No, not like them."

He lightly flicked his tongue along her lip, making her shiver.

"No staircase?" he guessed as he entered the room.

Nicole shook her head. Her reason was far more basic than that. "They didn't have a happy ending." The feel of his chest against her cheek stirred her and made her feel safe at the same time. She couldn't remember ever being this happy. "I like happy endings."

The muscles in his stomach tightened as her words danced along his chest.

"So do I."

Dennis set her down. Now, he had to tell her now, away from the monitors. Now while his conscience goaded him on.

The words felt like lead in his mouth. "Nicole, there's something I have to tell you."

Something in his manner told her she didn't want to hear. She shook her head. "No, there's nothing you have to tell me. You just have to make love with me. Make love with me here and now, before I burn up and become a cinder."

Still there was doubt in his eyes. She had to make him understand.

"No one's ever looked at me the way you do. No one's ever treated me the way you do." She took his hand and laid it on her breast. "Can you feel that? That's my heart, Dennis. You've brought it back from the dead. Legally, that makes it yours."

She didn't know what she was saying. He couldn't let her go on like this. "Nicole—"

Her eyes implored him. "Don't make me ask again."

A man could only be so strong. He couldn't resist both her and himself. "I won't."

His mouth covered hers. The needs buffering his body blocked out his guilt. Tomorrow, he'd deal with it all tomorrow. Maybe tomorrow things would come to light that he could work with. And then she would forgive him this lie. This huge lie that had allowed him to enter her life in the first place.

He undressed her slowly, treating her like an unexpected gift he had received for Christmas. With his heart hammering in his ears, he watched her eyes for any sign that she wanted him to stop.

But all he saw there was encouragement.

He glided his palms along her body, glorying in the silky feel of her skin. It was like rich whipped cream, and he had a terrible yen for cream.

Nicole felt her skin tingle as he removed her T-shirt, pulling it up over her head and tossing it aside. There was desire in his eyes when he looked at her. Tender desire.

Had desire ever been tender? she wondered. It hadn't been with Craig, or with anyone else. But it was tender now. Tender and worshipful.

If someone had come and told her that she had died and gone to heaven, she would have believed it. Because nowhere on earth had she ever encountered anyone like Dennis.

They undressed one another, garment for garment, their hands reverently exploring each other's bodies. Each pass was sweet agony, stirring desires, creating more demands.

He took a step back and looked at her. She was beautiful. The smile that crept to her lips was shy and full of pleasure. "What?" he coaxed.

"When you look at me, I don't feel funny."

"That's good," he murmured against her temple, doing delicious things to her nervous system. "Because you don't look funny."

Within moments, they were sealed in one another's arms,

sealed to one another's bodies. Dennis clothed her in warm, openmouthed kisses that threatened to reduce her to the consistency of ice cream left out on the counter overnight.

They tumbled onto the bed, lost in a world of their own creation. A world they were both eager to explore. They touched, tasted, ignited and gloried in the discoveries.

Nicole wrapped herself around Dennis, wishing that time could stand still, that it could remain this way forever. There was an urgency drumming through her. She couldn't shake the feeling that, somehow, she was on borrowed time. It went far beyond the fact that the twins would be waking soon, far beyond logic.

She wanted forever, but she would settle for now. As long as now contained him.

Her body called to his. He wasn't going to be able to hold back much longer. Turning so that he was on top, he pushed the hair away from her face.

"Hey, what's your hurry?" He could feel his loins throbbing as she moved beneath him. "It's better if you go slowly."

She felt as if she were going to explode soon if he didn't take her. "Says who?

"Damned if I know." She sparked a fire in his body, in his very soul. Feeling her firm torso moving beneath his, it was almost more than he could manage to keep from taking her quickly.

But he wanted her to remember this. When she looked back on this, he wanted her to remember this with love, not with anger or shame. He wanted her to know that he loved her.

This was the only way he had to show her.

"Wait." Taking both her hands in his, Dennis held them above her head. Slowly, his body teased hers, preparing it for him.

"For what?" she asked thickly.

But he didn't answer. Instead, he showed her. His lips moved along her face, along her throat, along the upper planes above her breasts, sealing each inch with a kiss that flowered into another, and another.

Nicole twisted and turned, absorbing the sensation, trying to contain the anticipation that impatiently pounded all through her. Like her dream, she realized in a haze. Except this was better. Much better.

"Oh." The word was surrounded with a moan. "Wait for that. I see. I see."

How could she feel both drugged and energized at the same time? Able to leap tall buildings in a single bound and yet lie there and absorb the luscious sensation of his mouth upon her? And yet, she did.

Now, her body screamed. Now. And still he went on, making her mindless, making her eager.

Making her his.

She moved like accelerated poetry beneath him. His last shred of self-control was torn away. He had no choice left to him but to enter. To start the beginning of the end.

Nicole felt his eyes on her. She opened hers, wanting to see what was within them before he took her. Was he making love to her or to just a body?

Old fears died hard, she thought.

Nicole could have cried when she saw herself mirrored in his eyes. At that moment, he belonged to her and she to him. Everything that had come before no longer mattered.

Only this did.

She arched, mutely accepting him. He sheathed himself in her.

As one, they moved together to the summit. Two halves of a whole, searching for the same thing, eager to take one another there.

They climbed higher, higher, the tempo increasing, until they reached the peak together.

Nicole cried out his name, shuddering as the sensation echoed through her body. He gathered her closer to him, holding on to the moment.

She sighed. She'd never known such peace, such exhilaration before. It was always going to be like this, she promised herself. Always.

Chapter 13

He watched Nicole as she stretched languidly on the bed, like a cat beneath a sun-drenched window waking from a restful sleep. Just looking made him ache for her all over again, even though they had made love only minutes ago.

Dennis cupped her face in his hands, wishing he could somehow freeze-frame this moment forever. She looked up at him and made his heart twist within his chest.

He brushed his lips over hers. "If you grin any harder, you're going to split your face. Want to let me in on the joke?"

She liked the way his eyes caressed her, liked absolutely everything about him. There wasn't one thing she could point to as a fault. He was just too good to be true.

As he had just demonstrated when he had made love with her.

"No joke." She settled against his chest. The warmth of his skin along her cheek soothed her. Nicole couldn't remember when she had felt this safe, this protected. This wonderful. "It's just that the night after you fixed my garbage disposal, I dreamed about you."

He struggled to hold on to the moment just a little longer. Reality and duty waited just beyond the fringe, but for this small island of time, she was his. "Oh? Good dream or bad dream?"

She turned her head to look up into his eyes. Her own were dreamy, contented.

"A sexy dream. A very sexy dream." Barely touching his skin, Nicole began drawing tiny swirls along the light hairs on his chest, the path going lower and lower.

She was unmanning him all over again. He couldn't think when she was touching him like that. He caught her hand in his. "You didn't answer my question."

The grin receded into a seductive smile. "Good dream," she whispered.

She stretched again, her body rubbing along his. She definitely did have feline tendencies, he thought.

"It was the most erotic dream I've ever had." Without warning, she flipped around so that she could rest her chin on his torso, her eyes teasing his. "And it doesn't begin to compare to the real thing." Very slowly, she drew herself up, her body sliding along his. Tempting him. Tempting her.

Face-to-face, she feathered her fingers through his hair. "Tell me, do other women know what a great lover you are?"

With the most serious expression he could manage, Dennis shook his head. "No, I was a monk until the day I met you."

It certainly felt that way. No other woman had made him feel things to this degree. It was like being cast from a three-dimensional world into one with four, full of colors and sounds he had never been aware of before.

She took the information in stride. "Good, then I won't

have to kill anyone.'' And then she became a temptress all over again. ''I'd rather make love again anyway.''

Her energy was incredible. And somehow, it managed to nudge his to the fore. He felt insatiable. ''Not too tired?''

''Not too tired,'' Nicole echoed. She could be dead and not too tired for this. For him.

Dennis pulled her into his arms, his mouth coming down quickly, as if he knew that the borrowed time he was on was almost up.

Nicole had no idea what had brought about this change, from courtly, patient lover to rogue, but she liked it. She definitely liked it. She could feel her heart racing immediately as she greedily collected his kisses and reciprocated.

A distant wail grew louder in strength and intensity, penetrating the burning haze around them.

Dennis raised his head, listening. He looked down at the woman in his arms with heartfelt regret. ''I think Erika or Ethan has other ideas for us.''

Nicole sighed. Losing the shelter of his arms, she leaned back against the pillow to try to compose herself. Right now, the room was still spinning at a precarious speed.

''Motherhood is wonderful.''

He wondered if she was trying to convince herself or just be ironic.

Nicole swung her legs over the side of the bed as she reached for her shorts. They had been discarded on the edge of the bed. But Dennis stopped her as he grabbed her wrist. Pulling her to him again, he kissed her with a level of passion that literally snatched her breath away. When he released her, she remained very still, searching his face for some explanation.

It took a minute to find her tongue. And even then, she blew out a shaky breath first. ''What brought that on?''

''Nothing.'' Rising on his side, he avoided her eyes. ''I

just wanted you to remember when you look back that you enjoyed it."

What a strange thing to say. She pushed her arms through her T-shirt, then pulled it over her head. Nicole drew her hair out, looking at him curiously.

"Enjoyed it?" She laughed. Talk about understatements. "I don't think Webster has come up with enough words in his dictionary to adequately describe what just happened here on that bed."

Dressed, she turned and fingered the rumpled comforter.

He looked around for his shirt, then remembered that it was in the other room. Glancing at Nicole, he stopped. "What are you doing?"

Her eyes were innocent when she looked up at him. "Checking for scorch marks. I would have bet anything that we came close to burning this up."

He laughed. "That wouldn't be a bet that I would take." The wail coming from the nursery had been increased by one. Both the twins were up, demanding attention. Dennis strode out of the room. "I'll take Ethan, you take Erika."

Incredible. The man really was incredible. Nicole caught his hand, stopping him just short of the nursery. When he turned to look at her, she rose on her toes and lightly touched her lips to his. She was never going to get her fill of this man.

"And all three of us take you." *If you'll have us,* she added silently.

By now, it had settled into a familiar, comfortable routine. The twins were changed, fed and burped, then held and played with. Before long, their soft, long lashes were brushing against their cheeks as they drifted off to sleep again, also in unison.

Nicole looked at Dennis. He was sitting in the rocking chair with Erika, looking exactly the way she had pictured the father of her children would look when she had fantasized about such things. Eons ago when she was still innocent.

Did it get any better than this?

Dennis saw her looking at him. There was love in her eyes. Another moment to hold on to when things were bleak, he thought. He got up and very carefully placed Erika in the crib.

Crossing silently to Nicole, he looked down at the sleeping infant in her arms. "I'll put him to bed," he offered. "Why don't you go watch some television and relax?"

"If I was any more relaxed," she whispered, surrendering her son, "I would be pudding." Rising, she tiptoed out of the room.

Watching television had no appeal to her. She thought longingly of going back to bed with Dennis, but the next move was up to him. She had opened up the door to her heart and seduced him into entering. It was up to him to move in.

Besides, she had work to do. The apartment was getting to look really cluttered. She hadn't done any real cleaning since before she entered the hospital.

And there was something she had been meaning to do for a long time now, she thought suddenly.

When Dennis walked into the living room, he found it empty. Looking around, he saw Nicole out on the tiny patio. The storage closet door was open and she was taking boxes out of it, stacking them behind her.

The storage closet, he thought suddenly like a man waking up from a prolonged coma. He'd never searched the storage closet.

Dennis shoved his hands into his pockets and walked out onto the patio. Closing the screen door behind him, he peered into the top box. Inside were trophies rubbing against one another like passengers in an overcrowded subway car.

"What are you doing?"

She pulled out the last box. "Getting rid of a few things I should have tossed out before. Craig's trophies." They had no place in her life, especially now that Dennis was in it.

Once she'd been so proud of Craig for winning. Now she looked at the collection as symbols of the beginning of the end. An end to an existence that had turned out to be a fantasy in her mind alone. She could look at the lot of them completely detached now, devoid of any feeling she had once had for the man.

"They're not worth anything, certainly not to me or my children. There's no point in having them take up space." Craig's clothes had gone to charity, but these she was simply going to throw in the trash.

Dennis picked up a trophy and examined it. It seemed a waste just to throw them away. "No other family members to send them to?"

She shrugged. "None that I know of."

Alerted by a sudden buzzing noise next to her ear, Nicole ducked out of the way just in time as a bee circled her head.

Attracted by Dennis's blond hair, the bee moved on toward another target. "Watch out!" she cried, pulling on Dennis's arm.

He swung around, backing up against the stack of boxes. They went crashing down onto the patio. The trophies came spilling out, tumbling over one another, denting as they came in contact with the cement.

"Hey, I'm sorry."

The bee had flown off to gather pollen from the honeysuckle vine that was climbing along the wall just beyond the patio. Nicole stooped down to gather up the trophies and throw them back into the boxes.

"Nothing to be sorry about. They're going into the trash anyway."

Dennis picked up the large trophy at his feet. The black

felt on the bottom had come unglued and was partially hanging off the award. Curious, he examined it and found that the bottom was hollow. Slipping his finger inside, he felt around. The tip of his finger came in contact with something metallic that moved just out of his reach. He shook the trophy until the object fell out.

It was a small, silver key. Dennis bent down and picked it up. "Nicole, what's this?"

She dumped the last of the trophies back into the boxes. Maybe she wouldn't just put it in the Dumpster. Maybe they could be melted down for scrap metal. "What's what?" she asked absently.

"This."

Nicole turned around. Dennis was holding a key in the palm of his hand. She picked it up and inspected it. "Looks like a key to me. Where did you find it?"

He nodded toward the trophy on the ground. "Inside that. The felt must have come off when it fell out of the box." Obviously, Logan had hidden the key. Dennis could feel adrenaline revving up within his veins. "What do you think it's the key to?"

"I have no idea." She turned it over in her hand. "Hey, wait, yes I do." Maybe she was getting ahead of herself. "Or maybe I do," she amended. "There was a bill in the mail the other day for a safety deposit box. Maybe this fits into it."

That had to be it. He'd been right all along. Logan had hidden the disk close to home.

He filtered the excitement from his voice. "Safety deposit box?"

She nodded. "I thought it was odd at the time. I didn't even know Craig had one, and I can't imagine what he would have kept in it. It's not as if he had a will or an insurance policy to put away for safekeeping." Her mouth hardened. "Craig Logan didn't have anything to leave behind except grief."

She frowned, looking down at the key. "He must have hidden this the last time he was here. I remember he was out on the patio. He wouldn't answer me when I asked what he was doing. Told me to go away. I thought he was just reliving past glory." She was about to pocket it when Dennis took the key from her. Surprised, she looked at him quizzically. "What?"

"Don't you want to see if it fits the box?" When she looked at the key impassively, he added, "Aren't you curious about it?"

If it had to do with Craig, it meant one thing. "Anything connected to Craig could just mean trouble."

He played his cards very close to his chest. If he seemed unduly interested, it might arouse her suspicions. But he couldn't just let the matter drop, either. "Maybe whatever is in the safety deposit box is what Standish was looking for."

Nicole caught her breath. It felt as if it had been jammed in her throat. She hadn't thought about the break-in in days.

"Do you think—?"

"Worth a look." He handed her back the key. "Where's the bank?"

She shook her head. "Not too far away. It's a local bank." She paused, closing her hand around the key. She could feel her heart accelerating. Nicole raised her eyes to his. "Dennis, I think I'm scared."

He placed his arm around her shoulders. "Don't be. I'll go with you."

That helped a great deal. Maybe it was foolish, given her track record, but she did feel safe when she was with him, as if nothing could ever hurt her again. "What if what we find does turn out to be what he was looking for when he tore up my apartment?"

At least he didn't have to lie about this. "We'll take it to the proper authorities."

He followed her to the kitchen. Nicole went straight to the rack where she hung her keys. Just below it was the letter organizer. She took out all the envelopes stuffed into the slot marked Bills. Spreading them out on the kitchen table, she found the one from the bank.

"Here, this is it."

Dennis noted the address. The bank was located on the outskirts of the outdoor shopping mall he'd passed Christmas morning when he had followed Nicole to Marlene's house.

"This is close to Marlene. Why don't we take the twins to your sister and then go to the bank?" he suggested.

She was going to ask why they didn't just take the babies with them, but then realized that Dennis was right. She couldn't very well go through whatever was inside the safety deposit box if her arms were full of babies.

Nicole nodded. "All right."

"Go get them ready," he instructed. "I'll be right back."

"Where are you going?"

He was already at the door. "There's something I need to get." He closed the door before she could ask him what it was.

Once inside his apartment, he went straight to the bedroom and took his suitcase out of the closet. Turning the lock sideways, he lifted the false bottom. There was a small pistol and holster taped there. With practiced movements, he strapped the gun onto his calf, then carefully lowered his pant leg over it.

He tapped out Winston's telephone number on the keypad. Just as he figured, Winston's answering machine picked up.

"Winston, it's Lincoln. I think my hunch is paying off. I found a key to a safety deposit box inside one of Logan's trophies. We're going to the bank now. California Savings and Loan in Newport Beach on MacArthur. I'll let you know if the disk is there. If it is, tell Sherwood a simple apology'll do. Say, a full-page ad in the *L.A. Times.*"

The smile on his face was grim. Hanging up, he returned to Nicole's apartment. The holster's strap was rubbing against his shin, chafing his conscience. He could almost hear the sands running out in the hourglass.

Sally crossed her arms before her chest, a smug expression on her face. "I was wondering when you were going to get around to using me. Marlene's not here and I'm taking care of Robby."

"Oh." Nicole exchanged looks with Dennis. "Maybe we can—"

There was no way he was going to allow her to take the twins with them. Something didn't feel right, and he didn't want to endanger the babies. If he could, he would have talked Nicole out of going with him as well, but that would really arouse her suspicions. He was stuck playing out the hand the way it was dealt.

"Hey, did I say no?" Sally demanded. "Don't put words in my mouth." She took the baby carrier from Dennis. "Two more won't make any difference to me." She smiled at the infant in her arms. "Thinking of opening up my own day care center, I am." She indicated the coffee table. "Just set her down there. I'll take care of them."

Nicole set Erika's carrier on the table, tucking the blanket around the infant carefully. She turned toward Sally.

"Thanks. We'll be back in half an hour or so."

"I'll be here." Accompanying them to the door, Sally looked Dennis up and down slowly. "Taking her out for a quick bite?"

Amused despite the situation, Dennis grinned. "Running an errand," he corrected.

"I'm available nights, too." Sally told him. "Why don't you make an evening of it?"

Nicole leaned over as she pretended to brush a kiss on the wrinkled cheek. "Don't push it, Sally," she hissed in her ear.

"Someone has to," Sally said innocently. "You never did know a good thing when you saw it." She looked at Dennis and gave him an approving nod.

"Sally has never approved of anyone before," Nicole told him as they left. "This may be a first."

In more ways than one, Dennis thought as he opened the car door for her. *In more ways than one.*

The teller behind the safety deposit box counter at California Savings and Loan was polite, but distant. And quite firm. He handed the signature card Nicole had filled out back to her after checking it against his records.

"I'm afraid that Mr. Logan didn't authorize anyone else to have access to box number 117, Mrs. Logan. You'll have to return with him."

"But I can't, he's—"

Dennis cut in before Nicole could tell the man that Craig was dead. That would bring up another set of ramifications he didn't have time to deal with.

"Can I have a word with you?" he asked the man. "Alone?"

By his expression, the teller obviously didn't think there was anything further to talk about. But he acquiesced.

Nicole didn't understand. Why did Dennis want to talk to the teller alone?

"I'll be right back," Dennis promised. He gave her hand a squeeze.

She supposed this was one of those situations where she was just going to have to trust him, she thought. Trusting didn't come easily to her, but it was something she was very willing to learn if it meant having him in her life.

The teller walked out from behind the long desk and indicated an alcove used for consultations with the bank's customers.

His back to Nicole, Dennis took out his wallet and flipped it open to his identification. He kept his voice low.

"I'm with the Justice Department. We have reason to believe that there might be important evidence contained in that safety deposit box. Now I can go and get a court order to make you turn over that box to Mrs. Logan," he said mildly, "but I think you should know that there are certain other parties after that item as well and they might not go through the trouble of getting a court order to get what they want. Or even ask." He paused significantly. The alarmed look in the man's eyes told Dennis he understood exactly what he was saying. "It would be safer for everyone all around if you just let Mrs. Logan look into the box. She can verify who she is."

The teller was visibly shaken and concerned. "Who's going to verify you?"

"Commendably cautious." Dennis smiled easily. He gave the teller a telephone number. "Ask for Albert Sherwood. He can give you my description." The teller wrote the number down. Dennis rubbed his hand over the back of his neck. He couldn't shake the feeling that something was wrong. "Of course, that would be using up valuable time."

The teller frowned. He looked down at the photo ID in Dennis's wallet. He blew out a breath. "Okay, follow me."

He returned to the desk. "Come this way, please." The teller pressed a button underneath the counter, allowing them to enter the vault.

Nicole inserted the key Dennis found into the first lock and the teller put the bank's key into the second one. He turned them simultaneously, then drew out the box and handed it to Nicole.

"You can use that room over there."

He indicated a little room reserved to give the bank's clients privacy. Dennis opened the door for her, then closed it behind them.

"What did you say to him?" Nicole asked.

He shrugged casually. "I introduced him to a few presidents he found to his liking."

She stared at him. "You bribed him?"

It was close to the end, and he was still lying to her. Dennis was beginning to hate his job. "I thought it was worth the trouble. Open the box, Nicole."

She looked down at the long, black metal box. Why did she feel afraid?

"Here goes nothing," Nicole murmured. She flipped the box open.

There was nothing inside except for a small, white box. When she opened that, she found a black computer disk nestled inside.

Bingo.

Nicole took out the disk. There was no label on it, no indication what program ran it. "Do you think this is what they were looking for?"

As sure as God made little green apples. "Did Craig own a computer?"

Nicole laughed softly, but there was no humor in it. "He couldn't even work a typewriter."

"Then this is what they're looking for." Dennis took the disk from her, placed it back into the small white box and closed the lid. "Here, put this in your purse and let's go."

There was an unfamiliar note in his voice. Uneasy, she did as he instructed.

Dennis brought the safety deposit box out and handed it to the teller. "Thanks for your help."

"Always our pleasure," the man responded automatically. His expression didn't bear out his words.

Nicole didn't say anything until she had descended the three steps outside of the bank's entrance. She felt very confused. She hadn't really given Craig's connection with Standish any thought. Finding the disk changed all that.

"What was he doing with it?" she asked suddenly as they reached his car. "What was Craig doing with that disk? What's on it?"

"Things you have no business knowing," a sinister voice responded behind them.

Before Dennis could turn around, something hard was shoved up against his rib cage. He didn't have to guess what it was. The look of horror on Nicole's face told him.

"Nice and easy now. Let's take a walk around here, shall we?" Holding on to Nicole's arm and with the nose of his gun in Dennis's ribs, a man neither of them recognized directed them toward the deserted area behind the bank.

"What do you know, it paid off." The man laughed to himself. "I never had much patience with waiting. Maybe I should try it more often." His tone changed abruptly. It was deadly. "I'll take the disk, Mrs. Logan. It doesn't belong to you."

She looked at Dennis out of the corner of her eye. "I don't have it."

"Don't play games with me, Mrs. Logan. I don't like games." His expression turned menacing. "The only ones I like are the games played at Mr. Standish's casino. He's been waiting a long time to find that disk." The man shoved his gun harder against Dennis. "Now hand it over and maybe no one's going to get hurt."

She didn't believe that for a minute. He was going to take the disk and then shoot them without a qualm. She thought of her children and of the man she had fallen in love with. Life had just begun for her. She wasn't about to have it end.

Nicole began to reach into her purse. Dennis saw the stubborn look enter her eyes and knew that she was going to try something. He had to divert the attention to himself before she was hurt.

Moving abruptly, Dennis drove his elbow into the other man's throat. The gun went off. As the noise registered, Dennis felt something hot slamming into his shoulder, setting it on fire. The point-blank impact almost knocked him down.

"Get out of here, Nicole," he yelled. "Now!"

She saw the blood beginning to discolor his sleeve. She couldn't just leave Dennis here like this. It was her Standish wanted, her and the disk. Not him.

Nicole didn't remember thinking, only reacting. She swung her shoulder bag against the gunman's legs. The man buckled to the pavement.

"Bitch!" he roared as he went down.

It was all the time Dennis needed. He pulled out his own gun and trained it on the other man. It was over in a matter of seconds. All the waiting, all the planning, all the deceit, it all ended here.

Dennis held the gun on the man. Staring down the bore, he still managed a wolfish grin. "Hey, no harm done. She's got something that belongs to Mr. Standish, that's all. A man has the right to claim what's his." He began to rise, but a simple movement from Dennis's gun and he remained where he was.

"Not always," Dennis said. "You're under arrest."

"You're making a citizen's arrest?" Nicole asked, stunned. What was he doing with a gun? None of this was making any sense to her.

"No, it's a little more complicated than that." He looked at the man on the ground. "What's your name?"

"Martin. Pete Martin," the man barked.

"All right, Pete Martin, I'm placing you under arrest."

"Under whose authority, Boy Scout?" the man sneered. He eyed the small handgun, waiting for an opportunity to disarm Dennis.

His arm really stung. Dennis held the gun with both hands to keep it steady. "The Justice Department's."

The man looked at him warily. The situation was beginning to become clear. "On what charge?"

"Carrying a concealed weapon, attempted robbery and racketeering to start with. I figure the disk will tell us anything else we need to know."

Dennis saw the look on Nicole's face. The moment of triumph was lost

Nicole could only stare at Dennis, her mouth hanging open. She felt as if she'd been kicked in the stomach.

Chapter 14

The sound of sirens still filled her ears. The red lights atop the ambulance danced in synchronized rhythm as people wove in and out of the scene before her eyes.

This was all so surreal.

It felt as if it were happening to someone else, not her. As if she were watching a huge movie screen and had somehow gotten sucked into the story without realizing how or when.

Nicole stared at Dennis. Her throat felt dry. Who was he? Who was this man she had so foolishly taken to her heart and her bed? She had no idea, only that he wasn't who he had told her he was. He was worse than a stranger. He was someone who had lied to her.

People were milling all around him. Someone was taking instructions from him. The paramedics his partner Winston had called were just finishing bandaging up Dennis's arm. At least, she thought the man's name was Dennis.

Nicole no longer felt that she knew anything at all anymore.

Winston looked the other way while the paramedic had quickly wrapped Dennis's wound and waited until the attendant was finished before talking. Behind them, Dombrowski was cuffing Martin and reading him his rights amid a barrage of profanity.

"Lucky for you, I check my messages," he said, watching the small dot of red grow larger on Dennis's bandage. "Otherwise, things might have gone down differently."

Winston had arrived within moments after Dennis had placed Martin under arrest. The paramedics arrived on the scene a few minutes after that. In the ensuing melee, Dennis hadn't had a chance to say a single word to Nicole. But he could feel her eyes on him, tearing away the last tissue covering his guilt.

"Yeah," he muttered.

This had turned out all right, but something else might not. Something suddenly far more important to him than making a big arrest.

He turned to look in Nicole's direction. She was staring at him as if he were a stranger. Not that he could blame her, he supposed. Dennis crossed to her, sidestepping Dombrowski who was ushering Martin inside the car he and Winston had come in.

She hated him, he thought, looking into her yes. "Give him the disk, Nicole."

Her mouth hardened. The bastard. He'd played her for a fool all along. And she had let him.

"Sure." Her voice was cold, but not for long. Her anger and hurt heated up the words. "That was what you were after all along, wasn't it? The disk." Digging the white box out of her purse, she shoved it into his hands.

Dennis passed the box over to Winston. The latter opened it to check out the contents.

"I—" Dennis didn't know what to say, where to start. The look in her eyes cut him dead.

She didn't want to hear it. Didn't want to hear a single word from him. She'd already heard enough. "You must feel pretty good about yourself. Like a Canadian Mountie, you got your man. Or your disk." The words were bitter. "Never mind that you had to use someone in order to do it."

Each word she uttered felt sharp, drawing blood as it scraped along his conscience.

God, how was he ever going to make this right? All he knew was that he had to try. "Nicole—"

Winston shifted. "Why don't I leave you two to work this out alone?" He began edging away. He eyed Nicole nervously. "Sherwood's going to want to see you, Dennis."

Dennis didn't even turn around. The words washed right over him. "Right. Later."

"No, go." With the flat of her hand, Nicole pushed Dennis's chest, making him stumble backward toward Winston. "Go! You and I don't have anything to say to each other anymore."

The paramedic looked embarrassed as he tapped Dennis on the arm. "Look, buddy, I think we should take you to the emergency room to have that checked out." He nodded at the bandage he had just put on.

Dennis waved him away. The shoulder ached, but he would get over that. This was far more important. "I've got my own doctor."

Nicole looked at the paramedic. "I'd ask him to verify that if I were you. He tends to make up things."

Dennis scowled at the attendant, ending any further discussion. The man held up his hand and pushed a clipboard in front of Dennis.

"Okay, just sign here that you didn't want to go in and refused any further medical attention." He tapped the space.

Dennis quickly scribbled his name down on the end of

the paper. Nicole was walking away. He threw the pen down on the board and hurried after her.

"Nicole." She didn't stop until he caught her wrist. "Nicole, let me take you home."

She wasn't about to get into the car with him. She wasn't about to get into anything with him ever again. All she wanted was to get away from Dennis as fast as she could. "I'll call my sister."

"She's not home," he reminded her. Her stubbornness was getting on his nerves. He had to make her listen to him.

"I'll call somebody else. A taxi." She wrenched her hand away. "Just get away from me."

Dennis saw Winston shaking his head as he got into the driver's side of the car. The ambulance had already left. People who had poured out of the bank to see the excitement were drifting back inside. Within moments, they were alone.

He felt more alone than he had ever been in his life.

"Nicole, let me explain—" He tried to take her hand again, but she wouldn't let him.

"What's there to explain?" she demanded, her eyes blazing. How could he? How *could* he? She was ready to love him forever and he had been lying to her all along. "You had a job to do, and you did it." Her eyes narrowed as the hurt mounted within them. "I made it easy for you, didn't I?"

"No." He shook his head. "You made it damn hard. I didn't want to lie to you." Each lie he told had burned on his tongue.

She was through believing him. "Well, you seemed to do a hell of a bang-up job of it."

Nicole felt tears gathering in her eyes, but she was not going to let them go. She'd be damned if she'd let him think she was crying over him. She swallowed, trying to get past the lump that was growing in her throat.

"You must be at the top of your class. Mr. Neighborly.

'Let me fix your disposal, Nicole,''' she said, mimicking him. '''Let me get your mail, Nicole. Buy your furniture, Nicole.''' Her eyes were slits of betrayed fury. '''Get you to bed, Nicole.'''

He couldn't stand this anymore. She was ripping them both apart. ''Nicole—''

She held up her hand. ''No, no, you're right. That was me. I did that.'' She bit down hard on her lip to keep her voice from quavering. She was *not* going to cry. ''Opened up my stupid heart and my stupid bed to you.'' Boy, they made up songs about fools like her. ''And you fell right in, didn't you? No trouble at all.''

She turned on her heel, starting to walk away again. This time, he grabbed her roughly and swung her around. The action hurt his shoulder, but only registered distantly. Her words hurt a great deal more.

''Let me get a word in, damn it.''

She threw back her head, her eyes flat. ''Why, so you can lie again? Sorry, my card's filled up. I can't take any more lies.'' She broke free. ''Now you can go to your almighty Justice Department and have a good laugh over this.'' She whispered the last words, afraid that her voice would break.

Is that what she really thought? He would have given her more credit than that. ''I'm not laughing.''

For a moment, she almost believed him. But that would have made her twice the fool that she already was. And she was through playing the fool.

''Too bad. I will be,'' she told him. ''Every time I think of what an idiot I was to fall for you. That I actually thought that you were different than all the others.'' She laughed harshly. ''Want a real laugh? I thought that you were the best thing that ever happened to me.''

She grew solemn. She felt so empty, as if there were

nothing left to hang on to. But there was. She still had her children. She had to remember that.

"Maybe you were," she said half to herself. "Because you finally taught me not to believe in dreams."

He couldn't stand to see her like this. She looked as if her soul had been stolen from her. "Nicole, this wasn't supposed to happen this way. None of it."

As if she could believe him. "But it did," she returned. She was tired. Too tired to go on talking. Too tired to go on having her heart torn out of her. "Everyone in my life has walked out on me in one way or another." Her voice was dead, devoid of any feeling. Just as she was. "I suggest you follow that pattern."

"Nicole—"

But she turned away from him. Head held high, she walked to the front of the bank to make her telephone call. She needed a taxi to take her to Marlene's house. And away from here.

"You don't have to lean on the bell," Sally complained as she opened the door. She looked outside and down the driveway. "So, where is he?"

"I shot him," Nicole snapped. At least, she wanted to. She wanted to pound on him until her fists and his body were numb. The way her soul felt right now. Numb, like the survivor of a bombing. She looked around the room. "Where are the twins, Sally? I have to go."

The girl looked terrible. "The hell you do. You're spending the night here."

Nicole swung around, the deadness receding as anger took over. Anger at being hurt. Anger at the world. It focused on the small woman standing in front of her.

"I'm not ten years old anymore, Sally. You can't tell me what to do."

The woman placed her hands on her hips.

"I don't care how old you are. I'll always be older. And I will always be the one in charge." There was to be no arguing with her. "Now, you're staying and that's that. You're in no condition to be driving home, especially not with the children."

If they weren't here, they had to be in the nursery. Nicole began walking out of the room. "I've got a taxi waiting."

Sally caught Nicole by the shoulders. Smaller than the other woman, Sally was still a power to be reckoned with.

"I don't care. Send him away. Marlene'll be home in a few minutes—"

Emotionally exhausted, Nicole gave in. Up to a point. "All right, I'll stay. But I don't want to talk to Marlene. I don't want to talk to anyone, Sally." She tried to shrug the woman's hold off, but Sally continued to hold on to her.

Sally searched Nicole's face. "Hurt you that badly, did he?"

Unable to maintain her bravado any longer, Nicole dissolved into tears. For a moment, she clung to Sally, crying her heart out. "Big time."

Sally stroked Nicole's head. "I'll kill him."

Nicole raised her head. She shook it, brushing back tears. "It was my fault. I left myself wide open. But not anymore. Not anymore." It was a promise she meant to keep.

Nicole hardly slept that night. Each time she closed her eyes, she saw his face. How could he have looked at her that way and lied so well? He looked so innocent, so truthful. She would have believed him if he had said the moon was made of green cheese.

Which was what he was banking on, she thought miserably.

Nicole spent most of the night in the nursery, tending to the twins and Robby whenever they woke up. Sally tried to make her go to bed, but Nicole remained steadfast. She insisted on taking care of them on her own, without any help.

She was never going to need help again, never going to rely on anyone again for anything, Nicole vowed fiercely to herself. If you depended on someone, you only left yourself wide open for pain.

And she was never going to hurt again.

Marlene had protested, then relented. Perhaps this was Nicole's way of working through everything. In the morning, she would talk to her. For now, she left her sister's gaping wound alone.

But when morning arrived, it brought other surprises to their door.

The door chimes rang at eight. Marlene had decided to go into work late, allowing herself time to talk to Nicole. Nicole had continued to reject any attempts to discuss the problem and Marlene was growing concerned. The last thing on her mind was a visitor.

It was too early for any deliveries or salespeople. Who—?

When Sally opened the door, she was completely unprepared for the visitor who was standing on the doorstep. The older woman was rendered speechless. Mutely, she stepped back, taking the door with her. "Mrs. Bailey?" she breathed.

Laura Bailey smiled shyly at the housekeeper who was as much of a fixture at the house as the richly carved front door.

"Yes, Sally, it's me," she answered in a soft, hushed voice made that much more quiet by the fear that palpitated within her. Fear that it was too late. Fear of rejection. "It's me. Is it all right if I come in? I'd like to see the girls."

Sally didn't say a word. She only nodded, her hazel eyes huge as she turned to lead the way into the living room.

"Who is it, Sall—?"

Marlene's voice drifted away as she saw the woman with Sally. A tall, slender blonde whose face had eluded the mark of time. Only her eyes showed what she had lived through. And they were incredibly sad.

"Mother?" Shock drenched Marlene. Her voice came out in a whisper.

The woman who stood there, dressed in a beige suit, looked like an updated version of the photograph Marlene kept on her nightstand.

But how could it be?

Laura couldn't help the tears that rose to her eyes. They glistened like scattered jewels.

All these years, all these sad, lonely, wasted years, she had envisioned this moment. She had been far too fearful to make it become reality. Even after she had heard that James had died, fear had paralyzed her, preventing her from approaching her daughters.

What would they think after all these years if she walked back into their lives?

"Yes, it's me."

Laura did the only thing she could. She opened her arms to her daughter. And prayed.

It took Marlene only a moment. Marlene, who never bore a grudge against anyone, felt as if Christmas had just exploded within her chest. She fell into her mother's arms. The two women hugged each other fiercely, trying to make up for all the lost years in that one embrace.

Laura sobbed against her daughter's hair.

"Oh, God," Marlene cried. "What are you doing here?"

Laura drew back, wanting to look at Marlene's face. Wanting to absorb every nuance. "I came to see you, to ask you for your forgiveness."

That went without saying. She had never hated her mother, only ached for her comforting presence. "But why now?"

"I had a visitor last night—" Laura stopped as she saw her other daughter enter the room.

Nicole's eyes were red rimmed from crying, from trying to wash Dennis's touch out of her life. Her expression immediately hardened as she recognized the woman beside Marlene.

"What are you doing here?" Unlike Marlene, her voice was cold, harsh.

Laura felt uncomfortable all over again. The relief she'd experienced moments ago was now a thing of the past. She had her father's eyes, Laura thought, looking at her youngest child. Laura tried to remember what Dennis had said to her last night.

"I came to clear something up."

Why now? Was her past going to continue to insist on haunting her? First Craig, now her mother. Was there no peace anymore? Nicole ran her hands along her arms, feeling cold. She looked to Sally for help, but the woman remained mutely on the outskirts. This was a family matter.

"After all these years, I don't think there's anything to clear up."

Laura nodded. She wanted to gather Nicole to her breast, but was afraid. Nicole had always been the emotional one. "He said you'd probably say that."

Nicole felt as if she were frozen to the floor. "'He?'"

"Dennis Lincoln," Laura explained. "He came to me last night and said—"

How much more tangled was this going to get? Was her mother somehow involved in all this, too?

"How do you know Dennis?" Nicole demanded.

"I don't," Laura explained quickly. She heard the hurt in her daughter's voice and ached for her. Had she done this to her? Wanting to do right, had she jut made things worse? "He tracked me down."

Nicole no longer believed anything she was told. "Why?"

Laura took a deep breath to fortify herself against the anger in her daughter's voice. "Because he said you needed to see me. Needed to see me more than I needed to remain away."

He was still interfering in her life, messing with her mind. Damn him for living. "Well, I don't," Nicole said. "So you can just go away again."

"Nicole!" Marlene cried. She'd let her sister go on, knowing how hurt she was, how much she'd been hurt when their mother had left. But she wasn't going to allow Nicole to push her away now.

Nicole turned to Marlene. How could she just accept their mother back, after what she had done to them? "She's been gone all these years and we've managed just fine without her."

"Have we?" Marlene asked pointedly.

Nicole felt as if the remainder of her world were crumbling, but she raised her chin defiantly. "Yes."

Being gentle with her hadn't helped at all. It was time to get tough. "Sit down and shut up, Nicole. I want to hear what Mother has to say." Marlene looked at the woman who had long ago given up the claim to that title. "Why *did* you leave us and go away?"

Stung, Nicole slanted her sister a look. Marlene had never talked to her that way before. How could she side with Laura Bailey after what her departure had put them both through?

"Why did you take his money and sell us?" Nicole demanded.

Laura didn't understand the question. "Sell you? If anything, when I left, I bought you peace of mind."

Nicole shook her head. "I don't understand."

Marlene sat down on the sofa, pulling Nicole down beside her. "Neither do I."

Laura sat down on the wing chair opposite her daughters. She twisted her hands together in her lap. "This isn't easy for me."

"Not like walking out, huh?" Nicole asked bitterly.

Marlene shot her sister a silencing look.

But Laura didn't blame Nicole for the bitterness her daughter felt. She was entitled to it. They both were. It surprised her that Marlene didn't share Nicole's feelings. But then, Marlene had always been a kindhearted little thing.

Dennis hadn't said much when they'd talked. Only that Nicole needed her mother. Laura wet her lips and began.

"When I married your father, I was very young. Too young to realize what a mismatch we were." She smiled sadly. "I guess I had my own idealized version of marriage." But all that was in the past and she knew better now. "I could never please him, but I tried. I really tried. For eleven years." She sighed as she remembered. "Eleven years of rejection, of criticism, of being made to feel that I couldn't do anything right." She watched her daughters' faces carefully as she continued. "And then I met someone."

So that was it; she'd left them for a lover. "And ran off with him?" Nicole's question was almost a challenge.

"No." Laura tried not to think about the man in her past. It had been over with for years. "It might have been easier on me if I had, but no, I didn't." She searched their eyes for understanding. They had to be made to comprehend what it was like for her. "He was very kind to me. Said things I needed to hear. Things your father never said."

Marlene understood exactly what her mother must have felt. She'd worked for years for her father, wanting only a single word of approval. It had never come.

Laura didn't realize that she was smiling as she remembered Brent. "He made me feel special, as if I had something to offer a man."

Like Dennis, Nicole thought.

"I fell in love with him and had an affair." She held her head high. If nothing else, she still had her own integrity. "I'm not proud of that, but these things happen. I was afraid that one of you might find out." She looked from one to the other. "I would die before hurting you. So I broke it off. I sent him away. But not before your father found out."

If she closed her eyes, she could still see him. Still hear him. Raging. Calling her names that wounded her.

"He was furious that I could do such a thing to him. When he calmed down, he demanded a divorce." She shrugged helplessly. "I was almost relieved. But then he told me that he was going to keep all of you." Even now, her face turned pale as she relived that moment. "I felt as if he'd ripped out my heart. You were the only things I had worth living for."

"That's why you left?" It sounded like complete nonsense to Nicole. If you love someone, you stayed. You didn't leave.

So much hurt, Laura thought. So much pain. If she had to do it all over again, it would be different. She would dig in and fight. But she had been young then and there had been no one to turn to for support, no one to guide her.

"No, I left because he threatened to take me to court and involve me in the worst custody battle of the century." The smile was sad. "Those were his words. 'The worst custody battle of the century.' He was going to drag me down in front of you, prove how unfit I was to be a mother."

She rose, unable to watch their faces any longer. If they didn't forgive her now, then there was no purpose to her sacrifice.

"There was nothing to gain and everything to lose." She saw Sally standing in the entrance to the family room. There was genuine pity in the older woman's eyes. "I didn't care about my name, but I did care how that might hurt you. So I agreed to go." She said the words to the fireplace.

"For a hundred thousand dollars."

Laura swung around to face Nicole, confused. "What hundred thousand dollars?"

Maybe Nicole was being a fool again, but the surprise on her mother's face looked genuine. "The hundred thousand dollars Father said he paid you to leave us."

What a little, little man James had been. It wasn't enough to deny her her children; he had to destroy her in their eyes as well.

"Not a dime," Laura said fiercely. "I didn't take a dime from him." She crossed to her daughters. "How could I? That would be like...selling you." As she said the words, she realized why Nicole had accused her of that.

Nicole rose to her feet. "Then where were you all these years?"

The years she had remained away were all a blur now. "At first, I stayed away because of his threat. And as you grew older...after Robby died..." The very words burned in her throat. She hadn't been allowed to attend her son's funeral. She had gone later, to bid goodbye to her boy alone. "...I felt that you wouldn't understand. I was afraid of your rejection. Afraid of the look that's in your eyes right now."

She didn't want to believe, she didn't, Nicole thought. If she believed, she could be hurt all over again. "Why did you change your mind now?"

That was simple. She had wanted to return for so long. Last night, she'd been given an excuse. One she clung to.

"Because Dennis said you needed me. He came to me last night. He was very persistent." And for that, Laura was going to be eternally grateful to him. "He persuaded me to tell him what really happened. And then he surprised me. He said you cried out for me when you were in labor."

When Nicole didn't bother to deny it, Laura knew that it was true. Her heart swelled. She'd been right to return. "I knew that I had to put my own feelings aside." She stood between them. "I do love you. Both of you. And Robby."

Tears glistened in her eyes again. "You don't know what it's been like, all these years, just following your progress from a distance." But, hopefully, all that was in the past now. She smiled sadly.

Nicole thought of how she would feel, barred from her children. How awful it would be if she could never hold them in her arms again.

She looked deep into her mother's eyes and saw the truth. That all these years what she had believed was a lie. The way she saw life had been shaped by a lie. She hadn't been abandoned. Her mother had left her because she loved her.

Laura repeated what she had first said to Marlene. "So I've come now to ask your forgiveness. And to tell you that I've never stopped loving you."

Marlene was first. She went to her mother and hugged her. The two women cried openly. Laura looked toward Nicole and extended her arm.

With a sob, Nicole joined them.

In the distance, the sound of tiny wails began to drift down the stairs. Sally stood in the doorway and shook her head. "Three crying up there, three crying down here. What a place to work."

She wiped the corner of her eye with her apron and went to tend to the babies.

Chapter 15

The Mustang wasn't in the carport when she pulled up later that morning. The sense of urgency that had prompted her to leave the reunion with her mother now threatened to overwhelm her.

He was gone. She was too late.

The words drummed through her brain like a death knell. He wasn't just at work, or running an errand. He was gone.

Being reunited with her mother and discovering that the version of the past she had always thought was true had been nothing more than a fabrication by her father was like a huge awakening for Nicole. Like a tilted kaleidoscope whose pieces reformed a completely different picture, she suddenly saw her life in a totally altered way. She'd allowed her childhood to color the way she saw relationships. But that way was wrong, completely wrong. Her mother hadn't rejected her, she'd been trying to protect her by leaving. Nicole realized that she had wasted all this time feeling unloved when in actuality she had been loved a great deal.

So much so that her mother had made the ultimate sacrifice for her. Her mother had withdrawn from her life when she had wanted nothing more than to remain in it.

If she was so wrong about her mother, maybe she had been wrong about Dennis, too. Maybe she had been too quick to shut him out.

Maybe, just maybe, she had thought as she had driven quickly from her sister's house to her own, he could say something to redeem himself if she gave him the chance. Her mother, delighted to discover that she had grandchildren, was more than happy to become acquainted with Erika and Ethan while Nicole drove home to see Dennis.

But now he might not be there at all.

Her heart in her mouth, Nicole parked the car and hurried up to his apartment. She stopped dead before she reached it. His door was standing wide open. He'd never leave his door open like that.

The dread was almost insurmountable as she drew closer. "Dennis?"

There was no response to her call.

Nicole crossed the threshold, looking around. There was an emptiness that went beyond the fact that the kitchen had been stripped of its furnishings. He wasn't here, she thought. "Dennis?"

The living room was empty. The simple sofa and coffee table were gone. The huge TV set that had brought him into her life was no longer there as well. Refusing to accept what her eyes already knew to be true, Nicole ran into the bedroom.

It was vacant. There were imprints in the rug where the bed had stood only yesterday. The hollow feeling in the pit of her stomach threatened to swallow Nicole up as she sank down in the space where the bed had been.

He was gone and she had no way of finding him.

The noise in the other room had Nicole scrambling back

to her feet. Heart thudding madly against her ribs, she hurried into the living room, calling his name before she reached it.

"Dennis?"

The husky man in the paint-splattered, faded coveralls looked at her curiously. Two cans of paint were on the floor beside him.

"No, my name's John." He nodded needlessly at the roller in his hand. "I'm here to paint the apartment."

Nicole's heart felt like a huge lead weight in her chest. She walked past the man on legs that were oddly rubbery.

"I'd better get out of your way," she murmured as she left the apartment.

Dennis took a long drink and then set the mug down. Smoky Joe's certainly lived up to its name all right, he thought. The air was thick with the smell of smoke, beer and cheap perfume. It wasn't a place they came to with any frequency, but the atmosphere seemed to suit the mood that was hovering around him these last few days.

"Want my opinion?" Winston asked.

He wrapped his hands around the mug as he stared straight ahead. A woman with raven hair and a fuchsia dress made out of a scrap of material was grinding against her partner on the dance floor directly in his line of vision. He looked away.

"No."

Winston sighed as he sipped his own beer. "You need a personality transplant, Lincoln."

Dennis looked at his partner darkly, then turned his head away again.

It was like stepping through a minefield, Winston thought. Safest thing was to back away, but he cared about the man too much to keep his mouth shut.

"Back to the one you had before all this started." Lifting

the mug again, Winston watched Dennis over the dingy glass rim.

"Thanks, Dr. Freud."

Even the voice didn't sound as if it belonged to Dennis. He'd gone through a complete change since they had discovered the disk, Winston thought. Since he had left Nicole.

"I'll see what I can do," Dennis muttered into his mug.

"You know what you can do," Winston told him and earned an even darker scowl. He pressed on. "You don't act like a man who should be riding high right now." Winston leaned forward. He wanted to get this out quickly, before Dennis walked out on him. "Look, we actually caught the bad guys for a change. The disk turned out to be a gold mine of information." Keeping his voice low, his tone grew in intensity. "We even got the head guy, the man you said was responsible for your old man committing suicide."

That should have made him feel good, Dennis thought, finally seeing Trask behind bars where he belonged. The man had aged considerably in his rise up the power structure. Stripped of his trappings, his men, Trask had looked like a shriveled little old man. It should have made Dennis feel vindicated, triumphant. Something. It didn't.

Dennis took another sip. He didn't taste the beer. Only his own dissatisfaction. "Your point?"

Winston gripped Dennis's wrist. "My point is you don't act like a man who's temporarily Sherwood's fair-haired boy."

Dennis shrugged. "Maybe that doesn't matter to me anymore."

"Exactly." Dennis could see the concern mixed with growing frustration in Winston's eyes. "And maybe that means that you still have some unfinished business."

He didn't want to hear her name. He didn't want to hear anything about it. The look in Nicole's eyes outside the bank had cut him completely dead. She had made it clear that she didn't want anything to do with him. He just had to get on with his life, that's all.

"Drop it, Winston."

Winston remained steadfast. "Sorry. I can't. I have to work with you and right now, you're about as easy to work with as a bear with a burr lodged where the sun doesn't shine."

Dennis raised the mug to his lips. "Colorful."

Well, at least Dennis wasn't hitting him or storming out. Maybe he was making a breakthrough. "Accurate. Go talk to her."

He sighed. A little of the darkness crept away from his eyes. When it did, Winston saw the misery that existed there.

"She doesn't want to talk to me, Winston. She made that very clear."

Winston remembered the look on Nicole's face as he had backed away. "She was angry," he argued.

Angry didn't begin to describe what Dennis had seen on her face. "And what makes you think she's changed her mind?"

Winston knew that if Dennis walked away from this, he was never going to forgive himself.

"She's had time to cool off. Maybe she misses you." Winston's mouth curved as he thought of what he had witnessed on the monitors. He'd never seen his partner so content as when he was with Nicole. "Or that maid service you provided for her." He pushed the mug away as he leaned forward again. "Sherwood said you deserved a couple of days off for a job well-done. Why don't you take it and spend it with her?"

Did Winston think that hadn't crossed his mind a dozen times? With the same result each time. Dennis knew she wouldn't see him. "Because she won't even open the door to me."

Winston laughed shortly as he shook his head. "If you're going to let a locked door stop you, then you don't deserve to be in the Department."

Gaining physical access was one thing. Gaining emotional access was another. "It's not *that* locked door that I'm thinking about."

"If you can't unlock that one, then you're not the man I think you are."

Dennis said nothing. He stared into the inside of his empty mug for a long time. Empty, just the way he felt without her. Finally, he pushed back his chair and rose.

He looked down at Winston. "I guess there's no other way to make you shut up, is there?"

Winston's smile was smug. "Nope."

"Tell Sherwood I'll call in," Dennis instructed as he pushed the chair to the table.

Winston nodded. "See you around, partner. Tell her hi for me," he called after Dennis.

Dennis waved a dismissive hand behind him as he left.

She was getting good at it. Tired, but good. She'd managed to feed and change first one twin and then the other quickly enough so that the process didn't have to begin again as soon as she was finished. Both were now sleeping peacefully. One more thing to do before she could think of herself. Not that she wanted to think about herself or anything at all. The hectic pace she kept up was the only thing keeping her going right now.

Why hadn't he come back, damn him?

With a sigh, she filled the dog's dish and set it down before Romeo. The Labrador looked at the offering without interest. He uttered a low moan as he nosed the dish aside.

Nicole squatted down beside the animal. "I know just how you feel." She stroked the dog's head. "You miss him too, don't you? I'm sorry, Romeo, but he's deserted both of us. Don't waste your time thinking about him. Just move on. There's no sense in mooning around like a lovesick puppy. Forget him. That's what I'm doing."

The hell I am.

The doorbell rang. She wasn't expecting anyone. Her mother had gone back to her home in Santa Barbara with promises that they would all get together at the end of the month. There was Marlene's wedding to plan before things got back to normal.

When the bell rang again, she rose to her feet and crossed to the door. At this time of day, it was probably a persistent salesman.

Her words of dismissal disappeared when she looked through the peephole. With a cry of disbelief, she pulled open the door and threw herself into Dennis's arms.

Relief washed over him. Holding her close, he brought his mouth down to hers. God, but he had missed her.

This was what she had been dreaming about for the past several days. It was what she had been aching over every waking minute she immersed herself in her whirlwind routine. He was back. He was really back.

The next moment, a firecracker went off inside her brain, releasing explosions and with it, a realization. Nicole wedged a hand between them and pushed Dennis back. Her eyes narrowed as she glared at him. "I forgot."

The kiss and the one hundred and eighty-degree switch had him dizzy. "What?"

She scowled. "I'm still mad at you." How could he have walked away from her, stayed away so long and then come back as if nothing had happened?

He started to take her back into his arms. "I noticed."

With determination, she pushed against his chest again, holding him at bay. "No, I'm serious."

Before he could begin his defense, Romeo came running up and leaped all over him like an eighty-five pound puppy.

"Down, Romeo, down." After washing Dennis's face with his tongue, the dog obeyed. Dennis rubbed Romeo's head as he walked into the apartment.

Hurt feelings mingled with joy. Nicole planted her hands at her waist as she followed him. "You walked out on me," she accused.

He turned, confused. If he lived to be a hundred, he was never going to understand the species. "You told me to go."

"Not for this long." The longer he stayed away, the more certain she had become that he hadn't really cared at all. "Where have you been all this time?"

He shrugged. "Working. Tying up all the loose ends." They had enough evidence, thanks to Logan's disk, to put the key members of the Syndicate away for a very long time. "Trying to get over you." He cupped her cheek with his hand. He'd almost forgotten how the feel of her skin thrilled him. "It didn't work. Everywhere I looked, you were there. You were in my thoughts morning, noon and night." He dropped his hand to his side, unable to read her expression. "Winston says I've gotten to be hell to work with."

She was trying desperately to compose herself. To put everything in perspective when all she wanted to do was to wrap herself around him and hold on tight. "Then he is your partner?"

"Yes."

A small smile played on her lips. "At least that wasn't a lie."

He didn't know where to begin, or how. All the words he had rehearsed on his way here had become a vague fog in his brain. "No."

"But everything else was." She searched his face, wanting to know the truth no matter how much it hurt. She deserved the truth. And prayed that it was what she wanted to hear. "Was it all lies, Dennis? Was everything you told me a lie?"

Dennis shook his head. He wanted to take her back into his arms, but this had to be cleared away first. "No."

She raised her chin, taking a deep breath. Nicole proceeded like a tightrope walker across a high wire, one tiny, cautious step at a time. "Where did you draw the line?"

His eyes held hers. "I didn't lie about my family. Or about my past. I really do have a law degree." He took a step closer. "And I didn't lie about the way I feel about you. That part was very true."

She wanted to believe him so much. "Was making love with me part of your job?"

He smiled, remembering. "Making love with you was the most wonderful experience of my life. If that had been in my job description, I would have signed on when I was fifteen."

Despite the situation, she smiled. "I would have been eight."

"I would have waited." He touched her again, his fingers gliding along the line of her jaw. He saw something in her eyes that gave him hope. "Listen to me for a minute. I have to tell you something. Craig was in debt to the Syndicate. Heavily. I don't know how he managed it, but he stole the accountant's disk—"

That sounded so strange to her. "They have accountants?"

He grinned. "Sounds funny, doesn't it? But they're businessmen after a fashion. Anyway, he thought that was his insurance policy. They had other ideas."

Her eyes widened. "You mean—?"

He didn't relish this part, but she deserved the truth, all of it. "They killed him. The car was tampered with."

Nicole covered her mouth in horror. But there were no tears. They had long since left her.

"Unfortunately for them, whoever tampered with the car did it before they found out where Craig hid the disk."

"And that's where you came in," she said quietly.

"That's where I came in," he repeated. "The Department thought you had it, or knew where it was."

She had never known the trouble she could have been in. Nicole shook her head. "I never—"

Dennis stopped her. There was no need for excuses. "I know." He took a deep breath. "Nicole, I'm not sorry for doing my job. I'm only sorry that it hurt you."

She bit her lower lip, wavering. "I really do want to believe you, but—"

The hell with waiting. He couldn't separate the way he felt from his words. Dennis took her into his arms. "Look into my eyes, Nicole. What do you see?"

She looked up and saw her reflection in his pupils. "Me."

He nodded. "That's right." His arms tightened around her. "Only you."

If she was trying to hold out against him, she was losing the battle. She could feel her body calling to his. Struggling, she tried to maintain her composure. "Why did you go looking for my mother?"

That he could answer simply. "Because you told me you wanted her."

Nicole shook her head. "I was half out of my head with pain." Another man would have dismissed what she had said under those circumstances.

His eyes touched her face, caressing her. Making love to her. "Sometimes the truth comes out at times like that."

Maybe it did, she thought. She owed him for that. Owed him for a lot of things. "My mother thinks you're a terrific person."

He smiled then and it rose to his eyes. "Mothers always liked me."

She could easily believe that. He had the look of apple

pie and baseball about him. Nicole threaded her arms around his neck. "Daughters, too."

The sigh of relief that went through him was tremendous. "Then you forgive me?"

She cocked her head. "That all depends."

He saw the glint of humor in her eyes and knew that things were going to be all right from here on in. "On what?"

Nicole ran her tongue along her teeth, her eyes holding his. "On how you plan to make it up to me."

That was easy. "I plan to try for the rest of my life, Nic."

She hadn't expected him to look so serious. Her pulse quickened. "Are you saying what I think you're saying?"

They both knew he was. "I took a look at my streamlined life and realized that it was missing something. Actually, three somethings," he amended. The dog barked. He glanced in Romeo's direction. "Maybe four." And then he shut out everything else in the room except for her. "Nicole, I love you. I've never said that to anyone before, and I don't intend to say that to anyone else again, except maybe to Erika and Ethan. Because I do. I love all three of you, and I want you to be part of my life from here on in. Otherwise, it's not a life, it's just an existence. Marry me, Nicole."

Yes, yes! She raised her eyes innocently to his. "Would I be Mrs. Dennis Lincoln if I did?"

That was an odd question. "Yes. Why?"

"Just checking," she explained impishly. She wound her arms around his neck and rose on her toes. Her body fit neatly against his. "I just thought you might have given me an alias."

"No, I didn't lie about that, either. My name is really Dennis Lincoln."

"Good, I've gotten used to that. No more lies?"

He lowered his mouth to hers. "No more lies," he promised. "Ever."

She felt the last word against her lips as he pressed his mouth to hers. And she believed him. You had to believe a man who made you feel safe.

* * * * *

passionate powerful provocative love stories that fulfill your every desire